THE NIGGER OF THE 'NARCISSUS'

JOSEPH CONRAD was born Józef Teodor Konrad Korzeniowski in the Russian part of Poland in 1857. His parents were punished by the Russians for their Polish nationalist activities and both died while Conrad was still a child. In 1874 he left Poland for France and in 1878 began a career with the British merchant navy. He spent nearly twenty years as a sailor and did not begin writing novels until he was approaching forty. He became a British citizen in 1886 and settled permanently in England after his marriage to Jessie George in 1896.

Conrad is a writer of extreme subtlety and sophistication; works such as *Heart of Darkness, Lord Jim,* and *Nostromo* display technical complexities which have established Conrad as one of the first English 'Modernists'. He is also noted for the unprecedented vividness with which he communicates a pessimist's view of man's personal and social destiny in such works as *The Secret Agent, Under Western Eyes,* and *Victory.* Despite the immediate critical recognition that they received in his life-time Conrad's major novels did not sell, and he lived in relative poverty until the commercial success of *Chance* (1913) secured for him a wider public and an assured income. In 1923 he visited America, with great acclaim, and he was offered a knighthood (which he declined) shortly before his death in 1924. Since then his reputation has steadily grown and he is now seen as a writer who revolutionized the English novel and was arguably the most important single innovator of the twentieth century.

JACQUES BERTHOUD was born in Switzerland and educated mostly in South Africa. He has taught at the Universities of Natal (Pietermaritzburg), Southampton, and York, where he is now head of the Department of English and Related Literature. He is the author of *Joseph Conrad, the Major Phase,* and has edited Trollope's *Phineas Finn* for the World's Classics Series.

THE WORLD'S CLASSICS

JOSEPH CONRAD

The Nigger of the 'Narcissus'

A Tale of the Sea

Edited with an Introduction by
JACQUES BERTHOUD

Oxford   New York
OXFORD UNIVERSITY PRESS
1984

Oxford University Press, Walton Street, Oxford OX2 6DP

London New York Toronto
Delhi Bombay Calcutta Madras Karachi
Kuala Lumpur Singapore Hong Kong Tokyo
Nairobi Dar es Salaam Cape Town
Melbourne Auckland
and associated companies in
Beirut Berlin Ibadan Mexico City Nicosia

Oxford is a trade mark of Oxford University Press

British Library Cataloguing in Publication Data
Conrad, Joseph
The nigger of the 'Narcissus'.—(The World's classics)
I. Title II. Berthoud, Jacques 823'.912 [F] PR6005.04
ISBN 0–19–281623–3

Library of Congress Cataloging in Publication Data
Conrad, Joseph, 1857–1924.
The Nigger of the 'Narcissus'.
(The World's classics)
Bibliography: p.
I. Berthoud, Jacques. II. Title. III. Series.
PR6005.04N5 1984   823'.912   84–9668
ISBN 0–19–281623–3 (pbk.)

Printed in Great Britain by
Hazell Watson & Viney Limited
Aylesbury, Bucks

CONTENTS

CONTENTS

INTRODUCTION

Conrad and the Sea

I

DESPITE the apparent provocativeness of its title, *The Nigger of the 'Narcissus'* has always occupied a special place in the affections of its readers. When it came out, it was at once recognized as a classic of the sea, and it has retained that status ever since. Why this should be is not difficult to perceive. To begin with, the novel is at once the most succinct and the most complete narrative of a deep sea voyage in the English language, combining the rituals and patterns of an ideal event (departure-arrival, storm-calm, mutiny-authority, etc.) with the unpredictabilities and particularities of a properly historical episode. More subtly, it has all the nostalgic seductiveness of an achievement seen in retrospect, for in its story its author (for whom too it was a special favourite) weighs up the meaning of his life as a master-mariner, and does not find it wanting. But, most deeply of all, *The Nigger of the 'Narcissus'* is the kind of work that offers its readers the promise of happiness, for it suggests that life at sea is able to loosen the grip that historical necessity usually fastens on us, whether as original sin or as economic law. It shows that service at sea demands, and in the end receives, that self-denying solidarity so obstinately resisted by narcissistic mankind. Thus men are saved despite themselves, and the remorseless logic of history is cheated of its power to hurt.

The special gratitude with which readers remember this novel needs no further elaboration. Whether this response is legitimate—that is, whether it rests on a reading that is more than simplistic or evasive—is a different matter. Is it possible to represent life at sea as a kind of moral idyll without forfeiting all claims to historical realism? This question has produced a number of sceptical answers, the most recent and the most formidable of which has argued that in Conrad the sea is an ahistorical device for naturalizing an all-too-historical ideological position.[1] In this view, if you transpose into a maritime context ideas that on land would show up, say, as a socially determined élitism, they take on the guise of a necessary condition of life, under which the language of rights loses all purchase and the language of duty all opposition.

As far as *The Nigger of the 'Narcissus'* is concerned, this view is open to two initial objections. The first is that, ironically, far from being too historical, it is not historical enough. For example, it registers no hint of the degree to which Conrad's text belongs to the period in which it was written. We think of the 1890s as being aesthetic in character (Wilde, Beardsley, the Rhymers' Club); or, more penetratingly, as socialist (Sidney Webb, Bernard Shaw, the Labour Party); but it has every claim also to be regarded as the decade of the sea. The year in which Conrad's first novel, *Almayer's Folly*, was published (1895) saw the appearance of Froude's *English Seamen*; the following year (1896) produced not only *An Outcast of the Islands* but Kipling's *The Seven Seas*; the year after that (1897) produced, in addition to *The Nigger of the 'Narcissus'*, Newbolt's *Admirals All* and Kipling's *Captains Courageous*. It would scarcely be an exaggeration to suggest that by the end of the nineteenth century the sea had become a national obsession. To ignore this fact when approaching

---

[1] Fredric Jameson in *The Political Unconscious*, Methuen, 1981, Chapter 5.

its most significant instance is to begin by wrong-setting one's critical sights.

The second prima facie difficulty is that this view assumes without examination that moral confidence and historical realism are incompatible in the England of the 1890s. It appears to claim that any endorsement of the established historical situation must necessarily be un-progressively false—the product of ideological fantasies in conflict with the real currents of the time. Yet the exhilaration, to which over three generations of readers have by now testified, bears little resemblance to the complacency of wish-fulfilment. The novel has the vitality and substance of a text in touch with the central issues of its period, not with its evasions. In what follows, I shall try to show that in *The Nigger of the 'Narcissus'*, the sea does not serve to block 'history' out but on the contrary is the means by which it is let in; and that it is not despite but by virtue of the fact that the novel is a maritime classic that it is also able to become a late Victorian classic.

II

Memories of the triumphs of the Royal Navy over Napoleon's fleets have obscured the less glorious truth that during the early decades of the nineteenth century the British Merchant Marine, stuck in the traditions of the East India trade, was rendered obsolete by the technical and commercial initiative of the United States. Having developed the clipper—in all essentials the prototype of Conrad's *Narcissus*: a light, lean-hulled, high-masted wooden vessel, with a bow made to cut instead of hit the waves and a stern designed to slide through the water rather than squat in it—the Americans challenged British ships on every ocean of the globe, and captured almost the whole of the Atlantic and Pacific trades.[2] This sudden expansion of sea power brought about a comparable efflorescence of sea literature. From Cooper's *The Pilot* (1824) to Melville's *Moby Dick* (1851)—a mere quarter-century—American fiction transformed the imaginative representation of the sea in Western literature.[3] But this literary movement collapsed as abruptly as the maritime trade it had reflected. By the middle of the century, the United States had retreated behind a tariff wall, transferred her imperial ambitions from the Eastern seaboard to the Western prairies, and started to prepare for a civil war. Meanwhile, British engineers were developing the marine engine; and in less than four decades British steamships had in their turn succeeded in driving American sailing ships off the face of the waters.

The transformation of the British Merchant Marine was inspired by two political decisions. In 1850 Lord Russell's Whig ministry, ideologically committed to the doctrine of free trade, repealed the Navigation Laws, which had protected British ships for over two centuries, and established Marine Boards in order to raise standards of efficiency and sobriety for officers, and of conduct and welfare for ratings. The effect of these enactments was spectacular. By 1900 the British Merchant Marine comprised 50 per cent of the total mercantile tonnage of the world, and its employees, from being perhaps the most incompetent in Europe, had acquired a reputation un-

---

[2] R. H. Thornton, *British Shipping*, Cambridge, 1959, pp. 5–6. Of the several books on the relevant maritime history that I consulted, Thornton's proved by far the liveliest, the best written, and the most useful.

[3] For an instructive study of this literary movement, see Thomas Philbrick, *James Fenimore Cooper and the Development of American Sea Fiction*, Harvard University Press, 1961.

rivalled for navigational skill and professional reliability.[4]
Such a fleet was of course far in excess of the country's
supply of seamen. As the composition of the *Narcissus*'s
crew indicates, a substantial proportion of the men on
British ships had to be recruited abroad. That a Pole like
Conrad should have been drawn into a service requiring
staff and respected for its competence is less sociologically
inexplicable that is commonly thought. Indeed, Conrad's
entire naval career, with its pursuit of Board of Trade
certificates, its deep-sea commissions to Australia and the
Far East, and its pride in the traditions of the Red Ensign,
accurately reflects the spirit of the Merchant Service at its
apogee.

We know, of course, that the national myths of an island
gravitate to its coastline; but specifically English myths (at
least on the evidence of the literature of the nineteenth
century) settled on the Royal Navy. Whether in the popular
novels of Captain Marryat on the 'old navy' that imposed
the continental blockade and of Charles Kingsley on the
Tudor buccaneers who fought the Armada, or whether in
the flood of patriotic verse pouring out of four generations
of poetasters, from Thomas Campbell at one end to Henry
Newbolt at the other end of the century, it is the military
ship that gets the praise. One of the indirect effects of this
is that the Merchant Service was left relatively free of the
worst prejudices of nationalism. Thus when, as the century
wore on, it came to rival the Royal Navy in the regard of
the country, it did not wholly succumb to the contagion of
jingoism. Conrad's oddly ambiguous attitudes towards the
country of his adoption, compounded as they were of pride
and irony, gratitude and exasperation, reflect the ambigui-
ties of his personal story; but they also express the spirit of

---

[4] All statistics in this introduction are taken from the 'Shipping' entry
of the *Encyclopaedia Britannica*, Ninth Edition, 1910.

the service to which he devoted sixteen years of his life. He would have felt quite alien on the deck of a frigate; on the poop of a merchantman he was able to feel as much at home as anywhere, for the traditions of the Merchant Marine were international as well as British—at one and the same time dependent on the law of commercial self-interest and animated by a self-sufficient code of conduct. The span of Conrad's life coincided almost exactly with an historical phase in which the trade of the world multiplied several times in volume, complexity and interdependence, and in which British ships, carrying about half this trade and over a third of all trade between foreign countries, could not but reflect the ideological expansiveness implied in these conditions.

The degree to which Conrad has been able to admit these complexities into his novel has not been sufficiently recognized. *The Nigger of the 'Narcissus'* resists any simple identification of itself with a patriotic idea. Distinguishing between land and sea, it associates the mythology of nationalism with England herself, evoking in the sunlight and wind of the Channel approaches that eager, boyish, adventurous love of country so fancied by the Victorian imperialist and so irritating to the contemporary intellectual. But we soon discover that the land itself, which, we are warned, 'towered up immense and strong, guarding priceless traditions *and untold suffering* ... *ignoble* virtues and splendid *transgressions*' (pp. 162–3, my italics), cannot sustain this kind of enthusiasm. What was initially offered to us as 'the great flagship of the race' reveals, as the *Narcissus* is drawn up the Thames, that it contains the infernal expanses of the world's most industrialized capital. On land, the patriotic myth is hopelessly entangled in the commercial and social realities of imperialism; at sea it loses even its partial potency. The crew of the *Narcissus* does not, of course, cease to notice national and racial distinctions once the anchor has been weighed. The Russian Finn Wamibo, for example, is so culturally displaced that he never quite becomes humanly decipherable to his companions; and the West Indian Negro Wait seems to them almost repulsively exotic when they first set eyes on him (p. 18). But even these differences are not allowed to become decisive. Wamibo's participation in Wait's rescue is convincingly presented as an unforced act of solidarity; and even when Wait decides to drop out, he is not ostracized, as it were, by the narrator, but actually made more human, shown to engage more deeply the loyalty of at least one member of the crew, and rendered more sympathetic to readers admitted into the privacy of his thoughts and feelings.

If racialist and nationalist prejudice enters the novel, it does so through a figure which the entire narrative is designed to repudiate. That Conrad should have made Donkin the self-appointed defender of seamen's rights has often been interpreted as connivance in the conservatism that inheres in all hierarchies. Be that as it may, it also generates a less advertised—but in this reading a more significant—irony: that professions of solidarity may in fact be expressions of *ressentiment*. Donkin's first public action in the forecastle is to insult the Russian Finn: 'These damned furriners should be kept under', he proclaims (p. 13); and thereafter his talk is laced with gratuitous racial abuse: 'You blooming square-head!' (to Wamibo); 'You fat-headed Dutchman!' (to the Scandinavian Nielsen); 'You black-faced swine!' (to James Wait). It is in Wait's interests, as he conceives them, not to take these insults seriously; but by associating with Donkin he becomes caught in the mechanism of self-destroying complicity and pays the price: as he lies helplessly dying, the defender of his rights robs him of his life's savings. The viciousness of this deed has been felt by every reader—but not the racial hatred that makes it possible. In a previous scene, the evangelical cook, Podmore, in his eagerness to save the dying man from damnation, had given way to what looked like an incoherent racialism: 'The black soul—blacker—body—rot—Devil . . .'. But this is Manichean and apocalyptic imagery, not genetic and social. Donkin suffers from the authentic complaint. He calls the dying Wait 'a black, rotten encumbrance' and 'a hateful nigger'; and when he hears him mutter that a white girl he knows 'would chuck—any toff—for a coloured gentleman', his response of 'scandalized . . . disgust' (p. 149) has prompted every miscegenation law of the past eighty years. Donkin is not a misunderstood socialist; he is, quite precisely, a National Socialist. He places the language of egalitarian rights in the service of an ideology fuelled by inferiority feelings and the lust of domination. This perspective on Donkin shows Conrad to have been much more politically prescient, much more responsive to the stirrings of the political current, than he is generally regarded as being at this stage in his career.

III

Attention to the novel's historical context prompts a number of adjustments to its received interpretation. One of these I have already tried to make: that the novel's notorious distinction between sea and land does not license the interpretation of the sea as a non-historical space in which a naive patriotism can perform its evolutions unchecked. I shall now turn to another: that the novel's equally famous distinction between sail and steam cannot be used to endorse a naive social conservatism. I shall not deny that *The Nigger of the 'Narcissus'* is a passionate farewell to the age of sail—only that this farewell takes the form of sentimental nostalgia for an idealized past.

I have already indicated that the development of the marine engine was the decisive factor in Britain's success in overcoming American competition in the second half of the nineteenth century. Once steam engines had been made efficient enough not to require an entire cargo of fuel to keep them going, the disappearance of sail became inevitable, for steamers could be built on a much larger scale than sailing ships (there is an optimum limit to the spread of canvas), and could be run with greater regularity, economy and safety. When Conrad was born, the annual rate of steamship construction in Britain had equalled that of sail; by the time he was writing *The Nigger of the 'Narcissus'*, three times as many steamers as sailing ships were being built, representing twenty times the tonnage. Whatever resistance sailing ships had been able to offer, particularly on the long haul to Australia, on which they could take advantage of the prevailing winds, had collapsed.

That the steamship is no less worthy a literary subject than the sailing ship, a number of contemporary master-pieces, including Conrad's *Typhoon* and Kipling's 'M'Andrew's Hymn', testify. Indeed, the vogue for album verses on the romance of sail that filled the anthologies of our grandparents indicates that the steamer might well be the likelier motif of the two. Conrad's impatience with his own reputation as a writer of sea tales shows his sensitivity to the danger of this stereotype. It also suggests why, more than any other maritime novelist of his time, he was able to bring his real experience of sail into his writing. One illustration will have to suffice. When he joined the Merchant Service the demand for speed on the more distant routes had been conceded. Before so-called clean winds—that is, winds that do not gust—the spread of canvas required for speed was not dangerous, though it was uncomfortable. Before erratic squalls, however, it would turn a full-rigged ship into what has been called 'about the most dangerous vehicle invented by man'.[5] To judge by its historical model, the deck of the loaded *Narcissus* was no more than forty-nine inches above the ocean—though it would have been shielded by five-foot bulwarks.[6] Under a captain like Allistoun who, being responsive to the demands of the age, 'loved his ship and drove her unmercifully', the *Narcissus* before a favourable wind would have her main deck almost continuously awash, and her crew (to quote the narrator) would be compelled to 'turn in wet' and 'turn out stiff'. In bad weather, however, any attempt to maintain speed would involve the very real risk of being blown over. If this happened—as it did, of course, to the *Narcissus*—the decision not to cut the masts in the hope of righting the ship by bringing the spars to windward would double the danger of foundering. And if the operation succeeded—as it did in the case of the *Narcissus*—the ship was by no means secure. Every reader will remember the sentence with which Conrad closes his storm scene. Referring to old Singleton, who had been at the helm for nearly thirty hours, he writes: 'He steered with care'. In the context this laconic statement achieves a stunning symbolic effect. But that it also carries an unrhetorical precision of reference is seldom appreciated. To steer a sailing ship in a high following wind requires concentration and courage, for as the ship dips forward in response to an overtaking wave, it will start a yaw (or swing) which, if not instantly corrected, will go out of control, turn the ship broadside, and expose it once again to the full weight of wind and water.[7]

---

[5] Thornton, op cit., p. 48.

[6] Gerald Morgan, 'The Book of the ship *"Narcissus"*', in Robert Kimbrough, ed., *The Nigger of the 'Narcissus'* (hereafter *NN*), Norton, 1979, p. 202.

[7] Basil Lubbock, as quoted by Thornton, op. cit., p. 49.

If Conrad chose the sailing ship as his subject, therefore, it was less for its romantic possibilities than because it allowed him to give greater reality to his representation of man's encounter with the sea. To drive a sailing ship is to confront nature directly. The hardships and deprivations incurred, to which he does full justice, forge a stronger link between the sailor and the element. In a short essay entitled 'Tales of the Sea', published a year after *The Nigger*, Conrad distinguishes between Fenimore Cooper and Captain Marryat on the grounds that for the latter the sea is nothing more than a frame for the exploits of naval midshipmen, while for the former it 'interpenetrates with life; it is in a subtle way a factor in the problem of existence, and for all its greatness, it is always in touch with the men, who, bound on errands of war or gain, traverse its immense solitudes'.[8]

Conrad shows this interpenetration at its most complete in his evocation of those seamen, survivors from the past, whom his narrator calls 'the everlasting children of the mysterious sea'—in contrast to the new generation of sailors, 'the grown-up children of the discontented earth', who are not so assimilated. In this he exploits one of Fenimore Cooper's major innovations. Referring in the essay from which I have just quoted to Cooper's first novel, *The Pilot* (written in part to correct the nautical deficiencies of Scott's *The Pirate*), Conrad describes its most memorable character, the old mariner Long Tom Coffin, as 'a monumental seaman with the individuality of life and the significance of a type'.[9] In his laconic speech, thickly brined with sea terms, his strength in an emergency, his prejudices based on experience, his oracular seamanship, and a love for his ship so unreserved that he chooses to go

[8] *Notes on Life and Letters*, Dent, 1949, p. 55.
[9] Ibid., p. 56.

down with her,[10] Long Tom is the prototype of Conrad's no less memorable Singleton. The secret of Singleton's unity of being, as Conrad said to Cunninghame Graham (who had proposed to improve Singleton with an education), is that 'he was in perfect accord with his life'. Any education beyond that which equipped him for the conditions of his profession would only serve to foment the doubts and divisions of self-consciousness. As he was, he could remain 'simple and great like an elemental force'.[11] We meet Singleton in Bombay Harbour deciphering the prose of Bulwer Lytton's *Pelham*—a novel devoted to promoting the figure of the *dandy*! We leave him in a London Board of Trade office—incapable of signing his wage-receipt. But maladjustment to the land is adjustment to the sea: under sail he is equal to any test which men in fear and revolt, and the elements in storm and calm, can propose. Judged one way he is an illiterate clown; judged another he is a surviving fragment of an epic age.

In creating Long Tom Coffin, Cooper sought to establish a new fictional type: the independent, self-respecting seaman more worthy of the democratic virtue of a young republic than the brutalized sea-peasantry of an *ancien régime* novelist like Smollett. No such political ancestry can be discerned in Singleton; yet in the novel he performs an unambiguous social function. Conrad insists in his treatment of him that his lack of conventional status is quite irrelevant to our assessment of him. Master of a craft that was already old in Homer's time, he has the dignity of his ancient calling. Such dignity would have been much more difficult to acquire on a steamer, for steam brought a new rating into being: an employee rather than a craftsman,

---

[10] See Philbrick, op. cit., Chapter 2.

[11] C. T. Watts, ed., *Joseph Conrad's Letters to R. B. Cunninghame Graham*, Cambridge, 1969, pp. 53–4.

without traditional skills, for (as R. H. Thornton has
pointed out) 'the job of shovelling coal into a furnace is not
seafaring'.[12] On a ship like the *Narcissus*, however, where
all employees cannot but practise seafaring, an egalitarian
pressure makes itself felt. The crew in its entirety participates in a common task and endures common hardships.
Whether driving the ship or the crew, the two mates work
with the men, sharing their watch and leading them aloft.
Thus it is that in merchant ships 'where the sense of
hierarchy is weak ... all feel themselves equal before the
unconcerned immensity of the sea and the exacting appeal
of the work' (p. 16). Conrad does not try to evade the
question of social inequality; on the contrary, he goes out
of his way to illustrate how readily the conversation of the
crew runs to defining the characteristics of a 'gentleman',
or to discussing the endeavours of reformist societies on
their behalf. Yet the point of these conversations is not the
crew's social predicament, but how unimplicated they feel
in what they are talking about, and thus how casually and
even humorously they can treat it. It is indeed in the
unselfconscious, practical, egalitarian tradition of the
Merchant Service in the last days of sail that Conrad found
a social image for one of his most original and durable
ideas—solidarity.

IV

It would seem, then, that in *The Nigger of the 'Narcissus'* the
sea does not serve to inhibit honest examination of political
and social questions. To understand how far this novel is
representative of the final phase of Victorianism, however,
we have to take the argument a stage further. It is not
enough to show that the sea is not inimical to history; it is

---

[12] Thornton, op. cit., p. 70.

also necessary to demonstrate that for Conrad the sea is *itself* an historical concept.

One of the reasons for regarding this novel as a sea-classic is that it presents the sea as an independent character in the narrative. No other novel published in England has attempted a more ambitious portrayal of the ocean. Under different seasons and latitudes, changing lights of day and night, contrasting states of agitation and stillness, and from a whole variety of visual perspectives, the sea emerges from Conrad's writing as a stupendously impersonal reality. Conrad's exploitation of animistic epithets has encouraged the view that he regarded the sea in allegorical terms. But the epithets themselves do not add up to allegory; paradoxically, they undo it. 'Incorruptible', 'unconcerned', 'mysterious', 'smiling', 'roaring', 'mischievous', 'disdainful', 'immortal', 'tormented', 'pitiless', 'august', 'heartless': such adjectives, as they accumulate, create an image of the sea as a living thing, but wholly resistant to human thought—that is, capable only of being represented, not of being interpreted. Indeed, its major attribute might be said to be its resistance to symbolization. Now even this conception of the sea is culturally determined —which is not to say, of course, that it is a mere projection, unrelated to the object it claims to represent. What it *does* suggest is that there could be other ways of regarding it: as a source of food, as an image of fecundity, as a pathway to adventure, as a repository of wonders and prodigies.

Conrad's conception of the sea as nature in its least accommodating form completes a tradition originally launched by Byron. As everybody used to know, the fourth canto of *Childe Harold's Pilgrimage* concludes with an invocation to the sea that transformed the mind of Europe on this subject. For Byron, the shore marks the boundary beyond which man's effectiveness ceases. The ocean's contemptuous destruction of his mightiest fleets and its sublime indifference to the passing of his empires makes it in all its phases—'calm or convulsed—in breeze or gale or storm'—the 'glass' and 'image' of eternity.[13] In this perspective, to adventure onto the waters is to be brought up against the mystery of man's origins and destination. On land, protected by the postponements and deferrals of civilized life, he can for a while nourish the illusion that he is not alone, that his hopes are not vain and his speech not unintelligible. But the sea which on all sides merges into 'the illimitable silence of all creation' (p. 147) permits no such evasion. Late-nineteenth-century man, intensely religious by nature but delivered by his science into a godless universe, finds in the sailor not a symbol but an extreme case of his own predicament. The irrelevance of consciousness to matter—one of the great themes of the age—is inscribed into every episode of *The Nigger of the 'Narcissus'*. Man is defined by his maladjustment to life: thus the *Narcissus* bears 'an intolerable load of regrets and hopes' (p. 30)—intolerable because man's longing for past or future happiness finds no support outside himself and because his knowledge of his own mortality has no bearing on his fate.

We have noticed that Conrad commended Cooper for depicting the sea as 'in a subtle way a factor in the problem of existence'. If this is so, it is because it first forces man to register his existential predicament, and then offers him the chance of a reprieve. His predicament is his knowledge that his life is fugitive and solitary. The crew of the *Narcissus* may not find it easy to face their mortality steadily; but the novel continuously reminds *us* of it. A sustained succession of images doubles the seamen with

[13] *Childe Harold's Pilgrimage*, Book IV, stanzas 178–84. For a Romantic narrative of an ocean crossing much closer in detail to Conrad, see Chateaubriand, *Mémoires d'Outre-Tombe*, Book VI, Chapter 2 (Pléiade ed.).

the shades they will become. The forecastle berths look
like 'narrow niches for coffins in a ... mortuary'; they
'yawn black like graves tenanted by uneasy corpses'; the
Captain stands on the poop 'like a phantom above the
grave'; the First Mate crawls among the huddled sailors
'like an animal prowling among corpses'; men sleeping in
the moonlight on deck make 'dark mounds' like 'neglected
graves'. . . . Sleeping or waking, men are sheathed in death.
Very little pressure is required, therefore, to make them
feel the vertigo of mortality. The merest suspicion that the
sick Negro might really be entertaining a sinister 'visitor' is
enough to blow 'undreamt of subtleties' into their hearts.
And this contagion is destructive: once received, it turns
whole men into incomplete beings, dissolving self into
yearning and identity into aspiration. As the title of the
novel suggests, Wait converts sailors into narcissists. The
only remedy, therefore, is obligatory action. Since a human
life consists in rising above, offering resistance to, the
indifference of nature, to long for life is in fact (as the
narrator puts it) to long for unrest. Since the sea 'commands that toil be long and unceasing', it is well qualified
for this remedial role. Thus it does not long permit the
crew 'to meditate at ease upon the complicated and acrid
savour of existence' (p. 90). At once curse and cure, it
redeems them in spite of themselves.

   The alternatives of diseased introspection and un-
reflecting action find an extreme representation in Wait
and Singleton. This of course is well known. What is
perhaps not so obvious is the degree to which death is the
issue between them. The crisis in Singleton's life comes
after his long ordeal at the wheel, when he is forced to
concede the inevitability of his decay—that is, of his defeat
by the sea. 'He looked on the immortal sea with a groping
perception of its heartless might; he saw it unchanged,
black and foaming under the eternal scrutiny of the stars;
he heard its impatient voice calling to him out of a pitiless

vastness full of unrest, of turmoil, and of terror' (p. 99). The crisis in Wait's life, equally appropriately, comes with the calm. Treated by Donkin as if he were already a corpse, he is obliged to savour the full bitterness of his dissolution. For Singleton, death is an external antagonist, for Wait an internal corruption. These alternatives, which resolve themselves into two ways of being, Conrad articulates in two contrasting forms of language—the symbolic and the technical.

In *The Nigger of the 'Narcissus'* the symbolic mode is used when men decide to turn a reality that contradicts their desires into a symbol or surrogate for a more acceptable imaginary alternative. In this restricted sense, symbols become verbal projections—wish-fulfilling solutions of the kind proffered by what the narrator calls 'the obstinate clamour of sages', and scarcely less tainted than Podmore's intoxicated visions of salvation. The identification of such symbols (a favourite pastime of certain Conrad commentators who pursue their task in exactly the wrong direction) is what the crew naturally falls to when released from the necessities of work. They fall back heavily into themselves, the whole of their life turns into ambiguity before their eyes, and their will to act melts into an indefinable discontent. Such are the conditions of the symbolic mode; their effects are no less predictable. The men transform a dying man, who pretends to be ill when he looks well and well when he is moribund, into a fetish, a guru, an idol. This process is subtly rendered by the whole narrative— most strikingly perhaps in the men's rescue of Wait, when they feel that they are not only performing the rescue of a comrade but also participating in a ritual of resurrection; most explicitly after Wait has been restored to his re-painted cabin, which at night has 'the brilliance of a silver shrine where a black idol, reclining under its blanket, blinked its weary eyes and received our homage' (p. 105). Wait has become symbolic; that is to say, significant not in terms of himself, of what is happening to him, but in terms of the anxieties which he and his fate awaken in the crew.

Technical language, that is, the technical vocabulary of seafaring, on the other hand, is language stripped of all symbolic ambiguity because it has to serve a specific practical end. In *The Mirror of the Sea* Conrad claims that in its uncompromising adaptation to the reality of facts technical language confers a kind of moral integrity on its users. One does not have to believe this to see that the moral crises of the novel repeatedly present themselves as a collision between the two languages. Singleton is the only member of the crew to tackle directly Wait's 'awful and veiled familiar'.—'Are you dying?' he asks the startled and confused Negro. And when he receives a shakily affirmative reply: 'Well, get on with your dying', he declares, 'don't make a blamed fuss *with that job*. We can't help you' (p. 42, my italics). The incongruousness of Singleton's phrase is not a symptom of slack characterization; it is the product of a fictional tactic requiring symbolic questions to provoke technical answers. When Donkin, that *agent provocateur* of moral malaise, foments the beginning of a mutiny, and the men, summoned on deck, are bluntly asked by Allistoun: 'What do you want?', they suddenly find that they have lost all the words they know 'in the immensity of their vague and burning desire'. The narrator comments: 'They knew what they wanted, but they could not find anything worth saying' (pp. 132–7). It is perfectly consistent with Conrad's strategy in this novel that the Captain should close this episode by forcing Donkin to restore the belaying pin, which he had used as a missile the night before, to its proper—that is, its technical—place in the fore-rigging.[14]

---

[14] *Moby Dick* exploits this effect on a massive scale. I suspect, however, that Conrad's hostility to that novel has to do with the fact that the relationship between the two 'languages' in Melville is less dramatic than philosophical, given his far greater commitment to the symbolic mode.

Although *The Nigger of the 'Narcissus'* seems to enact the victory of the technical over the symbolic, it is important to see that this victory would be deprived of all significance if the symbolic mode were thought to be nothing but a pointless aberration. Both modes constitute a response to a prior common challenge—that of the sea. For that reason, they are not merely antagonists; they can be regarded as entering into a kind of dialogue with each other. To develop this suggestion would not be appropriate here.[15] It should be noted, however, that this 'dialogue' is composed of languages spoken by the same person—the participating narrator who tells his tale retrospectively, and who is therefore at one and the same time the seaman who has completed the voyage (and thus in possession of its final significance) and also the seaman caught in the un-predictabilities of process (and thus uncertain of what to think or do). In this elementary sense both languages are interdependent. Symbolic language gives expression to a craving for meaning; technical language makes possible an embodiment of meaning. Without technical language the demand for meaning would become vacuous; without the demand for meaning technical language would remain mere technique, and the voyage of the *Narcissus* nothing more interesting than an accomplished fact.

What I have called the 'dialogue' between these two voices is Conrad's solution to a dilemma which must be finally recognized as historical. Of course this solution, which accounts for the novel's irresistible buoyancy of tone, may be possible only locally and for a limited time; but the dilemma to which it responds is more generally typical. I have tried to show that in this novel it is provoked by an animistic conception of the sea whose origins I have traced to the Romantic period, and which embodies a

---

[15] The possibilities of this sort of analysis are brilliantly explored in M. M. Bakhtin's *The Dialogic Imagination*, ed. Michael Holquist, Austin University Press, 1982.

conception of the material universe pervasive in nineteenth-century thought. What could be more natural, then, than that it should awaken an historical response? In *The Nigger of the 'Narcissus'* the sea, far from neutralizing history, actually brings it to life, for it makes possible the articulation of two major voices of the Victorian age: the language of symbolism, in which we hear the poignancy of a lost metaphysic, and the language of technique, in which we recognize the confidence of a pragmatism responsible for many conquests and crimes, and much construction amidst much destruction.

NOTE ON THE TEXT

THE bibliographical history of *The Nigger of the 'Narcissus'* is analysed in detail by Kenneth Davis and Donald Rude in 'The Transmission of the Text of *The Nigger of the "Narcissus"*' in *Conradiana* V (1973), and by Robert Kimbrough in his critical edition of *The Nigger of the 'Narcissus'* published by W. W. Norton and Co. (1979). The main sequence is as follows:

(i) Manuscript, completed on 19 February 1897, with a few corrections added shortly after. (It survives virtually complete in the library of the Rosenbach Foundation, Philadelphia.)

(ii) Typescript, with minor corrections, made in Spring 1897. (Two fragments survive, one at Colgate University, the other in ' the Rosenbach Foundation.)

(iii) Presentation and copyright copies. Seven were printed on 29 July 1897; on one of these (now at Colgate University) Conrad made a few corrections.

(iv) Serial publication, in five monthly instalments (not corresponding to the chapter divisions) in the *New Review*, August–December 1897, from the type-settings of (iii).

(v) First American publication in book form, entitled *The Children of the Sea: A Tale of the Forecastle*, on 30 November 1897 by Dodd, Meade and Co., New York.

(vi) First English publication in book form, entitled *The Nigger of the 'Narcissus', a Tale of the Forecastle*, on 2 December 1897 by Heinemann, London, with a few textual refinements.

(vii) Corrected Text, made by Conrad in April 1916 from (vi) for the 'definitive, limited' Collected Edition planned by Heinemann.

(viii) Collected Edition, published by Heinemann in 1921.

(ix) Popular Edition, published by Dent from (vi), (vii) and (viii) in 1950.

(x) Critical Edition, based on (viii) and fully collated with (i) to (vii), by Robert Kimbrough, published by W. W. Norton and Co. in 1979.

The present edition is not a critical edition. It is based on the Dent text (ix) compared with the Collected Edition (viii) and the Norton edition (x). The conservative emendations made to the base text, listed below, remove a few inconsistencies of punctuation and typographical errors, correct one or two grammatical mistakes where they do not affect the idiosyncratic flavour of Conrad's style, and occasionally confirm readings from the Collected Edition. In some cases, marked (N), I have accepted the authority of the Norton edition.

6.7	*sat* for *set*
23.24	*out* for *hout*
23.25	*out* for *hout*
23.29	*Irish* for *Hirish*
26.3	*chain-cable* for *chain cable*
30.11	*uneventful* for *eventful* (N)
32.11	*bitts* for *bits*
51.12	*officially* for *technically* (N)
55.5	*upwards,* for *upwards;*
69.20	*lie down* for *lay down*
72.2	*cleat* for *cleet* (*cleat* on 65.8)
92.25	*head-earings* for *head-earrings*
94.17	*battered and* for *battered, and*
97.23	'. . . *hallo.*' for '. . . *hallo*'
98.24	'. . . *break 'im up.*' for '. . . *break 'im up*'
102.12	*courageously to* for *to courageously*
104.12	*glove* for *globe* (N)
106.17	*of course. . . .* for *of course . . .*
108.30	*at once* for *to once*
121.20	*imposed* for *hymposed*
123.29	'*Don't!*'— for '*Don't!*'
123.33	'*Drop it!*'— for '*Drop it!*'
125.12	'*All right. . . .*' for '*All right . . .*'

126.7   *withdrew.... * for *withdrew ...*
137.17   *Years ago—* for *Years ago;*
151.5   *Yer nobody!* for *Yer nobody.*
151.19   *disturbing:* for *disturbing;*
152.16   *as* for *has*
170.1   *Ye're* for *Yer* (N)

A full account of the bibliographical history of the *Preface* is provided by Thomas Lavoie in 'Textual History and Textual Notes: the "Preface"', in the Norton edition. David R. Smith, in *Conrad's Manifesto: Preface to a Career* (Philadelphia, 1966), has transcribed the manuscript and printed it with Conrad's foreword to the 1914 Doubleday 'Deep Sea' edition of Conrad's works, entitled 'To My Readers in America'. The summary that follows indicates the importance the *Preface* held for Conrad.

(i) Manuscript, written immediately after the completion of the novel, in Spring 1897 (now in the Rosenbach Foundation).

(ii) Typescript, which introduces minor punctuation changes, and omits the fourth-to-last paragraph of the manuscript on the advice of Edward Garnett, as being too self-deprecatory (now in the Colgate University Library).

(iii) Afterword, printed immediately after the final (December) instalment of the *New Review* serialization.

(iv) Pamphlet, amended by Conrad and printed at his instigation by Lovick, Hythe, Kent, in 1902.

(v) Essay, under the title 'The Art of Fiction', published in *Harper's Weekly*, New York, on 13 May 1905.

(vi) Pamphlet, under the title *Joseph Conrad on the Art of Writing*, together with 'To My Readers in America' (see above), published by Doubleday, New York, in April 1914.

(vii) Preface, to *The Nigger of the 'Narcissus'*, in the Collected Edition, Heinemann, 1921.

The following text is based on the 1950 Dent edition, collated with the 1921 Collected Edition. There are substantial differences in punctuation between the two texts. A few emendations have been made, as follows:

viii.21   *hearts:* for *hearts,*
ix.25   *sentences,* for *sentences*
ix.35   *who,* for *who*
x.7   *see!* for *see.*
x.8   *everything!* for *everything.*
x.28   *fate—* for *fate,*
xi.3   *of),* for *of,)*
xi.8   *Art for Art* for *Art for Art,*
xi.11   *at times, and faintly,* for *at times and faintly*
xi.16   *arms;* for *arms,*

The deleted paragraph, originally placed between paragraphs 8 and 9 of the *Preface* in its final form, read as follows:

It may seem strange if not downright suspicious that so much should be said in introduction to the unimportant tale of the sea which follows. It may also appear the height of conceit or folly since every word of the preface may be brought in judgment against the work it is meant to introduce. But a preface—if anything—is spoken in perfect good faith, as one speaks to friends, and in the hope that the unprovoked confidence shall be treated with scrupulous fairness. And, after all, everyone desires to be understood; We all with mutual indulgence give way to the pressing need of explaining ourselves—the politician, the prophet, the fool, the bricklayer they all do it: and if so then why not the writer of tales who is, as far as I know, no greater criminal than any of these. It is true that the disclosure of the aim otherwise than by the effective effort towards it is a confession of weakness. Yet in the reign of art such an avowal is not so fatal as it would be elsewhere. For in art alone of all the enterprises of men there is a meaning in endeavour disassociated from success and merit—if any merit there be—is not wholly centred in achievement but may be faintly discerned in the aim.

SELECT BIBLIOGRAPHY

DENT's Collected Edition, 1946—(based on the Uniform Edition, 1923–8) has all Conrad's works except for *The Inheritors* and *The Nature of a Crime* (which are largely Ford Madox Ford's), *The Sisters*, and the dramatizations. *Congo Diary and Other Uncollected Pieces* (ed. Zdzisław Najder, 1978) contains Conrad's Congo notebooks, *The Sisters*, *The Nature of a Crime*, and other pieces.

The most important editions of Conrad's letters are as follows: William Blackburn (ed.), *Joseph Conrad: Letters to William Blackwood and David J. Meldrum* (1958), G. Jean-Aubry, *Joseph Conrad: Life and Letters* (1927), Zdzisław Najder (ed.), *Conrad's Polish Background: Letters to and from Polish Friends* (1964), C. T. Watts (ed.), *Joseph Conrad's Letters to R. B. Cunninghame Graham* (1969). There are further collections of letters edited by Richard Curle (1928), Edward Garnett (1928), J. A. Gee and P. J. Sturm (1940), D. B. J. Randall (1968), and G. Jean-Aubry (1930).

There are many biographies and personal memoirs of Conrad; the most important memoirs are those by Jessie Conrad (1926 and 1935), Richard Curle (1928), and Ford Madox Ford (1924), and there are further memoirs by Borys Conrad (1970) and John Conrad (1981). The best biographies of Conrad are those by Jocelyn Baines (1960), G. Jean-Aubry (1957), Bernard Meyer (a 'Psychoanalytic' biography, 1967), and Roger Tennant (1981), and there are large critical biographies by Frederick Karl (1979) and Ian Watt (*Conrad in the Nineteenth Century*, 1980).

There are biographically related studies which make substantial use of background or manuscript material of which the most important are J. D. Gordan, *Joseph Conrad: The Making of a Novelist* (1941), Norman Sherry, *Conrad's Eastern World* (1966) and *Conrad's Western World* (1971). There are further relevant studies by Jerry Allen (1965), Edward Crankshaw (1930), Richard Curle (1914), R. R. Hodges (1967), R. L. Mégroz (1931), Gustav Morf (1930 and 1976), J. H. Retinger (1941), and Norman Sherry (1972).

A very large number of critical books have now been published on

Conrad. The ones to be most strongly recommended are Jacques Berthoud, *Joseph Conrad: The Major Phase* (1978), H. M. Daleski, *Joseph Conrad: The Way of Dispossession* (1977), A. J. Guerard, *Conrad the Novelist* (1958), Jeremy Hawthorn, *Joseph Conrad: Language and Fictional Self-Consciousness* (1979), and E. K. Hay, *The Political Novels of Joseph Conrad* (1963). There are other studies of interest by C. B. Cox (1974), Avrom Fleishman (1967), Douglas Hewitt (1952), Bruce Johnson (1971), Paul Kirschner (1968), and Thomas Moser (1957). There are important essays on Conrad in Graham Hough, *Image and Experience* (1960), J. Hillis Miller, *Poets of Reality* (1966), and Norman Sherry (ed.), *Conrad: The Critical Heritage* (1973) and *Joseph Conrad: A Commemoration* (1976).

A CHRONOLOGY OF JOSEPH CONRAD

1857	3 December: Born Józef Teodor Konrad Korzeniowski, of Polish parents in the Ukraine.
1861	His father, poet and translator Apollo Korzeniowski, arrested for patriotic conspiracy.
1862	Conrad's parents exiled to Vologda, Russia; their son accompanies them.
1865	Death of his mother.
1869	Death of Apollo Korzeniowski in Kraków; Conrad comes under the protection of his uncle, Tadeusz Borbrowski.
1874	Leaves Poland for Marseilles to become a trainee seaman with the French merchant navy.
1876	As a 'steward' on the *Sainte-Antoine*, becomes acquainted with Dominic Cervoni (who appears in *The Mirror of the Sea* and *The Arrow of Gold* and is the source for Nostromo, and Peyrol in *The Rover*).
1877	Possibly involved in smuggling arms to the Spanish 'Carlists' from Marseilles.
1878	March: Shoots himself in the chest in Marseilles but is not seriously injured; as a direct result of this suicide attempt his uncle clears his debts. April: Joins his first British ship, the *Mavis*, and later in the same year joins *The Skimmer of the Sea*. Would have become liable for Russian military service if he had stayed with the French merchant navy.
ʿ1886	Becomes a British citizen and passes the examination for a Master's certificate.
1887	Is injured on the *Highland Forest* and hospitalized in Singapore.
1887–8	Gets to know the Malay archipelago as an officer of the *Vidar*.
1888	Master of the *Otago*, his only command.

1889 Resigns from the *Otago*, settles briefly in London and begins to write *Almayer's Folly*. Begins a lasting friendship with Marguerite Poradowska.

1890 Works in the Belgian Congo for the Société Anonyme pour le Commerce du Haut-Congo.

1891–3 His pleasantest experience at sea, as an officer of the *Torrens*; meets John Galsworthy, who is among the passengers and becomes a loyal friend.

1893 Autumn: Meets Jessie George.

1894 February: Death of Tadeusz Bobrowski. October: *Almayer's Folly* accepted by Unwin. Meets Edward Garnett, Unwin's reader and an influential literary friend.

1895 *Almayer's Folly* published.

1896 *An Outcast of the Islands* published. Becomes acquainted with H. G. Wells. 24 March: marriage to Jessie George. Begins work on *The Rescue*.

1897 *The Nigger of the 'Narcissus'* published. Meets Henry James and R. B. Cunninghame Graham (to be a close friend and the source for Gould in *Nostromo*).

1898 *Tales of Unrest* ('Karain', 'The Idiots', 'An Outpost of Progress', 'The Return', 'The Lagoon') published. Enters into collaboration with Ford Madox Ford (then Hueffer). Takes over from Ford the lease of a Kentish farmhouse, 'The Pent'. Friendship with Stephen Crane. Borys Conrad born.

1898–9 'Heart of Darkness' serialized in *Blackwood's*.

1899 J. B. Pinker becomes Conrad's literary agent.

1899–1900 *Lord Jim* serialized in *Blackwood's*.

1900 Stephen Crane dies. *Lord Jim* published as a book.

1901 *The Inheritors* (collaboration with Ford) published.

1902 *Youth: and Two Other Stories* ('Youth', 'Heart of Darkness', 'The End of the Tether') published.

1903 *Typhoon: And Other Stories* ('Typhoon', 'Amy Foster', 'Falk', 'Tomorrow') and *Romance* (collaboration with Ford) published.

1904 Jessie Conrad injures her knees and is partially disabled for life. *Nostromo* published.

1906 Meets Arthur Marwood, who becomes his closest friend John Conrad born. *The Mirror of the Sea* published.

1907   The Conrads move to The Someries, Luton Hoo. *The Secret Agent* published.

1908   *A Set of Six* ('Gaspar Ruiz', 'The Informer', 'The Brute', 'An Anarchist', 'The Duel', 'Il Conde') published.

1909   Quarrels with Ford over his contributions to *The English Review*. The Conrads move to a cottage at Aldington, near 'The Pent'.

1910   Completion of *Under Western Eyes* accompanied by a nervous breakdown; Conrad lies in bed holding 'converse with the characters' of the novel. On his recovery the Conrads move to Capel House, Orlestone.

1911   *Under Western Eyes* published.

1912   *A Personal Record* and *'Twixt Land and Sea* ('A Smile of Fortune', 'The Secret Sharer', 'Freya of the Seven Isles') published.

1913   *Chance* published.

1914   *Chance* has good sales, especially in America; the earlier work now finds a larger public. The Conrads visit Poland and are nearly trapped by the outbreak of war.

1915   *Within the Tides* ('The Planter of Malata', 'The Partner', 'The Inn of the Two Witches') and *Victory* published.

1917   *The Shadow-Line* published. Conrad begins to write Author's Notes for a collected edition of his works.

1919   *The Arrow of Gold* published. The Conrads move to Oswalds, Bishopsbourne, near Canterbury.

1920   *The Rescue* published, 24 years after it was begun.

1921   Visit to Corsica for research on *Suspense*. Conrad in poor health. *Notes on Life and Letters* published.

1923   Conrad visits America and is lionized.

1924   May: Declines the offer of a knighthood. 3 August: Dies of a heart attack at Oswalds.

1924   *The Nature of a Crime* (collaboration with Ford) published.

1925   *Tales of Hearsay* ('The Warrior's Soul', 'Prince Roman', 'The Tale', 'The Black Mate') and *Suspense* published.

1926   *Last Essays* published.

1928   *The Sisters* (fragment) published.

THE NIGGER OF THE 'NARCISSUS'

A TALE OF THE SEA

To
Edward Garnett*
this tale
about my friends
of the sea

PREFACE

A work that aspires, however humbly, to the condition of art should carry its justification in every line. And art itself may be defined as a single-minded attempt to render the highest kind of justice to the visible universe, by bringing to light the truth, manifold and one, underlying its every aspect. It is an attempt to find in its forms, in its colours, in its light, in its shadows, in the aspects of matter and in the facts of life what of each is fundamental, what is enduring and essential—their one illuminating and convincing quality—the very truth of their existence. The artist, then, like the thinker or the scientist, seeks the truth and makes his appeal. Impressed by the aspect of the world the thinker plunges into ideas, the scientist into facts—whence, presently, emerging they make their appeal to those qualities of our being that fit us best for the hazardous enterprise of living. They speak authoritatively to our common-sense, to our intelligence, to our desire of peace or to our desire of unrest; not seldom to our prejudices, sometimes to our fears, often to our egoism—but always to our credulity. And their words are heard with reverence, for their concern is with weighty matters: with the cultivation of our minds and the proper care of our bodies, with the attainment of our ambitions, with the perfection of the means and the glorification of our precious aims.

It is otherwise with the artist.

Confronted by the same enigmatical spectacle the

artist descends within himself, and in that lonely region
of stress and strife, if he be deserving and fortunate,
he finds the terms of his appeal. His appeal is made
to our less obvious capacities: to that part of our nature
which, because of the warlike conditions of existence,
is necessarily kept out of sight within the more resisting
and hard qualities—like the vulnerable body within
a steel armour. His appeal is less loud, more profound,
less distinct, more stirring—and sooner forgotten.
Yet its effect endures forever. The changing wisdom
of successive generations discards ideas, questions facts,
demolishes theories. But the artist appeals to that
part of our being which is not dependent on wisdom;
to that in us which is a gift and not an acquisition—
and, therefore, more permanently enduring. He speaks
to our capacity for delight and wonder, to the sense of
mystery surrounding our lives; to our sense of pity, and
beauty, and pain; to the latent feeling of fellowship
with all creation—and to the subtle but invincible
conviction of solidarity that knits together the loneliness of innumerable hearts: to the solidarity in dreams,
in joy, in sorrow, in aspirations, in illusions, in hope,
in fear, which binds men to each other, which binds
together all humanity—the dead to the living and the
living to the unborn.

  It is only some such train of thought, or rather of
feeling, that can in a measure explain the aim of the
attempt, made in the tale which follows, to present
an unrestful episode in the obscure lives of a few indi-
viduals out of all the disregarded multitude of the bewildered, the simple and the voiceless. For, if any
part of truth dwells in the belief confessed above, it becomes evident that there is not a place of splendour or
a dark corner of the earth that does not deserve, if
only a passing glance of wonder and pity. The motive

then, may be held to justify the matter of the work; but this preface, which is simply an avowal of endeavour, cannot end here—for the avowal is not yet complete.

Fiction—if it at all aspires to be art—appeals to temperament. And in truth it must be, like painting, like music, like all art, the appeal of one temperament to all the other innumerable temperaments whose subtle and resistless power endows passing events with their true meaning, and creates the moral, the emotional atmosphere of the place and time. Such an appeal to be effective must be an impression conveyed through the senses; and, in fact, it cannot be made in any other way, because temperament, whether individual or collective, is not amenable to persuasion. All art, therefore, appeals primarily to the senses, and the artistic aim when expressing itself in written words must also make its appeal through the senses, if its high desire is to reach the secret spring of responsive emotions. It must strenuously aspire to the plasticity of sculpture, to the colour of painting, and to the magic suggestiveness of music—which is the art of arts. And it is only through complete, unswerving devotion to the perfect blending of form and substance; it is only through an unremitting never-discouraged care for the shape and ring of sentences, that an approach can be made to plasticity, to colour, and that the light of magic suggestiveness may be brought to play for an evanescent instant over the commonplace surface of words: of the old, old words, worn thin, defaced by ages of careless usage.

The sincere endeavour to accomplish that creative task, to go as far on that road as his strength will carry him, to go undeterred by faltering, weariness or reproach, is the only valid justification for the worker in prose. And if his conscience is clear, his answer to those who, in the

fulness of a wisdom which looks for immediate profit,
demand specifically to be edified, consoled, amused; who
demand to be promptly improved, or encouraged, or
frightened, or shocked, or charmed, must run thus:—
My task which I am trying to achieve is, by the power
of the written word to make you hear, to make you feel
—it is, before all, to make you *see*! That—and no more,
and it is everything! If I succeed, you shall find there
according to your deserts: encouragement, consolation,
fear, charm—all you demand—and, perhaps, also that
glimpse of truth for which you have forgotten to ask.

To snatch in a moment of courage, from the remorseless rush of time, a passing phase of life, is only the beginning of the task. The task approached in tenderness and faith is to hold up unquestioningly, without
choice and without fear, the rescued fragment before
all eyes in the light of a sincere mood. It is to show
its vibration, its colour, its form; and through its movement, its form, and its colour, reveal the substance of
its truth—disclose its inspiring secret: the stress and
passion within the core of each convincing moment.
In a single-minded attempt of that kind, if one be deserving and fortunate, one may perchance attain to
such clearness of sincerity that at last the presented
vision of regret or pity, of terror or mirth, shall awaken
in the hearts of the beholders that feeling of unavoidable solidarity; of the solidarity in mysterious origin,
in toil, in joy, in hope, in uncertain fate—which binds
men to each other and all mankind to the visible world.

It is evident that he who, rightly or wrongly, holds
by the convictions expressed above cannot be faithful
to any one of the temporary formulas of his craft. The
enduring part of them—the truth which each only im-
perfectly veils—should abide with him as the most
precious of his possessions, but they all: Realism,

Romanticism, Naturalism, even the unofficial sentimentalism (which like the poor, is exceedingly difficult
to get rid of), all these gods must, after a short period
of fellowship, abandon him—even on the very threshold
of the temple—to the stammerings of his conscience
and to the outspoken consciousness of the difficulties
of his work. In that uneasy solitude the supreme cry
of Art for Art itself, loses the exciting ring of its apparent immorality. It sounds far off. It has ceased
to be a cry, and is heard only as a whisper, often incomprehensible, but at times, and faintly, encouraging.

Sometimes, stretched at ease in the shade of a road-
side tree, we watch the motions of a labourer in a distant field, and after a time, begin to wonder languidly
as to what the fellow may be at. We watch the movements of his body, the waving of his arms; we see
him bend down, stand up, hesitate, begin again. It
may add to the charm of an idle hour to be told the
purpose of his exertions. If we know he is trying to
lift a stone, to dig a ditch, to uproot a stump, we look
with a more real interest at his efforts; we are disposed
to condone the jar of his agitation upon the restfulness
of the landscape; and even, if in a brotherly frame of
mind, we may bring ourselves to forgive his failure.
We understood his object, and, after all, the fellow has
tried, and perhaps he had not the strength—and perhaps he had not the knowledge. We forgive, go on our
way—and forget.

And so it is with the workman of art. Art is long
and life is short, and success is very far off. And thus,
doubtful of strength to travel so far, we talk a little
about the aim—the aim of art, which, like life itself,
is inspiring, difficult—obscured by mists. It is not
in the clear logic of a triumphant conclusion; it is not
in the unveiling of one of those heartless secrets which

are called the Laws of Nature.   It is not less great, but
only more difficult.

To arrest, for the space of a breath, the hands busy
about the work of the earth, and compel men entranced
by the sight of distant goals to glance for a moment at
the surrounding vision of form and colour, of sunshine
and shadows; to make them pause for a look, for a sigh,
for a smile—such is the aim, difficult and evanescent,
and reserved only for a very few to achieve.   But sometimes, by the deserving and the fortunate, even that
task is accomplished.   And when it is accomplished—
behold!—all the truth of life is there: a moment of
vision, a sigh, a smile—and the return to an eternal rest.

1897.   J. C.

THE NIGGER OF THE
'NARCISSUS'

. . . My Lord in his discourse discovered
a great deal of love to this ship.

Diary of Samuel Pepys

THE NIGGER OF THE "NARCISSUS"

THE
NIGGER OF THE "NARCISSUS"

CHAPTER ONE

MR. BAKER, chief mate of the ship *Narcissus*,* stepped in one stride out of his lighted cabin into the darkness of the quarter-deck. Above his head, on the break of the poop, the night-watchman rang a double stroke. It was nine o'clock. Mr. Baker, speaking up to the man above him, asked:—"Are all the hands aboard, Knowles?"

The man limped down the ladder, then said reflectively:—

"I think so, sir. All our old chaps are there, and a lot of new men has come. . . . . They must be all there."

"Tell the boatswain to send all hands aft," went on Mr. Baker; "and tell one of the youngsters to bring a good lamp here. I want to muster*our crowd."

The main deck was dark aft, but halfway from forward, through the open doors of the forecastle, two streaks of brilliant light cut the shadow of the quiet night that lay upon the ship. A hum of voices was heard there, while port and starboard, in the illuminated doorways, silhouettes of moving men appeared for a moment, very black, without relief, like figures cut out of sheet tin. The ship was ready for sea. The carpenter had driven in the last wedge of the main-

3

hatch battens, and, throwing down his maul,* had wiped his face with great deliberation, just on the stroke of five. The decks had been swept, the windlass oiled and made ready to heave up the anchor; the big tow-rope lay in long bights along one side of the main deck, with one end carried up and hung over the bows, in readiness for the tug that would come paddling and hissing noisily, hot and smoky, in the limpid, cool quietness of the early morning. The captain was ashore, where he had been engaging some new hands to make up his full crew; and, the work of the day over, the ship's officers had kept out of the way, glad of a little breathing-time. Soon after dark the few liberty-men* and the new hands began to arrive in shore-boats rowed by white-clad Asiatics, who clamoured fiercely for pay-ment before coming alongside the gangway-ladder. The feverish and shrill babble of Eastern language struggled against the masterful tones of tipsy seamen, who argued against brazen claims and dishonest hopes by profane shouts. The resplendent and bestarred peace of the East was torn into squalid tatters by howls of rage and shrieks of lament raised over sums ranging from five annas* to half a rupee;* and every soul afloat in Bombay Harbour* became aware that the new hands were joining the *Narcissus*.

Gradually the distracting noise had subsided. The boats came no longer in splashing clusters of three or four together, but dropped alongside singly, in a subdued buzz of expostulation cut short by a "Not a pice* more! You go to the devil!" from some man staggering up the accommodation-ladder—a dark figure, with a long bag poised on the shoulder. In the forecastle the new-comers, upright and swaying amongst corded boxes and bundles of bedding, made friends with the old hands, who sat one above another in the two tiers of bunks, gazing at their future shipmates with glances critical but friendly. The two forecastle lamps were turned up high, and shed an intense hard glare; shore-going round hats were pushed far on the backs of heads, or rolled about on the deck amongst the chain-cables; white collars, undone, stuck out on each side of red faces; big arms in white sleeves gesticulated; the growling voices hummed steady amongst bursts of laughter and hoarse calls. "Here, sonny, take that bunk! . . . Don't you do it! . . . What's your last ship? . . . I know her. . . . Three years ago, in Puget Sound.* . . . This here berth leaks, I tell you! . . . Come on; give us a chance to swing that chest! . . . Did you bring a bottle, any of you shore toffs? . . . Give us a bit of 'baccy. . . . I know her; her skipper drank himself to death. . . . He was a dandy boy! . . . Liked his lotion inside, he did! . . . No! . . . Hold your row, you chaps! . . . I tell you, you came on board a hooker,* where they get their money's worth out of poor Jack,* by——! . . ."

A little fellow, called Craik and nicknamed Belfast, abused the ship violently, romancing on principle, just to give the new hands something to think over. Archie, sitting aslant on his sea-chest, kept his knees out of the way, and pushed the needle steadily through a white patch in a pair of blue trousers. Men in black jackets and stand-up collars, mixed with men bare-footed, bare-armed, with coloured shirts open on hairy chests, pushed against one another in the middle of the forecastle. The group swayed, reeled, turning upon itself with the motion of a scrimmage, in a haze of tobacco smoke. All were speaking together, swearing at every second word. A Russian Finn, wearing a yellow shirt

with pink stripes, stared upwards, dreamy-eyed, from
under a mop of tumbled hair. Two young giants with
smooth, baby faces—two Scandinavians—helped each
other to spread their bedding, silent, and smiling placidly at the tempest of good-humoured and meaningless
curses. Old Singleton, the oldest able seaman in the
ship, sat apart on the deck right under the lamps, stripped to the waist, tattooed like a cannibal chief all over
his powerful chest and enormous biceps. Between the
blue and red patterns his white skin gleamed like satin;
his bare back was propped against the heel of the bowsprit, and he held a book at arm's length before his
big, sunburnt face. With his spectacles and a venerable white beard, he resembled a learned and savage
patriarch, the incarnation of barbarian wisdom serene
in the blasphemous turmoil of the world. He was
intensely absorbed, and as he turned the pages an
expression of grave surprise would pass over his rugged
features. He was reading "Pelham."* The popularity
of Bulwer Lytton in the forecastles of Southern-going
ships is a wonderful and bizarre phenomenon. What
ideas do his polished and so curiously insincere sentences
awaken in the simple minds of the big children who
people those dark and wandering places of the earth?
What meaning their rough, inexperienced souls can
find in the elegant verbiage of his pages? What excitement?—what forgetfulness?—what appeasement?
Mystery! Is it the fascination of the incomprehensible?—is it the charm of the impossible? Or are those
beings who exist beyond the pale of life stirred by his
tales as by an enigmatical disclosure of a resplendent
world that exists within the frontier of infamy and filth,
within that border of dirt and hunger, of misery and
dissipation, that comes down on all sides to the water's
edge of the incorruptible ocean, and is the only thing

they know of life, the only thing they see of surrounding land—those life-long prisoners of the sea? Mystery!
Singleton, who had sailed to the southward since
the age of twelve, who in the last forty-five years had
lived (as we had calculated from his papers) no more
than forty months ashore—old Singleton, who boasted,
with the mild composure of long years well spent, that
generally from the day he was paid off from one ship
till the day he shipped in another he seldom was in a
condition to distinguish daylight—old Singleton sat
unmoved in the clash of voices and cries, spelling
through "Pelham" with slow labour, and lost in an
absorption profound enough to resemble a trance. He
breathed regularly. Every time he turned the book
in his enormous and blackened hands the muscles of
his big white arms rolled slightly under the smooth
skin. Hidden by the white moustache, his lips, stained
with tobacco-juice that trickled down the long beard,
moved in inward whisper. His bleared eyes gazed
fixedly from behind the glitter of black-rimmed glasses.
Opposite to him, and on a level with his face, the ship's
cat sat on the barrel of the windlass in the pose of a
crouching chimera, blinking its green eyes at its old
friend. It seemed to meditate a leap on to the old
man's lap over the bent back of the ordinary seaman
who sat at Singleton's feet. Young Charley was lean
and long-necked. The ridge of his backbone made a
chain of small hills under the old shirt. His face of a
street-boy—a face precocious, sagacious, and ironic,
with deep downward folds on each side of the thin, wide
mouth—hung low over his bony knees. He was learn-
ing to make a lanyard knot with a bit of an old rope.
Small drops of perspiration stood out on his bulging
forehead; he sniffed strongly from time to time, glancing
out of the corners of his restless eyes at the old seaman,

who took no notice of the puzzled youngster muttering at his work.

The noise increased. Little Belfast seemed, in the heavy heat of the forecastle, to boil with facetious fury. His eyes danced; in the crimson of his face, comical as a mask, the mouth yawned black, with strange grimaces. Facing him, a half-undressed man held his sides, and, throwing his head back, laughed with wet eyelashes. Others stared with amazed eyes. Men sitting doubled up in the upper bunks smoked short pipes, swinging bare brown feet above the heads of those who, sprawling below on sea-chests, listened, smiling stupidly or scornfully. Over the white rims of berths stuck out heads with blinking eyes; but the bodies were lost in the gloom of those places, that re-sembled narrow niches for coffins in a whitewashed and lighted mortuary. Voices buzzed louder. Archie, with compressed lips, drew himself in, seemed to shrink into a smaller space, and sewed steadily, industrious and dumb. Belfast shrieked like an inspired Dervish:—
". . . So I seez to him, boys, seez I, 'Beggin' yer pardon, sorr,' seez I to that second mate of that steamer—'beggin' your-r-r pardon, sorr, the Board of Trade*must 'ave been drunk when they granted you your certificate!' 'What do you say, you——!' seez he, comin' at me like a mad bull . . . all in his white clothes; and I up with my tar-pot and cap-sizes it all over his blamed lovely face and his lovely jacket. . . . 'Take that!' seez I. 'I am a sailor, anyhow, you nosing, skipper-licking, useless, sooper-floos bridge-stanchion, you!' 'That's the kind of man I am!' shouts I. . . . You should have seed him skip, boys! Drowned, blind with tar, he was! So . . ."

"Don't 'ee believe him! He never upset no tar;

I was there!" shouted somebody. The two Norwegians sat on a chest side by side, alike and placid, resembling a pair of love-birds on a perch, and with round eyes stared innocently; but the Russian Finn, in the racket of explosive shouts and rolling laughter, remained motionless, limp and dull, like a deaf man without a backbone. Near him Archie smiled at his needle. A broad-chested, slow-eyed newcomer spoke deliberately to Belfast during an exhausted lull in the noise:—— "I wonder any of the mates here are alive yet with such a chap as you on board! I concloode they ain't that bad now, if you had the taming of them, sonny."

"Not bad! Not bad!" screamed Belfast. "If it wasn't for us sticking together. . . . . Not bad! They ain't never bad when they ain't got a chawnce, blast their black 'arts. . . ." He foamed, whirling his arms, then suddenly grinned and, taking a tablet of black tobacco out of his pocket, bit a piece off with a funny show of ferocity. Another new hand—a man with shifty eyes and a yellow hatchet face, who had been listening open-mouthed in the shadow of the midship locker—observed in a squeaky voice:—"Well, it's a 'omeward trip, anyhow. Bad or good, I can do it on my 'ed—s'long as I get 'ome. And I can look after my rights! I will show 'em!" All the heads turned towards him. Only the ordinary seaman and the cat took no notice. He stood with arms akimbo, a little fellow with white eyelashes. He looked as if he had known all the degradations and all the furies. He looked as if he had been cuffed, kicked, rolled in the mud; he looked as if he had been scratched, spat upon, pelted with unmentionable filth . . . and he smiled with a sense of security at the faces around. His ears were bending down under the weight of his battered felt hat. The torn tails of his black coat

flapped in fringes about the calves of his legs. He
unbuttoned the only two buttons that remained and
every one saw that he had no shirt under it. It was
his deserved misfortune that those rags which nobody
could possibly be supposed to own looked on him as
if they had been stolen. His neck was long and thin;
his eyelids were red; rare hairs hung about his jaws;
his shoulders were peaked and drooped like the broken
wings of a bird; all his left side was caked with mud
which showed that he had lately slept in a wet ditch.
He had saved his inefficient carcass from violent destruction by running away from an American ship*where,
in a moment of forgetful folly, he had dared to engage
himself; and he had knocked about for a fortnight
ashore in the native quarter, cadging for drinks, starving,
sleeping on rubbish-heaps, wandering in sunshine: a
startling visitor from a world of nightmares. He stood
repulsive and smiling in the sudden silence. This clean
white forecastle was his refuge; the place where he could
be lazy; where he could wallow, and lie and eat—and
curse the food he ate; where he could display his talents
for shirking work, for cheating, for cadging; where he
could find surely some one to wheedle and some one
to bully—and where he would be paid for doing all
this. They all knew him. Is there a spot on earth
where such a man is unknown, an ominous survival
testifying to the eternal fitness of lies and impudence?
A taciturn long-armed shellback,* with hooked fingers,
who had been lying on his back smoking, turned in his
bed to examine him dispassionately, then, over his
head, sent a long jet of clear saliva towards the door.
They all knew him! He was the man that cannot steer,
that cannot splice, that dodges the work on dark nights;
that, aloft, holds on frantically with both arms and
legs, and swears at the wind, the sleet, the darkness;

the man who curses the sea while others work. The
man who is the last out and the first in when all hands
are called. The man who can't do most things and
won't do the rest. The pet of philanthropists and self-
seeking landlubbers. The sympathetic and deserving
creature that knows all about his rights, but knows
nothing of courage, of endurance, and of the unex-
pressed faith, of the unspoken loyalty that knits together a ship's company. The independent offspring
of the ignoble freedom of the slums full of disdain and
hate for the austere servitude of the sea.

Some one cried at him: "What's your name?"—
"Donkin," he said, looking round with cheerful effront-
ery.—"What are you?" asked another voice.—"Why,
a sailor like you, old man," he replied, in a tone that
meant to be hearty but was impudent.—"Blamme if
you don't look a blamed sight worse than a broken-
down fireman," was the comment in a convinced
mutter. Charley lifted his head and piped in a cheeky
voice: "He is a man and a sailor"—then wiping his
nose with the back of his hand bent down industriously
over his bit of rope. A few laughed. Others stared
doubtfully. The ragged newcomer was indignant—
"That's a fine way to welcome a chap into a fo'c'sle,"
he snarled. "Are you men or a lot of 'artless canny-
bals?"—"Don't take your shirt off*for a word, shipmate," called out Belfast, jumping up in front, fiery,
menacing, and friendly at the same time.—"Is that
'ere bloke blind?" asked the indomitable scarecrow,
looking right and left with affected surprise. "Can't
'ee see I 'aven't got no shirt?"

He held both his arms out crosswise and shook the
rags that hung over his bones with dramatic effect.
" 'Cos why?" he continued very loud. "The bloody
Yankees been tryin' to jump my guts out*'cos I stood

up for my rights like a good 'un. I am an Englishman, I am. They set upon me an' I 'ad to run. That's why. A'n't yer never seed a man 'ard up? Yah! What kind of blamed ship is this? I'm dead broke. I 'aven't got nothink. No bag, no bed, no blanket, no shirt—not a bloomin' rag but what I stand in. But I 'ad the 'art to stand up agin' them Yankees. 'As any of you 'art enough to spare a pair of old pants for a chum?"

He knew how to conquer the naïve instincts of that crowd. In a moment they gave him their compassion, jocularly, contemptuously, or surlily; and at first it took the shape of a blanket thrown at him as he stood there with the white skin of his limbs showing his human kinship through the black fantasy of his rags. Then a pair of old shoes fell at his muddy feet. With a cry:— "From under," a rolled-up pair of canvas trousers, heavy with tar stains, struck him on the shoulder. The gust of their benevolence sent a wave of sentimental pity through their doubting hearts. They were touched by their own readiness to alleviate a shipmate's misery. Voices cried:—"We will fit you out, old man." Murmurs: "Never seed seech a hard case. . . . Poor beggar. . . . I've got an old singlet. . . . Will that be of any use to you? . . . Take it, matey. . . ." Those friendly murmurs filled the forecastle. He pawed around with his naked foot, gathering the things in a heap and looked about for more. Unemotional Archie perfunctorily contributed to the pile an old cloth cap with the peak torn off. Old Singleton, lost in the serene regions of fiction, read on unheeding. Charley, pitiless with the wisdom of youth, squeaked:—"If you want brass buttons for your new unyforms I've got two for you." The filthy object of universal charity shook his fist at the young-

ster.—"I'll make you keep this 'ere fo'c'sle clean,
young feller," he snarled viciously. "Never you fear.
I will learn you to be civil to an able seaman, you
ignerant ass." He glared harmfully, but saw Singleton
shut his book, and his little beady eyes began to roam
from berth to berth.—"Take that bunk by the door
there—it's pretty fair," suggested Belfast. So advised, he gathered the gifts at his feet, pressed them in
a bundle against his breast, then looked cautiously at
the Russian Finn, who stood on one side with an unconscious gaze, contemplating, perhaps, one of those
weird visions that haunt the men of his race.—"Get
out of my road, Dutchy," said the victim of Yankee
brutality. The Finn did not move—did not hear.
"Get out, blast ye," shouted the other, shoving him
aside with his elbow. "Get out, you blanked*deaf and
dumb fool. Get out." The man staggered, recovered
himself, and gazed at the speaker in silence.—"Those
damned furriners should be kept under," opined the
amiable Donkin to the forecastle. "If you don't
teach 'em their place they put on you like anythink."
He flung all his worldly possessions into the empty
bed-place, gauged with another shrewd look the risks
of the proceeding, then leaped up to the Finn, who
stood pensive and dull.—"I'll teach you to swell
around," he yelled. "I'll plug your eyes for you, you
blooming square-head."* Most of the men were now
in their bunks and the two had the forecastle clear to
themselves. The development of the destitute Donkin
aroused interest. He danced all in tatters before the
amazed Finn, squaring from a distance at the heavy,
unmoved face. One or two men cried encouragingly:
"Go it, Whitechapel!"*settling themselves luxuriously
in their beds to survey the fight. Others shouted:
"Shut yer row! . . . Go an' put yer 'ed in a

bag! . . . " The hubbub was recommencing. Suddenly many heavy blows struck with a handspike on the deck above boomed like discharges of small cannon through the forecastle. Then the boatswain's voice rose outside the door with an authoritative note in its drawl:—"D'ye hear, below there? Lay aft! Lay aft to muster all hands!"

There was a moment of surprised stillness. Then the forecastle floor disappeared under men whose bare feet flopped on the planks as they sprang clear out of their berths. Caps were rooted for amongst tumbled blankets. Some, yawning, buttoned waistbands. Half-smoked pipes were knocked hurriedly against wood-work and stuffed under pillows. Voices growled:— "What's up? . . . Is there no rest for us?" Donkin yelped:—"If that's the way of this ship, we'll 'ave to change all that. . . . You leave me alone. . . . I will soon. . . . " None of the crowd noticed him. They were lurching in twos and threes through the doors, after the manner of merchant Jacks who cannot go out of a door fairly, like mere landsmen. The votary of change followed them. Singleton, struggling into his jacket, came last, tall and fatherly, bearing high his head of a weather-beaten sage on the body of an old athlete. Only Charley remained alone in the white glare of the empty place, sitting between the two rows of iron links that stretched into the narrow gloom forward. He pulled hard at the strands in a hurried endeavour to finish his knot. Suddenly he started up, flung the rope at the cat, and skipped after the black tom which went off leaping sedately over chain compressors, with its tail carried stiff and upright, like a small flag pole.

Outside the glare of the steaming forecastle the serene purity of the night enveloped the seamen with its sooth-

ing breath, with its tepid breath flowing under the
stars that hung countless above the mastheads in a
thin cloud of luminous dust. On the town side the
blackness of the water was streaked with trails of light
which undulated gently on slight ripples, similar to
filaments that float rooted to the shore. Rows of
other lights stood away in straight lines as if drawn
up on parade between towering buildings; but on the
other side of the harbour sombre hills arched high their
black spines, on which, here and there, the point of a
star resembled a spark fallen from the sky. Far off,
Byculla*way, the electric lamps at the dock gates shone
on the end of lofty standards with a glow blinding and
frigid like captive ghosts of some evil moons. Scattered all over the dark polish of the roadstead, the ships
at anchor floated in perfect stillness under the feeble
gleam of their riding-lights, looming up, opaque and
bulky, like strange and monumental structures abandoned by men to an everlasting repose.

Before the cabin door Mr. Baker was mustering the
crew. As they stumbled and lurched along past the
mainmast, they could see aft his round, broad face
with a white paper before it, and beside his shoulder
the sleepy head, with dropped eyelids, of the boy, who
held, suspended at the end of his raised arm, the
luminous globe of a lamp. Even before the shuffle of
naked soles had ceased along the decks, the mate began
to call over the names. He called distinctly in a serious
tone befitting this roll-call to unquiet loneliness, to
inglorious and obscure struggle, or to the more trying
endurance of small privations and wearisome duties.
As the chief mate read out a name, one of the men
would answer: "Yes, sir!" or "Here!" and, detaching
himself from the shadowy mob of heads visible above
the blackness of starboard bulwarks, would step bare-

footed into the circle of light, and in two noiseless strides
pass into the shadows on the port side of the quarter-
deck. They answered in divers tones: in thick mutters,
in clear, ringing voices; and some, as if the whole thing
had been an outrage on their feelings, used an injured
intonation: for discipline is not ceremonious in merchant
ships, where the sense of hierarchy is weak, and where
all feel themselves equal before the unconcerned immensity of the sea and the exacting appeal of the work.

Mr. Baker read on steadily:—"Hansen—Campbell—
Smith—Wamibo. Now, then, Wamibo. Why don't
you answer? Always got to call your name twice."
The Finn emitted at last an uncouth grunt, and, stepping out, passed through the patch of light, weird and
gaudy, with the face of a man marching through a
dream. The mate went on faster:—"Craik—Singleton—Donkin. . . . O Lord!" he involuntarily
ejaculated as the incredibly dilapidated figure appeared
in the light. It stopped; it uncovered pale gums and
long, upper teeth in a malevolent grin.—"Is there anythink wrong with me, Mister Mate?" it asked, with a
flavour of insolence in the forced simplicity of its tone.
On both sides of the deck subdued titters were heard.—
"That'll do. Go over," growled Mr. Baker, fixing
the new hand with steady blue eyes. And Donkin
vanished suddenly out of the light into the dark group
of mustered men, to be slapped on the back and to hear
flattering whispers:—"He ain't afeard, he'll give
sport to 'em, see if he don't. . . . Reg'lar Punch
and Judy show. . . . Did ye see the mate start
at him? . . . Well! Damme, if I ever! . . . "

The last man had gone over, and there was a moment
of silence while the mate peered at his list.—"Sixteen,
seventeen," he muttered. "I am one hand short,
bo'sen," he said aloud. The big west-countryman at

his elbow, swarthy and bearded like a gigantic Spaniard, said in a rumbling bass:—"There's no one left forward, sir. I had a look round. He ain't aboard, but he may turn up before daylight."—"Ay. He may or he may not," commented the mate, "can't make out that last name. It's all a smudge. . . . That will do, men. Go below."

The distinct and motionless group stirred, broke up, began to move forward.

"Wait!" cried a deep, ringing voice.

All stood still. Mr. Baker, who had turned away yawning, spun round open-mouthed. At last, furious, he blurted out:—"What's this? Who said 'Wait'? What . . . "

But he saw a tall figure standing on the rail. It came down and pushed through the crowd, marching with a heavy tread towards the light on the quarter-deck. Then again the sonorous voice said with insistence:—"Wait!" The lamplight lit up the man's body. He was tall. His head was away up in the shadows of lifeboats that stood on skids above the deck. The whites of his eyes and his teeth gleamed distinctly, but the face was indistinguishable. His hands were big and seemed gloved.

Mr. Baker advanced intrepidly. "Who are you? How dare you . . . " he began.

The boy, amazed like the rest, raised the light to the man's face. It was black. A surprised hum—a faint hum that sounded like the suppressed mutter of the word "Nigger"—ran along the deck and escaped out into the night. The nigger seemed not to hear. He balanced himself where he stood in a swagger that marked time. After a moment he said calmly:—"My name is Wait—James Wait."

"Oh!" said Mr. Baker. Then, after a few seconds

of smouldering silence, his temper blazed out. "Ah! Your name is Wait. What of that? What do you want? What do you mean, coming shouting here?"

The nigger was calm, cool, towering, superb. The men had approached and stood behind him in a body. He overtopped the tallest by half a head. He said: "I belong to the ship." He enunciated distinctly, with soft precision. The deep, rolling tones of his voice filled the deck without effort. He was naturally scornful, unaffectedly condescending, as if from his height of six foot three he had surveyed all the vastness of human folly and had made up his mind not to be too hard on it. He went on:—"The captain shipped*me this morning. I couldn't get aboard sooner. I saw you all aft as I came up the ladder, and could see directly you were mustering the crew. Naturally I called out my name. I thought you had it on your list, and would understand. You misapprehended." He stopped short. The folly around him was confounded. He was right as ever, and as ever ready to forgive. The disdainful tones had ceased, and, breathing heavily, he stood still, surrounded by all these white men. He held his head up in the glare of the lamp— a head vigorously modelled into deep shadows and shining lights—a head powerful and misshapen with a tormented and flattened face—a face pathetic and brutal: the tragic, the mysterious, the repulsive mask of a nigger's soul.

Mr. Baker, recovering his composure, looked at the paper close. "Oh, yes; that's so. All right, Wait. Take your gear forward," he said.

Suddenly the nigger's eyes rolled wildly, became all whites. He put his hand to his side and coughed twice, a cough metallic, hollow, and tremendously loud; it resounded like two explosions in a vault; the dome of

the sky rang to it, and the iron plates of the ship's bulwarks seemed to vibrate in unison, then he marched
off forward with the others. The officers lingering
by the cabin door could hear him say: "Won't some
of you chaps lend a hand with my dunnage?* I've got
a chest and a bag." The words, spoken sonorously,
with an even intonation, were heard all over the ship,
and the question was put in a manner that made re-
fusal impossible. The short, quick shuffle of men carrying something heavy went away forward, but the tall
figure of the nigger lingered by the main hatch in a
knot of smaller shapes. Again he was heard asking:
"Is your cook a coloured gentleman?" Then a disappointed and disapproving "Ah! h'm!" was his comment upon the information that the cook happened
to be a mere white man. Yet, as they went all together
towards the forecastle, he condescended to put his head
through the galley door and boom out inside a magnificent "Good evening, doctor!"*that made all the saucepans ring. In the dim light the cook dozed on the
coal locker in front of the captain's supper. He
jumped up as if he had been cut with a whip, and dashed
wildly on deck to see the backs of several men going
away laughing. Afterwards, when talking about that
voyage, he used to say:—"The poor fellow had scared
me. I thought I had seen the devil." The cook
had been seven years in the ship with the same captain.
He was a serious-minded man with a wife and three
children, whose society he enjoyed on an average one
month out of twelve. When on shore he took his family
to church twice every Sunday. At sea he went to
sleep every evening with his lamp turned up full, a
pipe in his mouth, and an open Bible in his hand.
Some one had always to go during the night to put out
the light, take the book from his hand, and the pipe

from between his teeth. "For"—Belfast used to say, irritated and complaining—"some night, you stupid cookie, you'll swallow your ould clay, and we will have no cook."—"Ah! sonny, I am ready for my Maker's call . . . wish you all were," the other would answer with a benign serenity that was altogether imbecile and touching. Belfast outside the galley door danced with vexation. "You holy fool! I don't want you to die," he howled, looking up with furious, quivering face and tender eyes. "What's the hurry? You blessed wooden-headed ould heretic, the divvle will have you soon enough. Think of Us . . . of Us . . . of Us!" And he would go away, stamping, spitting aside, disgusted and worried; while the other, stepping out, saucepan in hand, hot, begrimed and placid, watched with a superior, cock-sure smile the back of his "queer little man" reeling in a rage. They were great friends.

Mr. Baker, lounging over the after-hatch, sniffed the humid night in the company of the second mate.— "Those West India niggers run fine and large—some of them . . . Ough! . . . Don't they? A fine, big man that, Mr. Creighton. Feel him on a rope. Hey? Ough! I will take him into my watch, I think." The second mate, a fair, gentlemanly young fellow, with a resolute face and a splendid physique, observed quietly that it was just about what he expected. There could be felt in his tone some slight bitterness which Mr. Baker very kindly set himself to argue away. "Come, come, young man," he said, grunting between the words. "Come! Don't be too greedy. You had that big Finn in your watch all the voyage. I will do what's fair. You may have those two young Scandinavians and I . . . Ough! . . . I get the nigger, and will take that . . .

Ough! that cheeky costermonger* chap in a black frock-coat. I'll make him . . . Ough! . . . make him toe the mark, or my . . . Ough! . . . name isn't Baker. Ough! Ough! Ough!"

He grunted thrice—ferociously. He had that trick of grunting so between his words and at the end of sentences. It was a fine, effective grunt that went well with his menacing utterance, with his heavy, bull-necked frame, his jerky, rolling gait; with his big, seamed face, his steady eyes, and sardonic mouth. But its effect had been long ago discounted by the men. They liked him; Belfast—who was a favourite, and knew it—mimicked him, not quite behind his back. Charley—but with greater caution—imitated his rolling gait. Some of his sayings became established, daily quotations in the forecastle. Popularity can go no farther! Besides, all hands were ready to admit that on a fitting occasion the mate could "jump down a fellow's throat in a reg'lar Western Ocean*style."

Now he was giving his last orders. "Ough! . . . You, Knowles! Call all hands at four. I want . . . Ough! . . . to heave short before the tug comes. Look out for the captain. I am going to lie down in my clothes. . . . Ough! . . . Call me when you see the boat coming. Ough! Ough! . . . The old man is sure to have something to say when he gets aboard," he remarked to Creighton. "Well, good-night. . . . Ough! A long day be-fore us to-morrow. . . . Ough! . . . Better turn in now. Ough! Ough!"

Upon the dark deck a band of light flashed, then a door slammed, and Mr. Baker was gone into his neat cabin. Young Creighton stood leaning over the rail, and looked dreamily into the night of the East. And he saw in it a long country lane, a lane of waving leaves and dancing sunshine. He saw stirring boughs of old trees outspread, and framing in their arch the tender, the caressing blueness of an English sky. And through the arch a girl in a light dress, smiling under a sunshade, seemed to be stepping out of the tender sky.

At the other end of the ship the forecastle, with only one lamp burning now, was going to sleep in a dim emptiness traversed by loud breathings, by sudden short sighs. The double row of berths yawned black, like graves tenanted by uneasy corpses. Here and there a curtain of gaudy chintz, half drawn, marked the resting-place of a sybarite. A leg hung over the edge very white and lifeless. An arm stuck straight out with a dark palm turned up, and thick fingers half closed. Two light snores, that did not synchronise, quarrelled in funny dialogue. Singleton stripped again—the old man suffered much from prickly heat— stood cooling his back in the doorway, with his arms crossed on his bare and adorned chest. His head touched the beam of the deck above. The nigger, half undressed, was busy casting adrift the lashing of his box, and spreading his bedding in an upper berth. He moved about in his socks, tall and noiseless, with a pair of braces beating about his calves. Amongst the shadows of stanchions and bowsprit, Donkin munched a piece of hard ship's bread, sitting on the deck with upturned feet and restless eyes; he held the biscuit up before his mouth in the whole fist and snapped his jaws at it with a raging face. Crumbs fell between his outspread legs. Then he got up.

"Where's our water-cask?" he asked in a contained voice.

Singleton, without a word, pointed with a big hand that held a short smouldering pipe. Donkin bent over

the cask, drank out of the tin, splashing the water,
turned round and noticed the nigger looking at him
over the shoulder with calm loftiness. He moved up
sideways.

"There's a blooming supper for a man," he whispered
bitterly. "My dorg at 'ome wouldn't 'ave it. It's
fit enouf for you an' me. 'Ere's a big ship's fo'c'sle!
. . . Not a blooming scrap of meat in the kids.
I've looked in all the lockers. . . . "

The nigger stared like a man addressed unexpectedly
in a foreign language. Donkin changed his tone:—
"Giv' us a bit of 'baccy, mate," he breathed out confidentially, "I 'aven't 'ad smoke or chew for the last
month. I am rampin' mad for it. Come on, old man!"

"Don't be familiar," said the nigger. Donkin
started and sat down on a chest near by, out of sheer
surprise. "We haven't kept pigs together," continued
James Wait in a deep undertone. "Here's your tobacco." Then, after a pause, he inquired:—"What
ship?"—"Golden State," muttered Donkin indistinctly,
biting the tobacco. The nigger whistled low.—"Ran?"
he said curtly. Donkin nodded: one of his cheeks
bulged out. "In course I ran," he mumbled. "They
booted the life out of one Dago chap on the passage
'ere, then started on me. I cleared out 'ere.— "Left
your dunnage behind?"—"Yes, dunnage and money,"
answered Donkin, raising his voice a little; "I got
nothink. No clothes, no bed. A bandy-legged little
Irish chap 'ere 'as give me a blanket. . . .
Think I'll go an' sleep in the fore topmast staysail
to-night."

He went on deck trailing behind his back a corner of
the blanket. Singleton, without a glance, moved
slightly aside to let him pass. The nigger put away his
shore togs and sat in clean working clothes on his box,

one arm stretched over his knees. After staring at
Singleton for some time he asked without emphasis:—
"What kind of ship is this? Pretty fair? Eh?"

Singleton didn't stir. A long while after he said,
with unmoved face:—"Ship! . . . Ships are all
right. It is the men in them!"

He went on smoking in the profound silence. The
wisdom of half a century spent in listening to the
thunder of the waves had spoken unconsciously through
his old lips. The cat purred on the windlass. Then
James Wait had a fit of roaring, rattling cough, that
shook him, tossed him like a hurricane, and flung him
panting with staring eyes headlong on his sea-chest.
Several men woke up. One said sleepily out of his
bunk: "'Struth! what a blamed row!"—"I have a
cold on my chest," gasped Wait.—"Cold! you call it,"
grumbled the man; "should think 'twas something
more. . . . "—"Oh! you think so," said the
nigger upright and loftily scornful again. He climbed
into his berth and began coughing persistently while he
put his head out to glare all round the forecastle.
There was no further protest. He fell back on the
pillow, and could be heard there wheezing regularly
like a man oppressed in his sleep.

Singleton stood at the door with his face to the light
and his back to the darkness. And alone in the dim
emptiness of the sleeping forecastle he appeared bigger,
colossal, very old; old as Father Time himself, who
should have come there into this place as quiet as a
sepulchre to contemplate with patient eyes the short
victory of sleep, the consoler. Yet he was only a child
of time, a lonely relic of a devoured and forgotten
generation. He stood, still strong, as ever unthinking;
a ready man with a vast empty past and with no future,
with his childlike impulses and his man's passions

already dead within his tattooed breast. The men who could understand his silence were gone—those men who knew how to exist beyond the pale of life and within sight of eternity. They had been strong, as those are strong who know neither doubts nor hopes. They had been impatient and enduring, turbulent and devoted, unruly and faithful. Well-meaning people had tried to represent those men as whining over every mouthful of their food; as going about their work in fear of their lives. But in truth they had been men who knew toil, privation, violence, debauchery—but knew not fear, and had no desire of spite in their hearts. Men hard to manage, but easy to inspire; voiceless men—but men enough to scorn in their hearts the sentimental voices that bewailed the hardness of their fate. It was a fate unique and their own; the capacity to bear it appeared to them the privilege of the chosen! Their generation lived inarticulate and indispensable, without knowing the sweetness of affections or the refuge of a home—and died free from the dark menace of a narrow grave. They were the everlasting children of the mysterious sea. Their successors are the grown-up children of a discontented earth. They are less naughty, but less innocent; less profane, but perhaps also less believing; and if they had learned how to speak they have also learned how to whine. But the others were strong and mute; they were effaced, bowed and enduring, like stone caryatides that hold up in the night the lighted halls of a resplendent and glorious edifice. They are gone now —and it does not matter. The sea and the earth are unfaithful to their children: a truth, a faith, a generation of men goes—and is forgotten, and it does not matter! Except, perhaps, to the few of those who believed the truth, confessed the faith—or loved the men.

A breeze was coming. The ship that had been lying tide-rode swung to a heavier puff; and suddenly the slack of the chain-cable between the windlass and the hawse-pipe clinked, slipped forward an inch, and rose gently off the deck with a startling suggestion as of unsuspected life that had been lurking stealthily in the iron. In the hawse-pipe the grinding links sent through the ship a sound like a low groan of a man sighing under a burden. The strain came on the windlass, the chain tautened like a string, vibrated—and the handle of the screw-brake moved in slight jerks. Singleton stepped forward.

Till then he had been standing meditative and un-thinking, reposeful and hopeless, with a face grim and blank—a sixty-year-old child of the mysterious sea. The thoughts of all his lifetime could have been ex-pressed in six words, but the stir of those things that were as much part of his existence as his beating heart called up a gleam of alert understanding upon the stern-ness of his aged face. The flame of the lamp swayed, and the old man, with knitted and bushy eyebrows, stood over the brake, watchful and motionless in the wild saraband of dancing shadows. Then the ship, obedient to the call of her anchor, forged ahead slightly and eased the strain. The cable relieved, hung down, and after swaying imperceptibly to and fro dropped with a loud tap on the hard wood planks. Singleton seized the high lever, and, by a violent throw forward of his body, wrung out another half-turn from the brake. He recovered himself, breathed largely, and remained for awhile glaring down at the powerful and compact engine that squatted on the deck at his feet like some quiet monster—a creature amazing and tame.

"You . . . hold!" he growled at it master-fully, in the incult*tangle of his white beard.

CHAPTER TWO

NEXT morning, at daylight, the *Narcissus* went to sea.

A slight haze blurred the horizon. Outside the harbour the measureless expanse of smooth water lay sparkling like a floor of jewels, and as empty as the sky. The short black tug gave a pluck to windward, in the usual way, then let go the rope, and hovered for a moment on the quarter with her engines stopped; while the slim, long hull of the ship moved ahead slowly under lower topsails. The loose upper canvas blew out in the breeze with soft round contours, resembling small white clouds snared in the maze of ropes. Then the sheets were hauled home, the yards hoisted, and the ship became a high and lonely pyramid, gliding, all shining and white, through the sunlit mist. The tug turned short round and went away towards the land. Twenty-six pairs of eyes watched her low broad stern crawling languidly over the smooth swell between the two paddle-wheels that turned fast, beating the water with fierce hurry. She resembled an enormous and aquatic black beetle, surprised by the light, overwhelmed by the sunshine, trying to escape with ineffectual effort into the distant gloom of the land. She left a lingering smudge of smoke on the sky, and two vanishing trails of foam on the water. On the place where she had stopped a round black patch of soot remained, undulating on the swell—an unclean mark of the creature's rest.

The *Narcissus* left alone, heading south, seemed to

stand resplendent and still upon the restless sea, under the moving sun. Flakes of foam swept past her sides; the water struck her with flashing blows; the land glided away slowly fading; a few birds screamed on motionless wings over the swaying mastheads. But soon the land disappeared, the birds went away; and to the west the pointed sail of an Arab dhow*running for Bombay, rose triangular and upright above the sharp edge of the horizon, lingered and vanished like an illusion. Then the ship's wake, long and straight, stretched itself out through a day of immense solitude. The setting sun, burning on the level of the water, flamed crimson below the blackness of heavy rain clouds. The sunset squall, coming up from behind, dissolved itself into the short deluge of a hissing shower. It left the ship glistening from trucks to water-line, and with darkened sails. She ran easily before a fair monsoon,* with her decks cleared for the night; and, moving along with her, was heard the sustained and monotonous swishing of the waves, mingled with the low whispers of men mustered aft for the setting of watches; the short plaint of some block aloft; or, now and then, a loud sigh of wind.

Mr. Baker, coming out of his cabin, called out the first name sharply before closing the door behind him. He was going to take charge of the deck. On the homeward trip, according to an old custom of the sea, the chief officer takes the first night-watch—from eight till midnight. So Mr. Baker, after he had heard the last "Yes, sir!" said moodily, "Relieve the wheel and look-out"; and climbed with heavy feet the poop ladder to windward. Soon after Mr. Creighton came down, whistling softly, and went into the cabin. On the doorstep the steward lounged, in slippers, meditative, and with his shirt-sleeves rolled up to the armpits.

On the main deck the cook, locking up the galley doors, had an altercation with young Charley about a pair of socks. He could be heard saying impressively, in the darkness amidships: "You don't deserve a kindness. I've been drying them for you, and now you complain about the holes—and you swear, too! Right in front of me! If I hadn't been a Christian—which you ain't, you young ruffian—I would give you a clout on the head. . . . Go away!" Men in couples or threes stood pensive or moved silently along the bulwarks in the waist. The first busy day of a homeward passage was sinking into the dull peace of resumed routine. Aft, on the high poop, Mr. Baker walked shuffling and grunted to himself in the pauses of his thoughts. Forward, the look-out man, erect between the flukes of the two anchors, hummed an endless tune, keeping his eyes fixed dutifully ahead in a vacant stare. A multitude of stars coming out into the clear night peopled the emptiness of the sky. They glittered, as if alive above the sea; they surrounded the running ship on all sides; more intense than the eyes of a staring crowd, and as inscrutable as the souls of men.

The passage had begun, and the ship, a fragment detached from the earth, went on lonely and swift like a small planet. Round her the abysses of sky and sea met in an unattainable frontier. A great circular solitude moved with her, ever changing and ever the same, always monotonous and always imposing. Now and then another wandering white speck, burdened with life, appeared far off—disappeared; intent on its own destiny. The sun looked upon her all day, and every morning rose with a burning, round stare of undying curiosity. She had her own future; she was alive with the lives of those beings who trod her decks; like that earth which had given her up to the

sea, she had an intolerable load of regrets and hopes.
On her lived timid truth and audacious lies; and, like
the earth, she was unconscious, fair to see—and condemned by men to an ignoble fate. The august loneliness of her path lent dignity to the sordid inspiration
of her pilgrimage. She drove foaming to the southward,
as if guided by the courage of a high endeavour. The
smiling greatness of the sea dwarfed the extent of
time. The days raced after one another, brilliant and
quick like the flashes of a lighthouse, and the nights,
uneventful and short, resembled fleeting dreams.

The men had shaken into their places, and the half-
hourly voice of the bells ruled their life of unceasing
care. Night and day the head and shoulders of a seaman could be seen aft by the wheel, outlined high
against sunshine or starlight, very steady above the
stir of revolving spokes. The faces changed, passing
in rotation. Youthful faces, bearded faces, dark faces:
faces serene, or faces moody, but all akin with the
brotherhood of the sea; all with the same attentive
expression of eyes, carefully watching the compass or
the sails. Captain Allistoun, serious, and with an old
red muffler round his throat, all day long pervaded the
poop. At night, many times he rose out of the darkness of the companion, such as a phantom above a
grave, and stood watchful and mute under the stars, his
night-shirt fluttering like a flag—then, without a
sound, sank down again. He was born on the shores
of the Pentland Firth.* In his youth he attained the
rank of harpooner in Peterhead whalers.* When he
spoke of that time his restless grey eyes became still
and cold, like the loom of ice. Afterwards he went into
the East Indian trade* for the sake of change. He
had commanded the *Narcissus* since she was built.
He loved his ship, and drove her unmercifully; for his

secret ambition was to make her accomplish some day a brilliantly quick passage which would be mentioned in nautical papers. He pronounced his owner's name with a sardonic smile, spoke but seldom to his officers, and reproved errors in a gentle voice, with words that cut to the quick. His hair was iron-grey, his face hard and of the colour of pump-leather. He shaved every morning of his life—at six—but once (being caught in a fierce hurricane eighty miles southwest of Mauritius*) he had missed three consecutive days. He feared naught but an unforgiving God, and wished to end his days in a little house, with a plot of ground attached— far in the country—out of sight of the sea.

He, the ruler of that minute world, seldom descended from the Olympian heights of his poop. Below him—at his feet, so to speak—common mortals led their busy and insignificant lives. Along the main deck, Mr. Baker grunted in a manner bloodthirsty and innocuous; and kept all our noses to the grindstone, being—as he once remarked—paid for doing that very thing. The men working about the deck were healthy and contented—as most seamen are, when once well out to sea. The true peace of God begins at any spot a thousand miles from the nearest land; and when He sends there the messengers of His might it is not in terrible wrath against crime, presumption, and folly, but paternally, to chasten simple hearts—ignorant hearts that know nothing of life, and beat undisturbed by envy or greed.

In the evening the cleared decks had a reposeful aspect, resembling the autumn of the earth. The sun was sinking to rest, wrapped in a mantle of warm clouds. Forward, on the end of the spare spars, the boatswain and the carpenter sat together with crossed arms; two men friendly, powerful, and deep-chested. Beside them the short, dumpy sailmaker—who had been in the Navy—related, between the whiffs of his pipe, impossible stories about Admirals. Couples tramped backwards and forwards, keeping step and balance without effort, in a confined space. Pigs grunted in the big pigstye. Belfast, leaning thoughtfully on his elbow, above the bars, communed with them through the silence of his meditation. Fellows with shirts open wide on sunburnt breasts sat upon the mooring bitts, and all up the steps of the forecastle ladders. By the foremast a few discussed in a circle the characteristics of a gentleman. One said:—"It's money as does it." Another maintained:—"No, it's the way they speak." Lame Knowles stumped up with an unwashed face (he had the distinction of being the dirty man of the forecastle), and showing a few yellow fangs in a shrewd smile, explained craftily that he "had seen some of their pants." The backsides of them— he had observed—were thinner than paper from constant sitting down in offices, yet otherwise they looked first-rate and would last for years. It was all appearance. "It was," he said, "bloomin' easy to be a gentleman when you had a clean job for life." They disputed endlessly, obstinate and childish; they repeated in shouts and with inflamed faces their amazing arguments; while the soft breeze, eddying down the enormous cavity of the foresail, distended above their bare heads, stirred the tumbled hair with a touch passing and light like an indulgent caress.

They were forgetting their toil, they were forgetting themselves. The cook approached to hear, and stood by, beaming with the inward consciousness of his faith, like a conceited saint unable to forget his glorious reward; Donkin, solitary and brooding over his wrongs

on the forecastle-head, moved closer to catch the drift
of the discussion below him; he turned his sallow face
to the sea, and his thin nostrils moved, sniffing the
breeze, as he lounged negligently by the rail. In the
glow of sunset faces shone with interest, teeth flashed,
eyes sparkled. The walking couples stood still suddenly, with broad grins; a man, bending over a wash-
tub, sat up, entranced, with the soapsuds flecking his
wet arms. Even the three petty officers listened leaning back, comfortably propped, and with superior
smiles. Belfast left off scratching the ear of his favourite pig, and, open mouthed, tried with eager eyes
to have his say. He lifted his arms, grimacing and baf-
fled. From a distance Charley screamed at the ring:—
"I know about gentlemen morn'n any of you. I've
been intermit with 'em. . . . I've blacked their
boots." The cook, craning his neck to hear better, was
scandalised. "Keep your mouth shut when your elders
speak, you impudent young heathen—you." "All
right, old Hallelujah, I'm done," answered Charley,
soothingly. At some opinion of dirty Knowles, delivered with an air of supernatural cunning, a ripple of
laughter ran along, rose like a wave, burst with a startling roar. They stamped with both feet; they turned
their shouting faces to the sky; many, spluttering,
slapped their thighs; while one or two, bent double,
gasped, hugging themselves with both arms like men
in pain. The carpenter and the boatswain, without
changing their attitude, shook with laughter where they
sat; the sailmaker, charged with an anecdote about a
Commodore, looked sulky; the cook was wiping his
eyes with a greasy rag; and lame Knowles, astonished
at his own success, stood in their midst showing a slow
smile.

Suddenly the face of Donkin leaning high-shouldered

over the after-rail became grave. Something like a
weak rattle was heard through the forecastle door. It
became a murmur; it ended in a sighing groan. The
washerman plunged both his arms into the tub abruptly;
the cook became more crestfallen than an exposed back-
slider; the boatswain moved his shoulders uneasily;
the carpenter got up with a spring and walked away—
while the sailmaker seemed mentally to give his story
up, and began to puff at his pipe with sombre determination. In the blackness of the doorway a pair of eyes
glimmered white, and big, and staring. Then James
Wait's head protruding, became visible, as if suspended between the two hands that grasped a doorpost
on each side of the face. The tassel of his blue woollen
nightcap, cocked forward, danced gaily over his left
eyelid. He stepped out in a tottering stride. He
looked powerful as ever, but showed a strange and affected unsteadiness in his gait; his face was perhaps
a trifle thinner, and his eyes appeared rather startlingly
prominent. He seemed to hasten the retreat of depart-
ing light by his very presence; the setting sun dipped
sharply, as though fleeing before our nigger; a black
mist emanated from him; a subtle and dismal influence;
a something cold and gloomy that floated out and settled on all the faces like a mourning veil. The circle
broke up. The joy of laughter died on stiffened lips.
There was not a smile left among all the ship's company. Not a word was spoken. Many turned their
backs, trying to look unconcerned; others, with averted
heads, sent half-reluctant glances out of the corners of
their eyes. They resembled criminals conscious of
misdeeds more than honest men distracted by doubt;
only two or three stared frankly, but stupidly, with
lips slightly open. All expected James Wait to say
something, and, at the same time, had the air of know-

ing beforehand what he would say. He leaned his back against the doorpost, and with heavy eyes swept over them a glance domineering and pained, like a sick tyrant overawing a crowd of abject but untrustworthy slaves.

No one went away. They waited in fascinated dread. He said ironically, with gasps between the words:—

"Thank you . . . chaps. You . . . are nice . . . and . . . quiet . . . you are! Yelling so . . . before . . . the door. . . ."

He made a longer pause, during which he worked his ribs in an exaggerated labour of breathing. It was intolerable. Feet were shuffled. Belfast let out a groan; but Donkin above blinked his red eyelids with invisible eyelashes, and smiled bitterly over the nigger's head.

The nigger went on again with surprising ease. He gasped no more, and his voice rang, hollow and loud, as though he had been talking in an empty cavern. He was contemptuously angry.

"I tried to get a wink of sleep. You know I can't sleep o' nights. And you come jabbering near the door here like a blooming lot of old women. . . . You think yourselves good shipmates. Do you? . . . Much you care for a dying man!"

Belfast spun away from the pigstye. "Jimmy," he cried tremulously, "if you hadn't been sick I would——"

He stopped. The nigger waited awhile, then said, in a gloomy tone:—"You would. . . . What? Go an' fight another such one as yourself. Leave me alone. It won't be for long. I'll soon die. . . . It's coming right enough!"

Men stood around very still and with exasperated

eyes. It was just what they had expected, and hated to hear, that idea of a stalking death, thrust at them many times a day like a boast and like a menace by this obnoxious nigger. He seemed to take a pride in that death which, so far, had attended only upon the ease of his life; he was overbearing about it, as if no one else in the world had ever been intimate with such a companion; he paraded it unceasingly before us with an affectionate persistence that made its presence indubitable, and at the same time incredible. No man could be suspected of such monstrous friendship! Was he a reality—or was he a sham—this ever-expected visitor of Jimmy's? We hesitated between pity and mistrust, while, on the slightest provocation, he shook before our eyes the bones of his bothersome and infamous skeleton. He was for ever trotting him out. He would talk of that coming death as though it had been already there, as if it had been walking the deck outside, as if it would presently come in to sleep in the only empty bunk; as if it had sat by his side at every meal. It interfered daily with our occupations, with our leisure, with our amusements. We had no songs and no music in the evening, because Jimmy (we all lovingly called him Jimmy, to conceal our hate of his accomplice) had managed, with that prospective decease of his, to disturb even Archie's mental balance. Archie was the owner of the concertina; but after a couple of stinging lectures from Jimmy he refused to play any more. He said:— "Yon's an uncanny joker. I dinna ken what's wrang wi' him, but there's something verra wrang, verra wrang. It's nae manner of use asking me. I won't play." Our singers became mute because Jimmy was a dying man. For the same reason no chap—as Knowles remarked—could "drive in a nail to hang his few poor rags upon," without being made aware of the enormity

he committed in disturbing Jimmy's interminable last
moments. At night, instead of the cheerful yell, "One
bell! Turn out! Do you hear there? Hey! hey! hey!
Show leg!" the watches were called man by man, in
whispers, so as not to interfere with Jimmy's, possibly,
last slumber on earth. True, he was always awake, and
managed, as we sneaked out on deck, to plant in our
backs some cutting remark that, for the moment, made
us feel as if we had been brutes, and afterwards made us
suspect ourselves of being fools. We spoke in low tones
within that fo'c'sle as though it had been a church. We
ate our meals in silence and dread, for Jimmy was capricious with his food, and railed bitterly at the salt
meat, at the biscuits, at the tea, as at articles unfit for
human consumption—"let alone for a dying man!"
He would say:—"Can't you find a better slice of meat
for a sick man who's trying to get home to be cured—
or buried? But there! If I had a chance, you fellows
would do away with it. You would poison me. Look
at what you have given me!" We served him in his
bed with rage and humility, as though we had been the
base courtiers of a hated prince; and he rewarded us
by his unconciliating criticism. He had found the
secret of keeping for ever on the run the fundamental
imbecility of mankind; he had the secret of life, that
confounded dying man, and he made himself master
of every moment of our existence. We grew desperate,
and remained submissive. Emotional little Belfast
was for ever on the verge of assault or on the verge of
tears. One evening he confided to Archie:—"For a
ha'penny I would knock his ugly black head off—the
skulking dodger!" And the straightforward Archie
pretended to be shocked! Such was the infernal spell
which that casual St. Kitt's nigger had cast upon our
guileless manhood! But the same night Belfast stole

from the galley the officers' Sunday fruit pie, to tempt
the fastidious appetite of Jimmy. He endangered not
only his long friendship with the cook but also—as it
appeared—his eternal welfare. The cook was overwhelmed with grief; he did not know the culprit but he
knew that wickedness flourished; he knew that Satan
was abroad amongst those men, whom he looked upon
as in some way under his spiritual care. Whenever
he saw three or four of us standing together he would
leave his stove, to run out and preach. We fled from
him; and only Charley (who knew the thief) affronted
the cook with a candid gaze which irritated the good
man. "It's you, I believe," he groaned, sorrowful
and with a patch of soot on his chin. "It's you. You
are a brand for the burning! No more of your socks
in my galley." Soon, unofficially, the information was
spread about that, should there be another case of
stealing, our marmalade (an extra allowance: half a
pound per man) would be stopped. Mr. Baker ceased
to heap jocular abuse upon his favourites, and grunted
suspiciously at all. The captain's cold eyes, high up
on the poop, glittered mistrustful, as he surveyed us
trooping in a small mob from halyards to braces for the
usual evening pull at all the ropes. Such stealing in a
merchant ship is difficult to check, and may be taken
as a declaration by men of their dislike for their officers.
It is a bad symptom. It may end in God knows what
trouble. The *Narcissus* was still a peaceful ship, but
mutual confidence was shaken. Donkin did not conceal his delight. We were dismayed.

Then illogical Belfast reproached our nigger with
great fury. James Wait, with his elbow on the pillow,
choked, gasped out:—"Did I ask you to bone*the
dratted thing? Blow your blamed pie. It has made
me worse—you little Irish lunatic, you!" Belfast,

with scarlet face and trembling lips, made a dash at him. Every man in the forecastle rose with a shout. There was a moment of wild tumult. Some one shrieked piercingly:—"Easy, Belfast! Easy! . . ." We expected Belfast to strangle Wait without more ado. Dust flew. We heard through it the nigger's cough, metallic and explosive like a gong. Next moment we saw Belfast hanging over him. He was saying plaint-ively:—"Don't! Don't, Jimmy! Don't be like that. An angel couldn't put up with ye—sick as ye are." He looked round at us from Jimmy's bedside, his com-ical mouth twitching, and through tearful eyes; then he tried to put straight the disarranged blankets. The unceasing whisper of the sea filled the forecastle. Was James Wait frightened, or touched, or repentant? He lay on his back with a hand to his side, and as motion-less as if his expected visitor had come at last. Belfast fumbled about his feet, repeating with emotion:— "Yes. We know. Ye are bad, but. . . . Just say what ye want done, and. . . . We all know ye are bad—very bad. . . ." No! Decidedly James Wait was not touched or repentant. Truth to say, he seemed rather startled. He sat up with incredible suddenness and ease. "Ah! You think I am bad, do you?" he said gloomily, in his clearest baritone voice (to hear him speak sometimes you would never think there was anything wrong with that man). "Do you? . . . Well, act according! Some of you haven't sense enough to put a blanket shipshape over a sick man. There! Leave it alone! I can die anyhow!" Belfast turned away limply with a gesture of discour-agement. In the silence of the forecastle, full of inter-ested men, Donkin pronounced distinctly:—"Well, I'm blowed!" and sniggered. Wait looked at him. He looked at him in a quite friendly manner. Nobody could tell what would please our incomprehensible invalid: but for us the scorn of that snigger was hard to bear.

Donkin's position in the forecastle was distinguished but unsafe. He stood on the bad eminence of a general dislike. He was left alone; and in his isolation he could do nothing but think of the gales of the Cape of Good Hope and envy us the possession of warm clothing and waterproofs. Our sea-boots, our oilskin coats, our well-filled sea-chests, were to him so many causes for bitter meditation: he had none of those things, and he felt instinctively that no man, when the need arose, would offer to share them with him. He was impudently cringing to us and systematically insolent to the officers. He anticipated the best results, for himself, from such a line of conduct—and was mistaken. Such natures forget that under extreme provocation men will be just—whether they want to be so or not. Donkin's insolence to long-suffering Mr. Baker became at last intolerable to us, and we rejoiced when the mate, one dark night, tamed him for good. It was done neatly, with great decency and decorum, and with little noise. We had been called—just before midnight— to trim the yards, and Donkin—as usual—made insulting remarks. We stood sleepily in a row with the forebrace in our hands waiting for the next order, and heard in the darkness a scuffly trampling of feet, an exclamation of surprise, sounds of cuffs and slaps, suppressed, hissing whispers:—"Ah! Will you!" . . . "Don't! . . . Don't!" . . . "Then behave." . . . "Oh! Oh! . . ." Afterwards there were soft thuds mixed with the rattle of iron things as if a man's body had been tumbling helplessly amongst the main-pump rods. Before we could realise the situation, Mr. Baker's voice was heard very near

and a little impatient:—"Haul away, men! Lay back
on that rope!" And we did lay back on the rope with
great alacrity. As if nothing had happened, the chief
mate went on trimming the yards with his usual and
exasperating fastidiousness. We didn't at the time
see anything of Donkin, and did not care. Had the
chief officer thrown him overboard, no man would have
said as much as "Hallo! he's gone!" But, in truth,
no great harm was done—even if Donkin did lose one
of his front teeth. We perceived this in the morning,
and preserved a ceremonious silence: the etiquette of
the forecastle commanded us to be blind and dumb in
such a case, and we cherished the decencies of our life
more than ordinary landsmen respect theirs. Charley,
with unpardonable want of *savoir vivre*,* yelled out:—
"'Ave you been to your dentyst? . . . Hurt ye,
didn't it?" He got a box on the ear from one of his
best friends. The boy was surprised, and remained
plunged in grief for at least three hours. We were
sorry for him, but youth requires even more discipline
than age. Donkin grinned venomously. From that
day he became pitiless; told Jimmy that he was a
"black fraud"; hinted to us that we were an imbecile
lot, daily taken in by a vulgar nigger. And Jimmy
seemed to like the fellow!

Singleton lived untouched by human emotions.
Taciturn and unsmiling, he breathed amongst us—in
that alone resembling the rest of the crowd. We were
trying to be decent chaps, and found it jolly difficult;
we oscillated between the desire of virtue and the fear
of ridicule; we wished to save ourselves from the pain of
remorse, but did not want to be made the contemptible
dupes of our sentiment. Jimmy's hateful accomplice
seemed to have blown with his impure breath undreamt-
of subtleties into our hearts. We were disturbed

and cowardly. That we knew. Singleton seemed to
know nothing, understand nothing. We had thought
him till then as wise as he looked, but now we dared,
at times, suspect him of being stupid—from old age.
One day, however, at dinner, as we sat on our boxes
round a tin dish that stood on the deck within the
circle of our feet, Jimmy expressed his general disgust
with men and things in words that were particularly
disgusting. Singleton lifted his head. We became
mute. The old man, addressing Jimmy, asked:—
"Are you dying?" Thus interrogated, James Wait
appeared horribly startled and confused. We all were
startled. Mouths remained open; hearts thumped,
eyes blinked; a dropped tin fork rattled in the dish;
a man rose as if to go out, and stood still. In less
than a minute Jimmy pulled himself together:—
"Why? Can't you see I am?" he answered shakily.
Singleton lifted a piece of soaked biscuit ("his teeth"—
he declared—"had no edge on them now") to his
lips.—"Well, get on with your dying," he said with
venerable mildness; "don't raise a blamed fuss with
us over that job. We can't help you." Jimmy fell
back in his bunk, and for a long time lay very still
wiping the perspiration off his chin. The dinner-tins
were put away quickly. On deck we discussed the
incident in whispers. Some showed a chuckling ex-
ultation. Many looked grave. Wamibo, after long
periods of staring dreaminess, attempted abortive
smiles; and one of the young Scandinavians, much tormented by doubt, ventured in the second dog-watch
to approach Singleton (the old man did not encourage
us much to speak to him) and ask sheepishly:—"You
think he will die?" Singleton looked up.—"Why, of
course he will die," he said deliberately. This seemed
decisive. It was promptly imparted to every one by

him who had consulted the oracle. Shy and eager, he would step up and with averted gaze recite his formula:—"Old Singleton says he will die." It was a relief! At last we knew that our compassion would not be misplaced, and we could again smile without misgivings—but we reckoned without Donkin. Donkin "didn't want to 'ave no truck with 'em dirty furriners." When Nilsen came to him with the news: "Singleton says he will die," he answered him by a spiteful "And so will you—you fat-headed Dutchman. Wish you Dutchmen were all dead—'stead comin' takin' our money inter your starvin' country." We were appalled. We perceived that after all Singleton's answer meant nothing. We began to hate him for making fun of us. All our certitudes were going; we were on doubtful terms with our officers; the cook had given us up for lost; we had overheard the boatswain's opinion that "we were a crowd of softies." We suspected Jimmy, one another, and even our very selves. We did not know what to do. At every insignificant turn of our humble life we met Jimmy overbearing and blocking the way, arm-in-arm with his awful and veiled familiar. It was a weird servitude.

It began a week after leaving Bombay and came on us stealthily like any other great misfortune. Every one had remarked that Jimmy from the first was very slack at his work; but we thought it simply the outcome of his philosophy of life. Donkin said:—"You put no more weight on a rope than a bloody sparrer." He disdained him. Belfast, ready for a fight, exclaimed provokingly:—"You don't kill yourself, old man!"—"Would you?" he retorted with extreme scorn—and Belfast retired. One morning, as we were washing decks, Mr. Baker called to him:—"Bring your broom over here, Wait." He strolled languidly.

"Move yourself! Ough!" grunted Mr. Baker; "what's the matter with your hind legs?" He stopped dead short. He gazed slowly with eyes that bulged out with an expression audacious and sad.—"It isn't my legs," he said, "it's my lungs." Everybody listened.—"What's . . . Ough! . . . What's wrong with them?" inquired Mr. Baker. All the watch stood around on the wet deck, grinning, and with brooms or buckets in their hands. He said mournfully:—"Going—or gone. Can't you see I'm a dying man? I know it!" Mr. Baker was disgusted. —"Then why the devil did you ship aboard here?"— "I must live till I die—mustn't I?" he replied. The grins became audible.—"Go off the deck—get out of my sight," said Mr. Baker. He was nonplussed. It was an unique experience. James Wait, obedient, dropped his broom, and walked slowly forward. A burst of laughter followed him. It was too funny. All hands laughed. . . . They laughed! . . . Alas!

He became the tormentor of all our moments; he was worse than a nightmare. You couldn't see that there was anything wrong with him: a nigger does not show. He was not very fat—certainly—but then he was no leaner than other niggers we had known. He coughed often, but the most prejudiced person could perceive that, mostly, he coughed when it suited his purpose. He wouldn't, or couldn't, do his work—and he wouldn't lie-up. One day he would skip aloft with the best of them, and next time we would be obliged to risk our lives to get his limp body down. He was reported, he was examined; he was remonstrated with, threatened, cajoled, lectured. He was called into the cabin to interview the captain. There were wild rumours. It was said he had cheeked the old man; it was said he had frightened him. Charley maintained that the "skipper, weepin,' 'as giv' 'im 'is blessin' an' a pot of jam.'' Knowles had it from the steward that the unspeakable Jimmy had been reeling against the cabin furniture; that he had groaned; that he had complained of general brutality and disbelief; and had ended by coughing all over the old man's meteorological journals which were then spread on the table. At any rate, Wait returned forward supported by the steward, who, in a pained and shocked voice, entreated us:—"Here! Catch hold of him, one of you. He is to lie-up." Jimmy drank a tin mugful of coffee, and, after bullying first one and then another, went to bed. He remained there most of the time, but when it suited him would come on deck and appear amongst us. He was scornful and brooding; he looked ahead upon the sea, and no one could tell what was the meaning of that black man sitting apart in a meditative attitude and as motionless as a carving.

He refused steadily all medicine; he threw sago and cornflour overboard till the steward got tired of bringing it to him. He asked for paregoric.* They sent him a big bottle; enough to poison a wilderness of babies. He kept it between his mattress and the deal lining of the ship's side; and nobody ever saw him take a dose. Donkin abused him to his face, jeered at him while he gasped; and the same day Wait would lend him a warm jersey. Once Donkin reviled him for half an hour; reproached him with the extra work his malingering gave to the watch; and ended by calling him "a black-faced swine." Under the spell of our accursed perversity we were horror-struck. But Jimmy positively seemed to revel in that abuse. It made him look cheerful— and Donkin had a pair of old sea boots thrown at him. "Here, you East-end trash," boomed Wait, "you may have that."

At last Mr. Baker had to tell the captain that James
Wait was disturbing the peace of the ship. "Knock
discipline on the head—he will, Ough," grunted Mr.
Baker. As a matter of fact, the starboard watch came
as near as possible to refusing duty, when ordered one
morning by the boatswain to wash out their forecastle.
It appears Jimmy objected to a wet floor—and that
morning we were in a compassionate mood. We
thought the boatswain a brute, and, practically, told
him so. Only Mr. Baker's delicate tact prevented an
all-fired row: he refused to take us seriously. He came
bustling forward, and called us many unpolite names
but in such a hearty and seamanlike manner that we
began to feel ashamed of ourselves. In truth, we
thought him much too good a sailor to annoy him will-
ingly: and after all Jimmy might have been a fraud—
probably was! The forecastle got a clean up that
morning; but in the afternoon a sick-bay was fitted up
in the deck-house. It was a nice little cabin opening
on deck, and with two berths. Jimmy's belongings
were transported there, and then—notwithstanding his
protests—Jimmy himself. He said he couldn't walk.
Four men carried him on a blanket. He complained
that he would have to die there alone, like a dog. We
grieved for him, and were delighted to have him removed from the forecastle. We attended him as
before. The galley was next door, and the cook looked
in many times a day. Wait became a little more
cheerful. Knowles affirmed having heard him laugh
to himself in peals one day. Others had seen him
walking about on deck at night. His little place, with
the door ajar on a long hook, was always full of tobacco
smoke. We spoke through the crack cheerfully,
sometimes abusively, as we passed by, intent on our
work. He fascinated us. He would never let doubt

die. He overshadowed the ship. Invulnerable in his promise of speedy corruption he trampled on our self-respect, he demonstrated to us daily our want of moral courage; he tainted our lives. Had we been a miserable gang of wretched immortals, unhallowed alike by hope and fear, he could not have lorded it over us with a more pitiless assertion of his sublime privilege.

CHAPTER THREE

MEANTIME the *Narcissus*, with square yards, ran out of the fair monsoon. She drifted slowly, swinging round and round the compass, through a few days of baffling light airs. Under the patter of short warm showers, grumbling men whirled the heavy yards from side to side; they caught hold of the soaked ropes with groans and sighs, while their officers, sulky and dripping with rain water, unceasingly ordered them about in wearied voices. During the short respites they looked with disgust into the smarting palms of their stiff hands, and asked one another bitterly:—"Who would be a sailor if he could be a farmer?" All the tempers were spoilt, and no man cared what he said. One black night, when the watch, panting in the heat and half-drowned with the rain, had been through four mortal hours hunted from brace to brace, Belfast declared that he would "chuck the sea for ever and go in a steamer." This was excessive, no doubt. Captain Allistoun, with great self-control, would mutter sadly to Mr. Baker:—"It is not so bad—not so bad," when he had managed to shove, and dodge, and manœuvre his smart ship through sixty miles in twenty-four hours. From the doorstep of the little cabin, Jimmy, chin in hand, watched our distasteful labours with insolent and melancholy eyes. We spoke to him gently—and out of his sight exchanged sour smiles.

Then, again, with a fair wind and under a clear sky, the ship went on piling up the South Latitude. She passed outside Madagascar and Mauritius without a

glimpse of the land. Extra lashings were put on the
spare spars. Hatches were looked to. The steward
in his leisure moments and with a worried air tried to
fit washboards to the cabin doors. Stout canvas was
bent with care. Anxious eyes looked to the westward, towards the cape of storms.* The ship began to
dip into a southwest swell, and the softly luminous sky
of low latitudes took on a harder sheen from day to
day above our heads: it arched high above the ship
vibrating and pale, like an immense dome of steel, reso-
nant with the deep voice of freshening gales. The sunshine gleamed cold on the white curls of black waves.
Before the strong breath of westerly*squalls the ship,
with reduced sail, lay slowly over, obstinate and yield-
ing. She drove to and fro in the unceasing endeavour
to fight her way through the invisible violence of the
winds: she pitched headlong into dark smooth hollows;
she struggled upwards over the snowy ridges of great
running seas; she rolled, restless, from side to side, like a
thing in pain. Enduring and valiant, she answered to
the call of men; and her slim spars waving for ever in
abrupt semicircles, seemed to beckon in vain for help
towards the stormy sky.

It was a bad winter off the Cape that year. The
relieved helmsmen came off flapping their arms, or
ran stamping hard and blowing into swollen, red fingers.
The watch on deck dodged the sting of cold sprays or,
crouching in sheltered corners, watched dismally the
high and merciless seas boarding the ship time after
time in unappeasable fury. Water tumbled in cata-
racts over the forecastle doors. You had to dash
through a waterfall to get into your damp bed. The
men turned in wet and turned out stiff to face the
redeeming and ruthless exactions of their glorious and
obscure fate. Far aft, and peering watchfully to wind-

ward, the officers could be seen through the mist of
squalls. They stood by the weather-rail, holding
on grimly, straight and glistening in their long coats;
and in the disordered plunges of the hard-driven ship,
they appeared high up, attentive, tossing violently
above the grey line of a clouded horizon in motionless
attitudes.

They watched the weather and the ship as men on
shore watch the momentous chances of fortune. Captain Allistoun never left the deck, as though he had
been part of the ship's fittings. Now and then the
steward, shivering, but always in shirt sleeves, would
struggle towards him with some hot coffee, half of
which the gale blew out of the cup before it reached
the master's lips. He drank what was left gravely in
one long gulp, while heavy sprays pattered loudly on
his oilskin coat, the seas swishing broke about his high
boots; and he never took his eyes off the ship. He
kept his gaze riveted upon her as a loving man watches
the unselfish toil of a delicate woman upon the slender
thread of whose existence is hung the whole meaning
and joy of the world. We all watched her. She was
beautiful and had a weakness. We loved her no less
for that. We admired her qualities aloud, we boasted
of them to one another, as though they had been our
own, and the consciousness of her only fault we kept
buried in the silence of our profound affection. She
was born in the thundering peal of hammers beating
upon iron, in black eddies of smoke, under a grey sky,
on the banks of the Clyde.* The clamorous and sombre
stream gives birth to things of beauty that float away
into the sunshine of the world to be loved by men.
The *Narcissus* was one of that perfect brood. Less
perfect than many perhaps, but she was ours, and, consequently, incomparable. We were proud of her. In

Bombay, ignorant landlubbers alluded to her as that "pretty grey ship." Pretty! A scurvy meed of commendation! We knew she was the most magnificent sea-boat ever launched. We tried to forget that, like many good sea-boats, she was at times rather crank.* She was exacting. She wanted care in loading and handling, and no one knew exactly how much care would be enough. Such are the imperfections of mere men! The ship knew, and sometimes would correct the presumptuous human ignorance by the wholesome discipline of fear. We had heard ominous stories about past voyages. The cook (officially a seaman, but in reality no sailor)—the cook, when unstrung by some misfortune, such as the rolling over of a saucepan, would mutter gloomily while he wiped the floor:— "There! Look at what she has done! Some voy'ge she will drown all hands! You'll see if she won't." To which the steward, snatching in the galley a moment to draw breath in the hurry of his worried life, would remark philosophically:—"Those that see won't tell, anyhow. I don't want to see it." We derided those fears. Our hearts went out to the old man when he pressed her hard so as to make her hold her own, hold to every inch gained to windward; when he made her, under reefed sails, leap obliquely at enormous waves. The men, knitted together aft into a ready group by the first sharp order of an officer coming to take charge of the deck in bad weather:—"Keep handy the watch," stood admiring her valiance. Their eyes blinked in the wind; their dark faces were wet with drops of water more salt and bitter than human tears; beards and moustaches, soaked, hung straight and dripping like fine seaweed. They were fantastically misshapen; in high boots, in hats like helmets, and swaying clumsily, stiff and bulky in glistening oilskins, they resembled men strangely equipped for some fabulous adventure. Whenever she rose easily to a towering green sea, elbows dug ribs, faces brightened, lips murmured:—"Didn't she do it cleverly," and all the heads turning like one watched with sardonic grins the foiled wave go roaring to leeward, white with the foam of a monstrous rage. But when she had not been quick enough and, struck heavily, lay over trembling under the blow, we clutched at ropes, and looking up at the narrow bands of drenched and strained sails waving desperately aloft, we thought in our hearts:—"No wonder. Poor thing!"

The thirty-second day out of Bombay began inauspiciously. In the morning a sea smashed one of the galley doors. We dashed in through lots of steam and found the cook very wet and indignant with the ship:— "She's getting worse every day. She's trying to drown me in front of my own stove!" He was very angry. We pacified him, and the carpenter, though washed away twice from there, managed to repair the door. Through that accident our dinner was not ready till late, but it didn't matter in the end because Knowles, who went to fetch it, got knocked down by a sea and the dinner went over the side. Captain Allistoun, looking more hard and thin-lipped than ever, hung on to full topsails and foresail, and would not notice that the ship, asked to do too much, appeared to lose heart altogether for the first time since we knew her. She refused to rise, and bored her way sullenly through the seas. Twice running, as though she had been blind or weary of life, she put her nose deliberately into a big wave and swept the decks from end to end. As the boatswain observed with marked annoyance, while we were splashing about in a body to try and save a worthless wash-tub:—"Every blooming thing in the ship is

going overboard this afternoon." Venerable Singleton
broke his habitual silence and said with a glance aloft:—
"The old man's in a temper with the weather, but it's
no good bein' angry with the winds of heaven." Jimmy
had shut his door, of course. We knew he was dry
and comfortable within his little cabin, and in our
absurd way were pleased one moment, exasperated the
next, by that certitude. Donkin skulked shamelessly,
uneasy and miserable. He grumbled:—"I'm perishin'
with cold outside in bloomin' wet rags, an' that 'ere
black sojer sits dry on a blamed chest full of bloomin'
clothes; blank his black soul!" We took no notice of
him; we hardly gave a thought to Jimmy and his
bosom friend. There was no leisure for idle probing
of hearts. Sails blew adrift. Things broke loose.
Cold and wet, we were washed about the deck while
trying to repair damages. The ship tossed about,
shaken furiously, like a toy in the hand of a lunatic.
Just at sunset there was a rush to shorten sail before
the menace of a sombre hail cloud. The hard gust of
wind came brutal like the blow of a fist. The ship
relieved of her canvas in time received it pluckily:
she yielded reluctantly to the violent onset; then,
coming up with a stately and irresistible motion,
brought her spars to windward in the teeth of the
screeching squall. Out of the abysmal darkness of
the black cloud overhead white hail streamed on her,
rattled on the rigging, leaped in handfuls off the yards,
rebounded on the deck—round and gleaming in the
murky turmoil like a shower of pearls. It passed
away. For a moment a livid sun shot horizontally
the last rays of sinister light between the hills of steep,
rolling waves. Then a wild night rushed in—stamped
out in a great howl that dismal remnant of a stormy
day.

There was no sleep on board that night. Most seamen remember in their life one or two such nights of a culminating gale. Nothing seems left of the whole universe but darkness, clamour, fury—and the ship. And like the last vestige of a shattered creation she drifts, bearing an anguished remnant of sinful mankind, through the distress, tumult, and pain of an avenging terror. No one slept in the forecastle. The tin oil-lamp suspended on a long string, smoking, described wide circles; wet clothing made dark heaps on the glistening floor; a thin layer of water rushed to and fro. In the bed-places men lay booted, resting on elbows and with open eyes. Hung-up suits of oil-skin swung out and in, lively and disquieting like reckless ghosts of decapitated seamen dancing in a tempest. No one spoke and all listened. Outside the night moaned and sobbed to the accompaniment of a continuous loud tremor as of innumerable drums beating far off. Shrieks passed through the air. Tremendous dull blows made the ship tremble while she rolled under the weight of the seas toppling on her deck. At times she soared up swiftly as if to leave this earth for ever, then during interminable moments fell through a void with all the hearts on board of her standing still, till a frightful shock, expected and sudden, started them off again with a big thump. After every dislocating jerk of the ship, Wamibo, stretched full length, his face on the pillow, groaned slightly with the pain of his tormented universe. Now and then, for the fraction of an intolerable second, the ship, in the fiercer burst of a terrible uproar, remained on her side, vibrating and still, with a stillness more appalling than the wildest motion. Then upon all those prone bodies a stir would pass, a shiver of suspense. A man would protrude his anxious head and a pair of eyes glistened

in the sway of light glaring wildly. Some moved their
legs a little as if making ready to jump out. But
several, motionless on their backs and with one hand
gripping hard the edge of the bunk, smoked nervously
with quick puffs, staring upwards, immobilised in a
great craving for peace.

At midnight, orders were given to furl the fore and
mizen topsails. With immense efforts men crawled
aloft through a merciless buffeting, saved the canvas
and crawled down almost exhausted, to bear in panting
silence the cruel battering of the seas. Perhaps for
the first time in the history of the merchant service the
watch, told to go below, did not leave the deck, as if
compelled to remain there by the fascination of a
venomous violence. At every heavy gust men, huddled together, whispered to one another:—"It can
blow no harder"—and presently the gale would give
them the lie with a piercing shriek, and drive their
breath back into their throats. A fierce squall seemed
to burst asunder the thick mass of sooty vapours; and
above the wrack of torn clouds glimpses could be caught
of the high moon rushing backwards with frightful
speed over the sky, right into the wind's eye. Many
hung their heads, muttering that it "turned their in-
wards out" to look at it. Soon the clouds closed up
and the world again became a raging, blind darkness
that howled, flinging at the lonely ship salt sprays and
sleet.

About half-past seven the pitchy obscurity round us
turned a ghastly grey, and we knew that the sun had
risen. This unnatural and threatening daylight, in
which we could see one another's wild eyes and drawn
faces, was only an added tax on our endurance. The
horizon seemed to have come on all sides within arm's
length of the ship. Into that narrowed circle furious

seas leaped in, struck, and leaped out. A rain of salt,
heavy drops flew aslant like mist. The main-topsail
had to be goose-winged, and with stolid resignation
every one prepared to go aloft once more; but the officers
yelled, pushed back, and at last we understood that no
more men would be allowed to go on the yard than
were absolutely necessary for the work. As at any
moment the masts were likely to be jumped out or
blown overboard, we concluded that the captain didn't
want to see all his crowd go over the side at once.
That was reasonable. The watch then on duty, led
by Mr. Creighton, began to struggle up the rigging.
The wind flattened them against the ratlines; then,
easing a little, would let them ascend a couple of steps;
and again, with a sudden gust, pin all up the shrouds
the whole crawling line in attitudes of crucifixion.
The other watch plunged down on the main deck to
haul up the sail. Men's heads bobbed up as the water
flung them irresistibly from side to side. Mr. Baker
grunted encouragingly in our midst, spluttering and
blowing amongst the tangled ropes like an energetic
porpoise. Favoured by an ominous and untrustworthy lull, the work was done without any one being
lost either off the deck or from the yard. For the
moment the gale seemed to take off, and the ship, as
if grateful for our efforts, plucked up heart and made
better weather of it.

At eight the men off duty, watching their chance,
ran forward over the flooded deck to get some rest.
The other half of the crew remained aft for their turn
of "seeing her through her trouble," as they expressed it.
The two mates urged the master to go below. Mr.
Baker grunted in his ear:—"Ough! surely now . . .
Ough! . . . confidence in us . . . nothing
more to do . . . she must lay it out or go.

Ough! Ough!" Tall young Mr. Creighton smiled
down at him cheerfully:—". . . She's as right
as a trivet!* Take a spell, sir." He looked at them
stonily with bloodshot, sleepless eyes. The rims of
his eyelids were scarlet, and he moved his jaw unceasingly with a slow effort, as though he had been masti-
cating a lump of india-rubber. He shook his head.
He repeated:—"Never mind me. I must see it out—I
must see it out," but he consented to sit down for a
moment on the skylight, with his hard face turned un-
flinchingly to windward. The sea spat at it—and
stoical, it streamed with water as though he had been
weeping. On the weather side of the poop the watch,
hanging on to the mizen rigging and to one another,
tried to exchange encouraging words. Singleton, at
the wheel, yelled out:—"Look out for yourselves!"
His voice reached them in a warning whisper. They
were startled.

A big, foaming sea came out of the mist; it made
the ship, roaring wildly, and in its rush it looked as
mischievous and discomposing as a madman with an
axe. One or two, shouting, scrambled up the rigging;
most, with a convulsive catch of the breath, held on
where they stood. Singleton dug his knees under the
wheel-box, and carefully eased the helm to the headlong
pitch of the ship, but without taking his eyes off the
coming wave. It towered close-to and high, like a wall
of green glass topped with snow. The ship rose to it
as though she had soared on wings, and for a moment
rested poised upon the foaming crest as if she had been
a great sea-bird. Before we could draw breath a heavy
gust struck her, another roller took her unfairly under
the weather bow, she gave a toppling lurch, and filled
her decks. Captain Allistoun leaped up, and fell;
Archie rolled over him, screaming:—"She will rise!"

She gave another lurch to leeward; the lower deadeyes
dipped heavily; the men's feet flew from under them,
and they hung kicking above the slanting poop. They
could see the ship putting her side in the water, and
shouted all together:—"She's going!" Forward the
forecastle doors flew open, and the watch below were
seen leaping out one after another, throwing their
arms up; and, falling on hands and knees, scrambled
aft on all fours along the high side of the deck, sloping
more than the roof of a house. From leeward the
seas rose, pursuing them; they looked wretched in a
hopeless struggle, like vermin fleeing before a flood;
they fought up the weather ladder of the poop one
after another, half naked and staring wildly; and as
soon as they got up they shot to leeward in clusters,
with closed eyes, till they brought up heavily with
their ribs against the iron stanchions of the rail; then,
groaning, they rolled in a confused mass. The immense
volume of water thrown forward by the last scend of
the ship had burst the lee door of the forecastle. They
could see their chests, pillows, blankets, clothing, come
out floating upon the sea. While they struggled back
to windward they looked in dismay. The straw beds
swam high, the blankets, spread out, undulated; while
the chests, waterlogged and with a heavy list, pitched
heavily like dismasted hulks, before they sank; Archie's
big coat passed with outspread arms, resembling a
drowned seaman floating with his head under water.
Men were slipping down while trying to dig their
fingers into the planks; others, jammed in corners,
rolled enormous eyes. They all yelled unceasingly:—
"The masts! Cut! Cut! . . ." A black squall
howled low over the ship, that lay on her side
with the weather yard-arms pointing to the clouds;
while the tall masts, inclined nearly to the horizon,

seemed to be of an immeasurable length. The carpenter
let go his hold, rolled against the skylight, and began
to crawl to the cabin entrance, where a big axe was kept
ready for just such an emergency. At that moment
the topsail sheet parted, the end of the heavy chain
racketed aloft, and sparks of red fire streamed down
through the flying sprays. The sail flapped once with
a jerk that seemed to tear our hearts out through our
teeth, and instantly changed into a bunch of fluttering
narrow ribbons that tied themselves into knots and
became quiet along the yard. Captain Allistoun struggled, managed to stand up with his face near the deck,
upon which men swung on the ends of ropes, like nest
robbers upon a cliff. One of his feet was on somebody's chest; his face was purple; his lips moved. He
yelled also; he yelled, bending down:—"No! No!"
Mr. Baker, one leg over the binnacle-stand, roared out:
—"Did you say no? Not cut?" He shook his head
madly. "No! No!" Between his legs the crawling
carpenter heard, collapsed at once, and lay full length
in the angle of the skylight. Voices took up the shout—
"No! No!" Then all became still. They waited
for the ship to turn over altogether, and shake them out
into the sea; and upon the terrific noise of wind and sea
not a murmur of remonstrance came out from those
men, who each would have given ever so many years
of life to see "them damned sticks go overboard!"
They all believed it their only chance; but a little hard-
faced man shook his grey head and shouted "No!"
without giving them as much as a glance. They were
silent, and gasped. They gripped rails, they had
wound ropes'-ends under their arms; they clutched
ringbolts, they crawled in heaps where there was foot-
hold; they held on with both arms, hooked themselves
to anything to windward with elbows, with chins, al-

most with their teeth: and some, unable to crawl away
from where they had been flung, felt the sea leap up,
striking against their backs as they struggled upwards.
Singleton had stuck to the wheel. His hair flew out
in the wind; the gale seemed to take its life-long adver-
sary by the beard and shake his old head. He wouldn't
let go, and, with his knees forced between the spokes,
flew up and down like a man on a bough. As Death
appeared unready, they began to look about. Donkin, caught by one foot in a loop of some rope, hung,
head down, below us, and yelled, with his face to the
deck:—"Cut! Cut!" Two men lowered themselves
cautiously to him; others hauled on the rope. They
caught him up, shoved him into a safer place, held
him. He shouted curses at the master, shook his fist
at him with horrible blasphemies, called upon us in
filthy words to "Cut! Don't mind that murdering
fool! Cut, some of you!" One of his rescuers struck
him a back-handed blow over the mouth; his head
banged on the deck, and he became suddenly very quiet,
with a white face, breathing hard, and with a few drops
of blood trickling from his cut lip. On the lee side
another man could be seen stretched out as if stunned;
only the washboard prevented him from going over the
side. It was the steward. We had to sling him up
like a bale for he was paralysed with fright. He had
rushed up out of the pantry when he felt the ship go
over, and had rolled down helplessly, clutching a china
mug. It was not broken. With difficulty we tore it
away from him, and when he saw it in our hands he was
amazed. "Where did you get that thing?" he kept
on asking us in a trembling voice. His shirt was blown
to shreds; the ripped sleeves flapped like wings. Two
men made him fast, and, doubled over the rope that
held him, he resembled a bundle of wet rags. Mr.

Baker crawled along the line of men, asking:—"Are you all there?" and looking them over. Some blinked vacantly, others shook convulsively; Wamibo's head hung over his breast; and in painful attitudes, cut by lashings, exhausted with clutching, screwed up in corners, they breathed heavily. Their lips twitched, and at every sickening heave of the overturned ship they opened them wide as if to shout. The cook, embracing a wooden stanchion, unconsciously repeated a prayer. In every short interval of the fiendish noises around he could be heard there, without cap or slippers, imploring in that storm the Master of our lives not to lead him into temptation. Soon he also became silent. In all that crowd of cold and hungry men, waiting wearily for a violent death, not a voice was heard; they were mute, and in sombre thoughtfulness listened to the horrible imprecations of the gale.

Hours passed. They were sheltered by the heavy inclination of the ship from the wind that rushed in one long unbroken moan above their heads, but cold rain showers fell at times into the uneasy calm of their refuge. Under the torment of that new infliction a pair of shoulders would writhe a little. Teeth chattered. The sky was clearing, and bright sunshine gleamed over the ship. After every burst of battering seas, vivid and fleeting rainbows arched over the drifting hull in the flick of sprays. The gale was ending in a clear blow, which gleamed and cut like a knife. Between two bearded shellbacks Charley, fastened with somebody's long muffler to a deck ring-bolt, wept quietly, with rare tears wrung out by bewilderment, cold, hunger, and general misery. One of his neighbours punched him in the ribs asking roughly:— "What's the matter with your cheek? In fine weather there's no holding you, youngster." Turning about

with prudence he worked himself out of his coat and
threw it over the boy. The other man closed up,
muttering:—"'Twill make a bloomin' man of you,
sonny." They flung their arms over and pressed
against him. Charley drew his feet up and his eyelids dropped. Sighs were heard, as men, perceiving
that they were not to be "drowned in a hurry," tried
easier positions. Mr. Creighton, who had hurt his
leg, lay amongst us with compressed lips. Some
fellows belonging to his watch set about securing him
better. Without a word or a glance he lifted his arms
one after another to facilitate the operation, and not a
muscle moved in his stern, young face. They asked
him with solicitude:—"Easier now, sir?" He answered
with a curt:—"That'll do." He was a hard young
officer, but many of his watch used to say they liked
him well enough because he had "such a gentlemanly
way of damning us up and down the deck." Others
unable to discern such fine shades of refinement,
respected him for his smartness. For the first time
since the ship had gone on her beam ends Captain
Allistoun gave a short glance down at his men. He
was almost upright—one foot against the side of the
skylight, one knee on the deck; and with the end of the
vang round his waist swung back and forth with his
gaze fixed ahead, watchful, like a man looking out for a
sign. Before his eyes the ship, with half her deck
below water, rose and fell on heavy seas that rushed
from under her flashing in the cold sunshine. We began
to think she was wonderfully buoyant—considering.
Confident voices were heard shouting:—"She'll do,
boys!" Belfast exclaimed with fervour:—"I would
giv' a month's pay for a draw at a pipe!" One or
two, passing dry tongues on their salt lips, muttered
something about a "drink of water." The cook, as

if inspired, scrambled up with his breast against the
poop water-cask and looked in. There was a little at
the bottom. He yelled, waving his arms, and two men
began to crawl backwards and forwards with the mug.
We had a good mouthful all round. The master shook
his head impatiently, refusing. When it came to
Charley one of his neighbours shouted:—"That bloomin' boy's asleep." He slept as though he had been
dosed with narcotics. They let him be. Singleton
held to the wheel with one hand while he drank, bending down to shelter his lips from the wind. Wamibo
had to be poked and yelled at before he saw the mug
held before his eyes. Knowles said sagaciously:—"It's
better'n a tot o' rum." Mr. Baker grunted:—"Thank
ye." Mr. Creighton drank and nodded. Donkin
gulped greedily, glaring over the rim. Belfast made
us laugh when with grimacing mouth he shouted:
—"Pass it this way. We're all taytottlers here."
The master, presented with the mug again by a crouching man, who screamed up at him:—"We all had a
drink, captain," groped for it without ceasing to look
ahead, and handed it back stiffly as though he could
not spare half a glance away from the ship. Faces
brightened. We shouted to the cook:—"Well done,
doctor!" He sat to leeward, propped by the water-
cask and yelled back abundantly, but the seas were
breaking in thunder just then, and we only caught
snatches that sounded like: "Providence" and "born
again." He was at his old game of preaching. We
made friendly but derisive gestures at him, and from
below he lifted one arm, holding on with the other,
moved his lips; he beamed up to us, straining his voice
—earnest, and ducking his head before the sprays.

Suddenly some one cried:—"Where's Jimmy?" and
we were appalled once more. On the end of the row

the boatswain shouted hoarsely:—"Has any one seed
him come out?" Voices exclaimed dismally:—
"Drowned—is he? . . . No! In his cabin!
. . . Good Lord! . . . Caught like a
bloomin' rat in a trap. . . . Couldn't open his
door . . . Aye! She went over too quick and
the water jammed it . . . Poor beggar! . . .
No help for 'im. . . . Let's go and see . . ."
"Damn him, who could go?" screamed Donkin.—
"Nobody expects you to," growled the man next
to him: "you're only a thing."—"Is there half a
chance to get at 'im?" inquired two or three men together. Belfast untied himself with blind impetuosity,
and all at once shot down to leeward quicker than a
flash of lightning. We shouted all together with dismay; but with his legs overboard he held and yelled
for a rope. In our extremity nothing could be terrible;
so we judged him funny kicking there, and with his
scared face. Some one begán to laugh, and, as if
hysterically infected with screaming merriment, all
those haggard men went off laughing, wild-eyed, like
a lot of maniacs tied up on a wall. Mr. Baker swung
off the binnacle-stand and tendered him one leg. He
scrambled up rather scared, and consigning us with
abominable words to the "divvle." "You are.
. . . Ough! You're a foul-mouthed beggar,
Craik," grunted Mr. Baker. He answered, stuttering
with indignation:—"Look at 'em, sorr. The bloomin'
dirty images! laughing at a chum going overboard.
Call themselves men, too." But from the break of
the poop the boatswain called out:—"Come along,"
and Belfast crawled away in a hurry to join him. The
five men, poised and gazing over the edge of the poop,
looked for the best way to get forward. They seemed
to hesitate. The others, twisting in their lashings,

turning painfully, stared with open lips. Captain Allistoun saw nothing; he seemed with his eyes to hold the ship up in a superhuman concentration of effort. The wind screamed loud in sunshine; columns of spray rose straight up; and in the glitter of rainbows bursting over the trembling hull the men went over cautiously, disappearing from sight with deliberate movements.

They went swinging from belaying pin to cleat above the seas that beat the half-submerged deck. Their toes scraped the planks. Lumps of green cold water toppled over the bulwark and on their heads. They hung for a moment on strained arms, with the breath knocked out of them, and with closed eyes—then, letting go with one hand, balanced with lolling heads, trying to grab some rope or stanchion further forward. The long-armed and athletic boatswain swung quickly, gripping things with a fist hard as iron, and remembering suddenly snatches of the last letter from his "old woman." Little Belfast scrambled in a rage spluttering "cursed nigger." Wamibo's tongue hung out with excitement; and Archie, intrepid and calm, watched his chance to move with intelligent coolness.

When above the side of the house, they let go one after another, and falling heavily, sprawled, pressing their palms to the smooth teak wood. Round them the backwash of waves seethed white and hissing. All the doors had become trap-doors, of course. The first was the galley door. The galley extended from side to side, and they could hear the sea splashing with hollow noises in there. The next door was that of the carpenter's shop. They lifted it, and looked down. The room seemed to have been devastated by an earthquake. Everything in it had tumbled on the bulkhead facing the door, and on the other side of that bulkhead there was Jimmy, dead or alive. The bench,

a half-finished meat-safe, saws, chisels, wire rods, axes,
crowbars, lay in a heap besprinkled with loose nails.
A sharp adze*stuck up with a shining edge that gleamed
dangerously down there like a wicked smile. The
men clung to one another peering. A sickening, sly
lurch of the ship nearly sent them overboard in a body.
Belfast howled "Here goes!" and leaped down. Archie
followed cannily, catching at shelves that gave way
with him, and eased himself in a great crash of ripped
wood. There was hardly room for three men to move.
And in the sunshiny blue square of the door, the boatswain's face, bearded and dark, Wamibo's face, wild
and pale, hung over—watching.

Together they shouted: "Jimmy! Jim!" From
above the boatswain contributed a deep growl: "You
. . . Wait!" In a pause, Belfast entreated:
"Jimmy, darlin', are ye aloive?" The boatswain said:
"Again! All together, boys!" All yelled excitedly.
Wamibo made noises resembling loud barks. Belfast
drummed on the side of the bulkhead with a piece of
iron. All ceased suddenly. The sound of screaming
and hammering went on thin and distinct—like a
solo after a chorus. He was alive. He was screaming
and knocking below us with the hurry of a man pre-
maturely shut up in a coffin. We went to work. We
attacked with desperation the abominable heap of
things heavy, of things sharp, of things clumsy to handle.
The boatswain crawled away to find somewhere a flying
end of a rope; and Wamibo, held back by shouts:—
"Don't jump! . . . Don't come in here, muddle-
head!"—remained glaring above us—all shining eyes,
gleaming fangs, tumbled hair; resembling an amazed
and half-witted fiend gloating over the extraordinary
agitation of the damned. The boatswain adjured us
to "bear a hand,"*and a rope descended. We made

things fast to it and they went up spinning, never to be seen by man again. A rage to fling things overboard possessed us. We worked fiercely cutting our hands, and speaking brutally to one another. Jimmy kept up a distracting row; he screamed piercingly, without drawing breath, like a tortured woman; he banged with hands and feet. The agony of his fear wrung our hearts so terribly that we longed to abandon him, to get out of that place deep as a well and swaying like a tree, to get out of his hearing, back on the poop where we could wait passively for death in incomparable repose. We shouted to him to "shut up, for God's sake." He redoubled his cries. He must have fancied we could not hear him. Probably he heard his own clamour but faintly. We could picture him crouching on the edge of the upper berth, letting out with both fists at the wood, in the dark, and with his mouth wide open for that unceasing cry. Those were loathsome moments. A cloud driving across the sun would darken the doorway menacingly. Every movement of the ship was pain. We scrambled about with no room to breathe, and felt frightfully sick. The boatswain yelled down at us:—"Bear a hand! Bear a hand! We two will be washed away from here directly if you ain't quick!" Three times a sea leaped over the high side and flung bucketfuls of water on our heads. Then Jimmy, startled by the shock, would stop his noise for a moment—waiting for the ship to sink, perhaps—and began again, distressingly loud, as if invigorated by the gust of fear. At the bottom the nails lay in a layer several inches thick. It was ghastly. Every nail in the world, not driven in firmly somewhere, seemed to have found its way into that carpenter's shop. There they were, of all kinds, the remnants of stores from seven voyages. Tin-tacks, copper tacks (sharp as needles), pump nails, with big heads, like tiny iron mushrooms; nails without any heads (horrible); French nails polished and slim.   They lay in a solid mass more inabordable*than a hedgehog.   We hesitated, yearning for a shovel, while Jimmy below us yelled as though he had been flayed.   Groaning, we dug our fingers in, and very much hurt, shook our hands, scattering nails and drops of blood.   We passed up our hats full of assorted nails to the boatswain, who, as if performing a mysterious and appeasing rite, cast them wide upon a raging sea.

We got to the bulkhead at last.   Those were stout planks.   She was a ship, well finished in every detail—the *Narcissus* was.   They were the stoutest planks ever put into a ship's bulkhead—we thought—and then we perceived that, in our hurry, we had sent all the tools overboard.   Absurd little Belfast wanted to break it down with his own weight, and with both feet leaped straight up like a springbok, cursing the Clyde shipwrights for not scamping their work.   Incidentally he reviled all North Britain, the rest of the earth, the sea—and all his companions.   He swore, as he alighted heavily on his heels, that he would never, never any more associate with any fool that "hadn't savee enough to know his knee from his elbow."   He managed by his thumping to scare the last remnant of wits out of Jimmy.   We could hear the object of our exasperated solicitude darting to and fro under the planks.   He had cracked his voice at last, and could only squeak miserably.   His back or else his head rubbed the planks, now here, now there, in a puzzling manner.   He squeaked as he dodged the invisible blows.   It was more heartrending even than his yells.   Suddenly Archie produced a crowbar.   He had kept it back; also a small hatchet.   We howled with satisfaction.   He struck a mighty blow and small chips flew at our eyes. The boatswain above shouted:—"Look out! Look out there. Don't kill the man. Easy does it!" Wamibo, maddened with excitement, hung head down and insanely urged us:—"Hoo! Strook 'im! Hoo! Hoo!" We were afraid he would fall in and kill one of us and, hurriedly, we entreated the boatswain to "shove the blamed Finn overboard." Then, all together, we yelled down at the planks:—"Stand from under! Get forward," and listened. We only heard the deep hum and moan of the wind above us, the mingled roar and hiss of the seas. The ship, as if overcome with despair, wallowed lifelessly, and our heads swam with that unnatural motion. Belfast clamoured:—"For the love of God, Jimmy, where are ye? . . . Knock! Jimmy darlint! . . . Knock! You bloody black beast! Knock!" He was as quiet as a dead man inside a grave; and, like men standing above a grave, we were on the verge of tears—but with vexation, the strain, the fatigue; with the great longing to be done with it, to get away, and lie down to rest somewhere where we could see our danger and breathe. Archie shouted:—"Gi'e me room!" We crouched behind him, guarding our heads, and he struck time after time in the joint of planks. They cracked. Suddenly the crowbar went halfway in through a splintered oblong hole. It must have missed Jimmy's head by less than an inch. Archie withdrew it quickly, and that infamous nigger rushed at the hole, put his lips to it, and whispered "Help" in an almost extinct voice; he pressed his head to it, trying madly to get out through that opening one inch wide and three inches long. In our disturbed state we were absolutely paralysed by his incredible action. It seemed impossible to drive him away. Even Archie at last lost his composure. "If ye don't clear oot I'll

drive the crowbar thro' your head," he shouted in a
determined voice. He meant what he said, and his
earnestness seemed to make an impression on Jimmy.
He disappeared suddenly, and we set to prising and
tearing at the planks with the eagerness of men trying
to get at a mortal enemy, and spurred by the desire to
tear him limb from limb. The wood split, cracked,
gave way. Belfast plunged in head and shoulders
and groped viciously. "I've got 'im! Got 'im," he
shouted. "Oh! There! . . . He's gone; I've
got 'im! . . . Pull at my legs! . . .
Pull!" Wamibo hooted unceasingly. The boatswain
shouted directions:—"Catch hold of his hair, Belfast;
pull straight up, you two! . . . Pull fair!"
We pulled fair. We pulled Belfast out with a jerk,
and dropped him with disgust. In a sitting posture,
purple-faced, he sobbed despairingly:—"How can I
hold on to 'is blooming short wool?" Suddenly
Jimmy's head and shoulders appeared. He stuck halfway, and with rolling eyes foamed at our feet. We
flew at him with brutal impatience, we tore the shirt
off his back, we tugged at his ears, we panted over
him; and all at once he came away in our hands as
though somebody had let go his legs. With the same
movement, without a pause, we swung him up. His
breath whistled, he kicked our upturned faces, he
grasped two pairs of arms above his head, and he
squirmed up with such precipitation that he seemed
positively to escape from our hands like a bladder full
of gas. Streaming with perspiration, we swarmed up
the rope, and, coming into the blast of cold wind,
gasped like men plunged into icy water. With burning
faces we shivered to the very marrow of our bones.
Never before had the gale seemed to us more furious,
the sea more mad, the sunshine more merciless and

mocking, and the position of the ship more hopeless
and appalling. Every movement of her was ominous
of the end of her agony and of the beginning of ours.
We staggered away from the door, and, alarmed by a
sudden roll, fell down in a bunch. It appeared to us
that the side of the house was more smooth than glass
and more slippery than ice. There was nothing to
hang on to but a long brass hook used sometimes to
keep back an open door. Wamibo held on to it and we
held on to Wamibo, clutching our Jimmy. He had
completely collapsed now. He did not seem to have
the strength to close his hand. We stuck to him
blindly in our fear. We were not afraid of Wamibo
letting go (we remembered that the brute was stronger
than any three men in the ship), but we were afraid of
the hook giving way, and we also believed that the ship
had made up her mind to turn over at last. But she
didn't. A sea swept over us. The boatswain spluttered:—"Up and away. There's a lull. Away aft
with you, or we will all go to the devil here." We
stood up surrounding Jimmy. We begged him to hold
up, to hold on, at least. He glared with his bulging
eyes, mute as a fish, and with all the stiffening knocked
out of him. He wouldn't stand; he wouldn't even as
much as clutch at our necks; he was only a cold black
skin loosely stuffed with soft cotton wool; his arms
and legs swung jointless and pliable; his head rolled
about; the lower lip hung down, enormous and heavy.
We pressed round him, bothered and dismayed;
sheltering him we swung here and there in a body;
and on the very brink of eternity we tottered all together with concealing and absurd gestures, like a lot
of drunken men embarrassed with a stolen corpse.

Something had to be done. We had to get him aft.
A rope was tied slack under his armpits, and, reaching

up at the risk of our lives, we hung him on the foresheet cleat. He emitted no sound; he looked as
ridiculously lamentable as a doll that had lost half its
sawdust, and we started on our perilous journey over
the main deck, dragging along with care that pitiful,
that limp, that hateful burden. He was not very
heavy, but had he weighed a ton he could not have
been more awkward to handle. We literally passed
him from hand to hand. Now and then we had to
hang him up on a handy belaying-pin, to draw a breath
and reform the line. Had the pin broken he would
have irretrievably gone into the Southern Ocean, but
he had to take his chance of that; and after a little
while, becoming apparently aware of it, he groaned
slightly, and with a great effort whispered a few words.
We listened eagerly. He was reproaching us with
our carelessness in letting him run such risks: "Now,
after I got myself out from there," he breathed out
weakly. "There" was his cabin. And he got himself
out. We had nothing to do with it apparently!
. . . No matter. . . . We went on and let
him take his chances, simply because we could not
help it; for though at that time we hated him more
than ever—more than anything under heaven—we
did not want to lose him. We had so far saved
him; and it had become a personal matter between us
and the sea. We meant to stick to him. Had we
(by an incredible hypothesis) undergone similar toil
and trouble for an empty cask, that cask would have
become as precious to us as Jimmy was. More precious, in fact, because we would have had no reason to
hate the cask. And we hated James Wait. We could
not get rid of the monstrous suspicion that this astounding black-man was shamming sick, had been malingering heartlessly in the face of our toil, of our scorn, of

our patience—and now was malingering in the face of
our devotion—in the face of death. Our vague and
imperfect morality rose with disgust at his unmanly lie.
But he stuck to it manfully—amazingly. No! It
couldn't be. He was at all extremity. His cantankerous
temper was only the result of the provoking invincible-
ness of that death he felt by his side. Any man may
be angry with such a masterful chum. But, then,
what kind of men were we—with our thoughts! Indignation and doubt grappled within us in a scuffle
that trampled upon the finest of our feelings. And
we hated him because of the suspicion; we detested him
because of the doubt. We could not scorn him safely—
neither could we pity him without risk to our dignity.
So we hated him, and passed him carefully from hand
to hand. We cried, "Got him?"—"Yes. All right.
Let go." And he swung from one enemy to another,
showing about as much life as an old bolster would do.
His eyes made two narrow white slits in the black face.
The air escaped through his lips with a noise like the
sound of bellows. We reached the poop ladder at
last, and it being a comparatively safe place, we lay
for a moment in an exhausted heap to rest a little.
He began to mutter. We were always incurably anxious to hear what he had to say. This time he mumbled
peevishly, "It took you some time to come. I began
to think the whole smart lot of you had been washed
overboard. What kept you back? Hey? Funk?"
We said nothing. With sighs we started again to drag
him up. The secret and ardent desire of our hearts
was the desire to beat him viciously with our fists about
the head; and we handled him as tenderly as though he
had been made of glass. . . .

The return on the poop was like the return of wan-
derers after many years amongst people marked by

the desolation of time. Eyes were turned slowly in
their sockets glancing at us. Faint murmurs were
heard, "Have you got 'im after all?" The well-
known faces looked strange and familiar; they seemed
faded and grimy; they had a mingled expression of
fatigue and eagerness. They seemed to have become
much thinner during our absence, as if all these men
had been starving for a long time in their abandoned
attitudes. The captain, with a round turn of a rope
on his wrist, and kneeling on one knee, swung with a
face cold and stiff; but with living eyes he was still
holding the ship up, heeding no one, as if lost in the
unearthly effort of that endeavour. We fastened up
James Wait in a safe place. Mr. Baker scrambled
along to lend a hand. Mr. Creighton, on his back,
and very pale, muttered, "Well done," and gave us,
Jimmy and the sky, a scornful glance, then closed his
eyes slowly. Here and there a man stirred a little, but
most of them remained apathetic, in cramped positions,
muttering between shivers. The sun was setting. A
sun enormous, unclouded and red, declining low as if
bending down to look into their faces. The wind
whistled across long sunbeams that, resplendent and
cold, struck full on the dilated pupils of staring eyes
without making them wink. The wisps of hair and
the tangled beards were grey with the salt of the sea.
The faces were earthy, and the dark patches under the
eyes extended to the ears, smudged into the hollows
of sunken cheeks. The lips were livid and thin, and
when they moved it was with difficulty, as though they
had been glued to the teeth. Some grinned sadly in
the sunlight, shaking with cold. Others were sad and
still. Charley, subdued by the sudden disclosure of
the insignificance of his youth, darted fearful glances.
The two smooth-faced Norwegians resembled decrepit

children, staring stupidly. To leeward, on the edge
of the horizon, black seas leaped up towards the glowing sun. It sank slowly, round and blazing, and the
crests of waves splashed on the edge of the luminous
circle. One of the Norwegians appeared to catch sight
of it, and, after giving a violent start, began to speak.
His voice, startling the others, made them stir. They
moved their heads stiffly, or turning with difficulty,
looked at him with surprise, with fear, or in grave
silence. He chattered at the setting sun, nodding his
head, while the big seas began to roll across the crimson disc; and over miles of turbulent waters the shadows of high waves swept with a running darkness the
faces of men. A crested roller broke with a loud hissing
roar, and the sun, as if put out, disappeared. The
chattering voice faltered, went out together with the
light. There were sighs. In the sudden lull that
follows the crash of a broken sea a man said wearily,
"Here's that blooming Dutchman gone off his chump."
A seaman, lashed by the middle, tapped the deck with
his open hand with unceasing quick flaps. In the
gathering greyness of twilight a bulky form was seen
rising aft, and began marching on all fours with the
movements of some big cautious beast. It was Mr.
Baker passing along the line of men. He grunted
encouragingly over every one, felt their fastenings.
Some, with half-open eyes, puffed like men oppressed
by heat; others mechanically and in dreamy voices
answered him, "Aye! aye! sir!" He went from one to
another grunting, "Ough! . . . See her through
it yet;" and unexpectedly, with loud angry outbursts,
blew up Knowles for cutting off a long piece from
the fall of the relieving tackle. "Ough!——Ashamed
of yourself——Relieving tackle——Don't you know
better!——Ough!——Able seaman! Ough!" The

lame man was crushed. He muttered, "Get som'think for a lashing for myself, sir."—"Ough! Lashing—— yourself. Are you a tinker or a sailor——What? Ough!——May want that tackle directly——Ough! ——More use to the ship than your lame carcass. Ough!——Keep it!——Keep it, now you've done it." He crawled away slowly, muttering to himself about some men being "worse than children." It had been a comforting row. Low exclamations were heard: "Hallo . . . Hallo." . . . Those who had been painfully dozing asked with convulsive starts, "What's up? . . . What is it?" The answers came with unexpected cheerfulness: "The mate is going bald-headed for lame Jack about something or other." "No!" . . . . "What 'as he done?" Some one even chuckled. It was like a whiff of hope, like a reminder of safe days. Donkin, who had been stupefied with fear, revived suddenly and began to shout:—"'Ear 'im; that's the way they tawlk to us. Vy donch 'ee 'it 'im—one ov yer? 'It 'im. 'It 'im! Comin' the mate over us. We are as good men as 'ee! We're all goin' to 'ell now. We 'ave been starved in this rotten ship, an' now we're goin' to be drowned for them black 'earted bullies! 'It 'im!" He shrieked in the deepening gloom, he blubbered and sobbed, screaming:—"'It 'im! 'It 'im!" The rage and fear of his disregarded right to live tried the steadfastness of hearts more than the menacing shadows of the night that advanced through the unceasing clamour of the gale. From aft Mr. Baker was heard:—"Is one of you men going to stop him—must I come along?" "Shut up!" . . . "Keep quiet!" cried various voices, exasperated, trembling with cold.—"You'll get one across the mug from me directly," said an invisible seaman, in a weary tone, "I won't let the mate have the trouble." He ceased and lay still with the silence of despair. On the black sky the stars, coming out, gleamed over an inky sea that, speckled with foam, flashed back at them the evanescent and pale light of a dazzling whiteness born from the black turmoil of the waves. Remote in the eternal calm they glittered hard and cold above the uproar of the earth; they surrounded the vanquished and tormented ship on all sides: more pitiless than the eyes of a triumphant mob, and as unapproachable as the hearts of men.

The icy south wind howled exultingly under the sombre splendour of the sky. The cold shook the men with a resistless violence as though it had tried to shake them to pieces. Short moans were swept unheard off the stiff lips. Some complained in mutters of "not feeling themselves below the waist;" while those who had closed their eyes, imagined they had a block of ice on their chests. Others, alarmed at not feeling any pain in their fingers, beat the deck feebly with their hands—obstinate and exhausted. Wamibo stared vacant and dreamy. The Scandinavians kept on a meaningless mutter through chattering teeth. The spare Scotchmen, with determined efforts, kept their lower jaws still. The West-country men lay big and stolid in an invulnerable surliness. A man yawned and swore in turns. Another breathed with a rattle in his throat. Two elderly hard-weather shellbacks, fast side by side, whispered dismally to one another about the landlady of a boarding-house in Sunderland, whom they both knew. They extolled her motherliness and her liberality; they tried to talk about the joint of beef and the big fire in the downstairs kitchen. The words dying faintly on their lips, ended in light sighs. A sudden voice cried into the cold night, "Oh Lord!" No one changed his position or took any notice

of the cry. One or two passed, with a repeated and
vague gesture, their hand over their faces, but most of
them kept very still. In the benumbed immobility
of their bodies they were excessively wearied by their
thoughts, which rushed with the rapidity and vividness
of dreams. Now and then, by an abrupt and startling
exclamation, they answered the weird hail of some illusion; then, again, in silence contemplated the vision
of known faces and familiar things. They recalled
the aspect of forgotten shipmates and heard the voice
of dead and gone skippers. They remembered the
noise of gaslit streets, the steamy heat of tap-rooms or
the scorching sunshine of calm days at sea.

Mr. Baker left his insecure place, and crawled, with
stoppages, along the poop. In the dark and on all
fours he resembled some carnivorous animal prowling
amongst corpses. At the break, propped to windward
of a stanchion, he looked down on the main deck. It
seemed to him that the ship had a tendency to stand
up a little more. The wind had eased a little, he
thought, but the sea ran as high as ever. The waves
foamed viciously, and the lee side of the deck disappeared under a hissing whiteness as of boiling milk,
while the rigging sang steadily with a deep vibrating
note, and, at every upward swing of the ship, the wind
rushed with a long-drawn clamour amongst the spars.
Mr. Baker watched very still. A man near him began
to make a blabbing noise with his lips, all at once and
very loud, as though the cold had broken brutally
through him. He went on:—"Ba—ba—ba—brrr—
brr—ba—ba."—"Stop that!" cried Mr. Baker, groping in the dark. "Stop it!" He went on shaking the
leg he found under his hand.—"What is it, sir?"
called out Belfast, in the tone of a man awakened suddenly; "we are looking after that 'ere Jimmy."—"Are

you? Ough! Don't make that row then. Who's that near you?"—"It's me—the boatswain, sir," growled the West-country man; "we are trying to keep life in that poor devil."—"Aye, aye!" said Mr. Baker. "Do it quietly, can't you."—"He wants us to hold him up above the rail," went on the boatswain, with irritation, "says he can't breathe here under our jackets."—"If we lift 'im, we drop 'im overboard," said another voice, "we can't feel our hands with cold."—"I don't care. I am choking!" exclaimed James Wait in a clear tone.—"Oh, no, my son," said the boatswain, desperately, "you don't go till we all go on this fine night."—"You will see yet many a worse," said Mr. Baker, cheerfully.—"It's no child's play, sir!" answered the boatswain. "Some of us further aft, here, are in a pretty bad way."—"If the blamed sticks had been cut out of her she would be running along on her bottom now like any decent ship, an' giv' us all a chance," said some one, with a sigh.—"The old man wouldn't have it . . . much he cares for us," whispered another.—"Care for you!" exclaimed Mr. Baker, angrily. "Why should he care for you? Are you a lot of women passengers to be taken care of? We are here to take care of the ship—and some of you ain't up to that. Ough! . . . What have you done so very smart to be taken care of? Ough! . . . Some of you can't stand a bit of a breeze without crying over it."—"Come, sorr. We ain't so bad," protested Belfast, in a voice shaken by shivers; "we ain't . . . brrr . . . "—"Again," shouted the mate, grabbing at the shadowy form; "again! . . . Why, you're in your shirt! What have you done?"—"I've put my oilskin and jacket over that half-dead nayggur—and he says he chokes," said Belfast, complainingly.—"You wouldn't call

me nigger if I wasn't half dead, you Irish beggar!"
boomed James Wait, vigorously.—"You . . . brrr
. . . You wouldn't be white if you were ever
so well . . . I will fight you . . . brrrr
. . . in fine weather . . brrr . . . with
one hand tied behind my back . . . brrrrrr
. . ."—"I don't want your rags—I want air,"
gasped out the other faintly, as if suddenly exhausted.

The sprays swept over whistling and pattering.
Men disturbed in their peaceful torpor by the pain of
quarrelsome shouts, moaned, muttering curses. Mr.
Baker crawled off a little way to leeward where a water-
cask loomed up big, with something white against it.
"Is it you, Podmore?" asked Mr. Baker, He had to
repeat the question twice before the cook turned,
coughing feebly.—"Yes, sir. I've been praying in
my mind for a quick deliverance; for I am prepared
for any call. . . . I——"—"Look here, cook,"
interrupted Mr. Baker, "the men are perishing with
cold."—"Cold!" said the cook, mournfully; "they
will be warm enough before long."—"What?" asked
Mr. Baker, looking along the deck into the faint sheen
of frothing water.—"They are a wicked lot," continued the cook solemnly, but in an unsteady voice,
"about as wicked as any ship's company in this sinful
world! Now, I"—he trembled so that he could hardly
speak; his was an exposed place, and in a cotton shirt,
a thin pair of trousers, and with his knees under his
nose, he received, quaking, the flicks of stinging, salt
drops; his voice sounded exhausted—"now, I—any
time . . . My eldest youngster, Mr. Baker
. . . a clever boy . . . last Sunday on
shore before this voyage he wouldn't go to church, sir.
Says I, 'You go and clean yourself, or I'll know the

reason why!' What does he do? . . . Pond Mr.
Baker—fell into the pond in his best rig, sir! . . .
Accident? . . . 'Nothing will save you, fine
scholar though you are!' says I. . . . Accident!
. . . I whopped him, sir, till I couldn't lift my
arm. . . ." His voice faltered. "I whopped
'im!" he repeated, rattling his teeth; then, after a while,
let out a mournful sound that was half a groan, half
a snore. Mr. Baker shook him by the shoulders.
"Hey! Cook! Hold up, Podmore! Tell me—is
there any fresh water in the galley tank? The ship is
lying along less, I think; I would try to get forward.
A little water would do them good. Hallo! Look out!
Look out!" The cook struggled.—"Not you, sir—
not you!" He began to scramble to windward.
"Galley! . . . my business!" he shouted.—
"Cook's going crazy now," said several voices. He
yelled:—"Crazy, am I? I am more ready to die than
any of you, officers incloosive—there! As long as she
swims I will cook! I will get you coffee."—"Cook,
ye are a gentleman!" cried Belfast. But the cook was
already going over the weather-ladder. He stopped
for a moment to shout back on the poop:—"As long
as she swims I will cook!" and disappeared as though
he had gone overboard. The men who had heard sent
after him a cheer that sounded like a wail of sick children. An hour or more afterwards some one said
distinctly: "He's gone for good."—"Very likely,"
assented the boatswain; "even in fine weather he was
as smart about the deck as a milch-cow*on her first
voyage. We ought to go and see." Nobody moved.
As the hours dragged slowly through the darkness Mr.
Baker crawled back and forth along the poop several
times. Some men fancied they had heard him exchange murmurs with the master, but at that time the

memories were incomparably more vivid than anything
actual, and they were not certain whether the murmurs
were heard now or many years ago. They did not
try to find out. A mutter more or less did not matter.
It was too cold for curiosity, and almost for hope.
They could not spare a moment or a thought from the
great mental occupation of wishing to live. And the
desire of life kept them alive, apathetic and enduring,
under the cruel persistence of wind and cold; while the
bestarred black dome of the sky revolved slowly above
the ship, that drifted, bearing their patience and their
suffering, through the stormy solitude of the sea.

Huddled close to one another, they fancied themselves utterly alone. They heard sustained loud noises,
and again bore the pain of existence through long hours
of profound silence. In the night they saw sunshine,
felt warmth, and suddenly, with a start, thought that
the sun would never rise upon a freezing world. Some
heard laughter, listened to songs; others, near the end
of the poop, could hear loud human shrieks, and opening their eyes, were surprised to hear them still, though
very faint, and far away. The boatswain said:—
"Why, it's the cook, hailing from forward, I think."
He hardly believed his own words or recognised his own
voice. It was a long time before the man next to him
gave a sign of life. He punched hard his other neigh-
bour and said:—"The cook's shouting!" Many did
not understand, others did not care; the majority further aft did not believe. But the boatswain and another man had the pluck to crawl away forward to see.
They seemed to have been gone for hours, and were
very soon forgotten. Then suddenly men who had
been plunged in a hopeless resignation became as if
possessed with a desire to hurt. They belaboured one
another with fists. In the darkness they struck per-

sistently anything soft they could feel near, and, with
a greater effort than for a shout, whispered excitedly:—
"They've got some hot coffee. . . . Boss'en
got it. . . ." "No! . . . Where?". . . .
"It's coming! Cook made it." James Wait moaned.
Donkin scrambled viciously, caring not where he kicked,
and anxious that the officers should have none of it.
It came in a pot, and they drank in turns. It was hot,
and while it blistered the greedy palates, it seemed
incredible. The men sighed out parting with the
mug:—"How 'as he done it?" Some cried weakly:—
"Bully for you, doctor!"

He had done it somehow. Afterwards Archie declared that the thing was "meeraculous." For many
days we wondered, and it was the one ever-interesting
subject of conversation to the end of the voyage. We
asked the cook, in fine weather, how he felt when he
saw his stove "reared up on end." We inquired, in
the north-east trade* and on serene evenings, whether
he had to stand on his head to put things right some-
what. We suggested he had used his bread-board for
a raft, and from there comfortably had stoked his
grate; and we did our best to conceal our admiration
under the wit of fine irony. He affirmed not to know
anything about it, rebuked our levity, declared himself,
with solemn animation, to have been the object of a
special mercy for the saving of our unholy lives. Fun-
damentally he was right, no doubt; but he need not
have been so offensively positive about it—he need not
have hinted so often that it would have gone hard with
us had he not been there, meritorious and pure, to receive the inspiration and the strength for the work of
grace. Had we been saved by his recklessness or his
agility, we could have at length become reconciled to
the fact; but to admit our obligation to anybody's

virtue and holiness alone was as difficult for us as for
any other handful of mankind. Like many benefactors
of humanity, the cook took himself too seriously, and
reaped the reward of irreverence. We were not un-
ungrateful, however. He remained heroic. His saying—*the* saying of his life—became proverbial in the
mouth of men as are the sayings of conquerors or sages.
Later, whenever one of us was puzzled by a task and
advised to relinquish it, he would express his determination to persevere and to succeed by the words:—"As
long as she swims I will cook!"

The hot drink helped us through the bleak hours
that precede the dawn. The sky low by the horizon
took on the delicate tints of pink and yellow like the
inside of a rare shell. And higher, where it glowed
with a pearly sheen, a small black cloud appeared, like
a forgotten fragment of the night set in a border of
dazzling gold. The beams of light skipped on the
crests of waves. The eyes of men turned to the east-
ward. The sunlight flooded their weary faces. They
were giving themselves up to fatigue as though they
had done for ever with their work. On Singleton's
black oilskin coat the dried salt glistened like hoar
frost. He hung on by the wheel, with open and lifeless
eyes. Captain Allistoun, unblinking, faced the rising
sun. His lips stirred, opened for the first time in
twenty-four hours, and with a fresh firm voice he cried,
"Wear ship!"

The commanding sharp tones made all these torpid
men start like a sudden flick of a whip. Then again,
motionless where they lay, the force of habit made some
of them repeat the order in hardly audible murmurs.
Captain Allistoun glanced down at his crew, and several, with fumbling fingers and hopeless movements,
tried to cast themselves adrift. He repeated im-

patiently, "Wear ship. Now then, Mr. Baker, get
the men along. What's the matter with them?"
—"Wear ship. Do you hear there?—Wear ship!"
thundered out the boatswain suddenly. His voice
seemed to break through a deadly spell. Men began
to stir and crawl.—"I want the fore-top-mast staysail run up smartly," said the master, very loudly;
"if you can't manage it standing up you must do it
lying down—that's all. Bear a hand!"—"Come along!
Let's give the old girl a chance," urged the boatswain.
—"Aye! aye! Wear ship!" exclaimed quavering
voices. The forecastle men, with reluctant faces,
prepared to go forward. Mr. Baker pushed ahead
grunting on all fours to show the way, and they followed
him over the break. The others lay still with a vile
hope in their hearts of not being required to move till
they got saved or drowned in peace.

After some time they could be seen forward appearing on the forecastle head, one by one in unsafe attitudes; hanging on to the rails, clambering over the
anchors; embracing the cross-head of the windlass or
hugging the fore-capstan. They were restless with
strange exertions, waved their arms, knelt, lay flat
down, staggered up, seemed to strive their hardest to
go overboard. Suddenly a small white piece of canvas
fluttered amongst them, grew larger, beating. Its
narrow head rose in jerks—and at last it stood distended and triangular in the sunshine.—"They have
done it!" cried the voices aft. Captain Allistoun let
go the rope he had round his wrist and rolled to leeward headlong. He could be seen casting the lee main
braces off the pins while the backwash of waves
splashed over him.—"Square the main yard!" he
shouted up to us—who stared at him in wonder. We
hesitated to stir. "The main brace, men. Haul!

haul anyhow! Lay on your backs and haul!" he screeched, half drowned down there. We did not believe we could move the main yard, but the strongest and the less discouraged tried to execute the order. Others assisted half-heartedly. Singleton's eyes blazed suddenly as he took a fresh grip of the spokes. Captain Allistoun fought his way up to windward.— "Haul men! Try to move it! Haul, and help the ship." His hard face worked suffused and furious. "Is she going off, Singleton?" he cried.—"Not a move yet, sir," croaked the old seaman in a horribly hoarse voice.—"Watch the helm, Singleton," spluttered the master. "Haul men! Have you no more strength than rats? Haul, and earn your salt."* Mr. Creighton, on his back, with a swollen leg and a face as white as a piece of paper, blinked his eyes; his bluish lips twitched. In the wild scramble men grabbed at him, crawled over his hurt leg, knelt on his chest. He kept perfectly still, setting his teeth without a moan, without a sigh. The master's ardour, the cries of that silent man inspired us. We hauled and hung in bunches on the rope. We heard him say with violence to Donkin, who sprawled abjectly on his stomach,—"I will brain you with this belaying pin if you don't catch hold of the brace," and that victim of men's injustice, cowardly and cheeky, whimpered:—"Are you goin' to murder us now," while with sudden desperation he gripped the rope. Men sighed, shouted, hissed meaningless words, groaned. The yards moved, came slowly square against the wind, that hummed loudly on the yard-arms.—"Going off, sir," shouted Singleton, "she's just started."—"Catch a turn with that brace. Catch a turn!" clamoured the master. Mr. Creighton, nearly suffocated and unable to move, made a mighty effort, and with his left hand managed to nip the rope.

—"All fast!" cried some one. He closed his eyes as if
going off into a swoon, while huddled together about
the brace we watched with scared looks what the ship
would do now.

She went off slowly as though she had been weary
and disheartened like the men she carried. She paid
off very gradually, making us hold our breath till we
choked, and as soon as she had brought the wind abaft
the beam she started to move, and fluttered our hearts.
It was awful to see her, nearly overturned, begin to
gather way and drag her submerged side through the
water. The dead-eyes of the rigging churned the
breaking seas. The lower half of the deck was full
of mad whirlpools and eddies; and the long line of the
lee rail could be seen showing black now and then in
the swirls of a field of foam as dazzling and white as a
field of snow. The wind sang shrilly amongst the
spars; and at every slight lurch we expected her to slip
to the bottom sideways from under our backs. When
dead before it she made the first distinct attempt to
stand up, and we encouraged her with a feeble and dis-
cordant howl. A great sea came running up aft and
hung for a moment over us with a curling top; then
crashed down under the counter and spread out on
both sides into a great sheet of bursting froth. Above
its fierce hiss we heard Singleton's croak:—"She is
steering!" He had both his feet now planted firmly
on the grating, and the wheel spun fast as he eased
the helm.—"Bring the wind on the port quarter and
steady her!" called out the master, staggering to his
feet, the first man up from amongst our prostrate heap.
One or two screamed with excitement:—"She rises!"
Far away forward, Mr. Baker and three others were
seen erect and black on the clear sky, lifting their arms,
and with open mouths as though they had been shout-

ing all together. The ship trembled, trying to lift
her side, lurched back, seemed to give up with a nerve-
less dip, and suddenly with an unexpected jerk swung
violently to windward, as though she had torn herself
out from a deadly grasp. The whole immense volume
of water, lifted by her deck, was thrown bodily across
to starboard. Loud cracks were heard. Iron ports
breaking open thundered with ringing blows. The
water topped over the starboard rail with the rush of
a river falling over a dam. The sea on deck, and the
seas on every side of her, mingled together in a deafening roar. She rolled violently. We got up and were
helplessly run or flung about from side to side. Men,
rolling over and over, yelled,—"The house will go!"
—"She clears herself!" Lifted by a towering sea
she ran along with it for a moment, spouting thick
streams of water through every opening of her wounded
sides. The lee braces having been carried away or
washed off the pins, all the ponderous yards on the
fore swung from side to side and with appalling rapidity
at every roll. The men forward were seen crouching
here and there with fearful glances upwards at the
enormous spars that whirled about over their heads.
The torn canvas and the ends of broken gear streamed
in the wind like wisps of hair. Through the clear
sunshine, over the flashing turmoil and uproar of the
seas, the ship ran blindly, dishevelled and headlong,
as if fleeing for her life; and on the poop we spun, we
tottered about, distracted and noisy. We all spoke at
once in a thin babble; we had the aspect of invalids
and the gestures of maniacs. Eyes shone, large and
haggard, in smiling, meagre faces that seemed to have
been dusted over with powdered chalk. We stamped,
clapped our hands, feeling ready to jump and do anything; but in reality hardly able to keep on our feet.

Captain Allistoun, hard and slim, gesticulated madly from the poop at Mr. Baker: "Steady these fore-yards! Steady them the best you can!" On the main deck, men excited by his cries, splashed, dashing aimlessly here and there with the foam swirling up to their waists. Apart, far aft, and alone by the helm, old Singleton had deliberately tucked his white beard under the top button of his glistening coat. Swaying upon the din and tumult of the seas, with the whole battered length of the ship launched forward in a rolling rush before his steady old eyes, he stood rigidly still, forgotten by all, and with an attentive face. In front of his erect figure only the two arms moved crosswise with a swift and sudden readiness, to check or urge again the rapid stir of circling spokes. He steered with care.

CHAPTER FOUR

ON MEN reprieved by its disdainful mercy, the immortal sea confers in its justice the full privilege of desired unrest. Through the perfect wisdom of its grace they are not permitted to meditate at ease upon the complicated and acrid savour of existence. They must without pause justify their life to the eternal pity that commands toil to be hard and unceasing, from sunrise to sunset, from sunset to sunrise; till the weary succession of nights and days tainted by the obstinate clamour of sages, demanding bliss and an empty heaven, is redeemed at last by the vast silence of pain and labour, by the dumb fear and the dumb courage of men obscure, forgetful, and enduring.

The master and Mr. Baker coming face to face stared for a moment, with the intense and amazed looks of men meeting unexpectedly after years of trouble. Their voices were gone, and they whispered desperately at one another.—"Any one missing?" asked Captain Allistoun.—"No. All there."—"Anybody hurt?"—"Only the second mate."—"I will look after him directly. We're lucky."—"Very," articulated Mr. Baker, faintly. He gripped the rail and rolled bloodshot eyes. The little grey man made an effort to raise his voice above a dull mutter, and fixed his chief mate with a cold gaze, piercing like a dart.— "Get sail on the ship," he said, speaking authoritatively and with an inflexible snap of his thin lips. "Get sail on her as soon as you can. This is a fair wind.* At once, sir—Don't give the men time to feel themselves.

They will get done up and stiff, and we will never
. . . We must get her along now" . . . He
reeled to a long heavy roll; the rail dipped into the
glancing, hissing water. He caught a shroud, swung
helplessly against the mate . . . "now we
have a fair wind at last——Make——sail." His head
rolled from shoulder to shoulder. His eyelids began
to beat rapidly. "And the pumps——pumps, Mr.
Baker." He peered as though the face within a foot
of his eyes had been half a mile off. "Keep the men
on the move to——to get her along," he mumbled
in a drowsy tone, like a man going off into a doze. He
pulled himself together suddenly. "Mustn't stand.
Won't do," he said with a painful attempt at a smile.
He let go his hold, and, propelled by the dip of the
ship, ran aft unwillingly, with small steps, till he
brought up against the binnacle stand. Hanging on
there he looked up in an objectless manner at Singleton,
who, unheeding him, watched anxiously the end of
the jib-boom—"Steering gear works all right?" he
asked. There was a noise in the old seaman's throat,
as though the words had been rattling together before
they could come out.—"Steers . . . like a little boat," he said, at last, with hoarse tenderness,
without giving the master as much as half a glance—
then, watchfully, spun the wheel down, steadied, flung
it back again. Captain Allistoun tore himself away
from the delight of leaning against the binnacle, and
began to walk the poop, swaying and reeling to preserve
his balance. . . .

The pump-rods, clanking, stamped in short jumps
while the fly-wheels turned smoothly, with great speed,
at the foot of the mainmast, flinging back and forth
with a regular impetuosity two limp clusters of men
clinging to the handles. They abandoned themselves,

swaying from the hip with twitching faces and stony eyes. The carpenter, sounding from time to time, exclaimed mechanically: "Shake her up! Keep her going!" Mr. Baker could not speak, but found his voice to shout; and under the goad of his objurgations, men looked to the lashings, dragged out new sails; and thinking themselves unable to move, carried heavy blocks aloft—overhauled the gear. They went up the rigging with faltering and desperate efforts. Their heads swam as they shifted their hold, stepped blindly on the yards like men in the dark; or trusted themselves to the first rope at hand with the negligence of exhausted strength. The narrow escapes from falls did not disturb the languid beat of their hearts; the roar of the seas seething far below them sounded continuous and faint like an indistinct noise from another world: the wind filled their eyes with tears, and with heavy gusts tried to push them off from where they swayed in insecure positions. With streaming faces and blowing hair they flew up and down between sky and water, bestriding the ends of yard-arms, crouching on foot-ropes, embracing lifts to have their hands free, or standing up against chain ties. Their thoughts floated vaguely between the desire of rest and the desire of life, while their stiffened fingers cast off head-earings,. fumbled for knives, or held with tenacious grip against the violent shocks of beating canvas. They glared savagely at one another, made frantic signs with one hand while they held their life in the other, looked down on the narrow strip of flooded deck, shouted along to leeward:" Light-to!" . . . "Haul out!" . . . "Make fast!" Their lips moved, their eyes started, furious and eager with the desire to be understood, but the wind tossed their words unheard upon the disturbed sea. In an unendurable and unending strain

they worked like men driven by a merciless dream to
toil in an atmosphere of ice or flame. They burnt and
shivered in turns. Their eyeballs smarted as if in the
smoke of a conflagration; their heads were ready to
burst with every shout. Hard fingers seemed to grip
their throats. At every roll they thought: Now I
must let go. It will shake us all off—and thrown
about aloft they cried wildly: "Look out there—catch
the end." . . . "Reeve clear" . . . "Turn
this block. . . . " They nodded desperately;
shook infuriated faces, "No! No! From down up."
They seemed to hate one another with a deadly hate.
The longing to be done with it all gnawed their breasts,
and the wish to do things well was a burning pain.
They cursed their fate, contemned their life, and wasted
their breath in deadly imprecations upon one another.
The sailmaker, with his bald head bared, worked fever-
ishly, forgetting his intimacy with so many admirals.
The boatswain, climbing up with marlinspikes and
bunches of spunyarn rovings, or kneeling on the yard
and ready to take a turn with the midship-stop, had
acute and fleeting visions of his old woman and the
youngsters in a moorland village. Mr. Baker, feeling
very weak, tottered here and there, grunting and inflexible, like a man of iron. He waylaid those who,
coming from aloft, stood gasping for breath. He ordered, encouraged, scolded. "Now then—to the main
topsail now! Tally on to that gantline. Don't stand
about there!"—"Is there no rest for us?" muttered
voices. He spun round fiercely, with a sinking heart.
—"No! No rest till the work is done. Work till you
drop. That's what you're here for." A bowed seaman at his elbow gave a short laugh.—"Do or die," he
croaked bitterly, then spat into his broad palms, swung
up his long arms, and grasping the rope high above

his head sent out a mournful, wailing cry for a pull all
together. A sea boarded the quarter-deck and sent
the whole lot sprawling to leeward. Caps, handspikes
floated. Clenched hands, kicking legs, with here and
there a spluttering face, stuck out of the white hiss of
foaming water. Mr. Baker, knocked down with the
rest, screamed—"Don't let go that rope! Hold on to
it! Hold!" And sorely bruised by the brutal fling,.
they held on to it, as though it had been the fortune of
their life. The ship ran, rolling heavily, and the topping crests glanced past port and starboard flashing
their white heads. Pumps were freed. Braces were
rove. The three topsails and foresail were set. She
spurted faster over the water, outpacing the swift rush
of waves. The menacing thunder of distanced seas
rose behind her—filled the air with the tremendous
vibrations of its voice. And devastated, battered
and wounded she drove foaming to the northward, as
though inspired by the courage of a high endeavour. . . .

The forecastle was a place of damp desolation.
They looked at their dwelling with dismay. It was
slimy, dripping; it hummed hollow with the wind, and
was strewn with shapeless wreckage like a half-tide
cavern in a rocky and exposed coast. Many had lost
all they had in the world, but most of the starboard
watch had preserved their chests; thin streams of
water trickled out of them, however. The beds were
soaked; the blankets spread out and saved by some nail
squashed under foot. They dragged wet rags from
evil-smelling corners, and wringing the water out,
recognised their property. Some smiled stiffly. Others
looked round blank and mute. There were cries of
joy over old waistcoats, and groans of sorrow over
shapeless things found among the splinters of smashed

bed boards. One lamp was discovered jammed under
the bowsprit. Charley whimpered a little. Knowles
stumped here and there, sniffing, examining dark places
for salvage. He poured dirty water out of a boot, and
was concerned to find the owner. Those who, overwhelmed by their losses, sat on the forepeak hatch,
remained elbows on knees, and, with a fist against each
cheek, disdained to look up. He pushed it under their
noses. "Here's a good boot. Yours?" They snarled,
"No—get out." One snapped at him, "Take it to
hell out of this." He seemed surprised. "Why?
It's a good boot," but remembering suddenly that he
had lost every stitch of his clothing, he dropped his find
and began to swear. In the dim light cursing voices
clashed. A man came in and, dropping his arms,
stood still, repeating from the doorstep, "Here's a
bloomin' old go! Here's a bloomin' old go!" A few
rooted anxiously in flooded chests for tobacco. They
breathed hard, clamoured with heads down. "Look
at that Jack!" . . . "Here! Sam! Here's my
shore-going rig spoilt for ever." One blasphemed
tearfully holding up a pair of dripping trousers. No
one looked at him. The cat came out from somewhere.
He had an ovation. They snatched him from hand
to hand, caressed him in a murmur of pet names.
They wondered where he had "weathered it out;" disputed about it. A squabbling argument began. Two
men brought in a bucket of fresh water, and all crowded
round it; but Tom, lean and mewing, came up with
every hair astir and had the first drink. A couple of
hands went aft for oil and biscuits.

Then in the yellow light and in the intervals of mop-
ping the deck they crunched hard bread, arranging to
"worry through somehow." Men chummed* as to
beds. Turns were settled for wearing boots and having

the use of oilskin coats. They called one another "old man" and "sonny" in cheery voices. Friendly slaps resounded. Jokes were shouted. One or two stretched on the wet deck, slept with heads pillowed on their bent arms, and several, sitting on the hatch, smoked. Their weary faces appeared through a thin blue haze, pacified and with sparkling eyes. The boatswain put his head through the door. "Relieve the wheel, one of you"—he shouted inside—"it's six. Blamme if that old Singleton hasn't been there more'n thirty hours. You are a fine lot." He slammed the door again. "Mate's watch on deck," said some one. "Hey, Donkin, it's your relief!" shouted three or four together. He had crawled into an empty bunk and on wet planks lay still. "Donkin, your wheel." He made no sound. "Donkin's dead," guffawed some one. "Sell 'is bloomin' clothes," shouted another. "Donkin, if ye don't go to the bloomin' wheel they will sell your clothes—d'ye hear?" jeered a third. He groaned from his dark hole. He complained about pains in all his bones, he whimpered pitifully. "He won't go," exclaimed a contemptuous voice, "your turn, Davis." The young seaman rose painfully squaring his shoulders. Donkin stuck his head out, and it appeared in the yellow light, fragile and ghastly. "I will giv' yer a pound of tobaccer," he whined in a conciliating voice, "so soon as I draw it from aft. I will—s'elp me . . ." Davis swung his arm backhanded and the head vanished. "I'll go," he said, "but you will pay for it." He walked unsteady but resolute to the door. "So I will," yelped Donkin, popping out behind him. "So I will—s'elp me . . . a pound . . . three bob they chawrge." Davis flung the door open. "You will pay my price . . . in fine weather," he shouted over his shoulder. One of the men unbut-

toned his wet coat rapidly, threw it at his head.
"Here, Taffy—take that, you thief!" "Thank you!"
he cried from the darkness above the swish of rolling
water. He could be heard splashing; a sea came on
board with a thump. "He's got his bath already,"
remarked a grim shellback. "Aye, aye!" grunted
others. Then, after a long silence, Wamibo made
strange noises. "Hallo, what's up with you?" said
some one grumpily. "He says he would have gone for
Davy," explained Archie, who was the Finn's inter-
preter generally. "I believe him!" cried voices.
. . . "Never mind, Dutchy . . . You'll
do, muddle-head. . . . Your turn will come
soon enough . . . You don't know when ye're
well off." They ceased, and all together turned their
faces to the door. Singleton stepped in, made two
paces, and stood swaying slightly. The sea hissed,
flowed roaring past the bows, and the forecastle trembled, full of deep murmurs; the lamp flared, swinging
like a pendulum. He looked with a dreamy and puzzled
stare, as though he could not distinguish the still men
from their restless shadows. There were awestruck
exclamations:—"Hallo, hallo." . . . "How does
it look outside now, Singleton?" Those who sat
on the hatch lifted their eyes in silence, and the next
oldest seaman in the ship (those two understood one
another, though they hardly exchanged three words in a
day) gazed up at his friend attentively for a moment,
then taking a short clay pipe out of his mouth, offered
it without a word. Singleton put out his arm towards
it, missed, staggered, and suddenly fell forward, crash-
ing down, stiff and headlong like an uprooted tree.
There was a swift rush. Men pushed, crying:—
"He's done!" . . . "Turn him over!" . . .
"Stand clear there!" Under a crowd of startled faces

bending over him he lay on his back, staring upwards
in a continuous and intolerable manner. In the breathless silence of a general consternation, he said in a grating murmur:—"I am all right," and clutched with his
hands. They helped him up, He mumbled despon-
dently:—"I am getting old . . . old."—"Not
you," cried Belfast, with ready tact. Supported on
all sides, he hung his head.—"Are you better?" they
asked. He glared at them from under his eyebrows
with large black eyes, spreading over his chest the
bushy whiteness of a beard long and thick.—"Old!
old!" he repeated sternly. Helped along, he reached
his bunk. There was in it a slimy soft heap of something that smelt, as does at dead low water a muddy
foreshore. It was his soaked straw bed. With a convulsive effort he pitched himself on it, and in the darkness of the narrow place could be heard growling
angrily, like an irritated and savage animal uneasy in
its den:—"Bit of breeze . . . small thing
. . . can't stand up . . . old!" He slept
at last, high-booted, sou'wester on head, and his
oilskin clothes rustled, when with a deep sighing groan
he turned over. Men conversed about him in quiet,
concerned whispers. "This will break 'im up." . . .
"Strong as a horse" . . . "Aye. But he ain't
what he used to be." . . . In sad murmurs
they gave him up. Yet at midnight he turned out to
duty as if nothing had been the matter, and answered
to his name with a mournful "Here!" He brooded
alone more than ever, in an impenetrable silence and
with a saddened face. For many years he had heard
himself called "Old Singleton," and had serenely accepted the qualification, taking it as a tribute of respect
due to a man who through half a century had measured
his strength against the favours and the rages of the

sea. He had never given a thought to his mortal self.
He lived unscathed, as though he had been indestructible, surrendering to all the temptations, weathering
many gales. He had panted in sunshine, shivered in
the cold; suffered hunger, thirst, debauch; passed
through many trials—known all the furies. Old! It
seemed to him he was broken at last. And like a
man bound treacherously while he sleeps, he woke up
fettered by the long chain of disregarded years. He
had to take up at once the burden of all his existence,
and found it almost too heavy for his strength. Old!
He moved his arms, shook his head, felt his limbs.
Getting old . . . and then? He looked upon
the immortal sea with the awakened and groping perception of its heartless might; he saw it unchanged,
black and foaming under the eternal scrutiny of the
stars; he heard its impatient voice calling for him out of
a pitiless vastness full of unrest, of turmoil, and of
terror. He looked afar upon it, and he saw an immensity tormented and blind, moaning and furious, that
claimed all the days of his tenacious life, and, when
life was over, would claim the worn-out body of its
slave. . . .

This was the last of the breeze. It veered quickly,
changed to a black south-easter,* and blew itself out,
giving the ship a famous shove to the northward into
the joyous sunshine of the trade. Rapid and white she
ran homewards in a straight path, under a blue sky
and upon the plain of a blue sea. She carried Singleton's completed wisdom, Donkin's delicate suscep-
tibilities, and the conceited folly of us all. The hours
of ineffective turmoil were forgotten; the fear and an-
guish of these dark moments were never mentioned
in the glowing peace of fine days. Yet from that time

our life seemed to start afresh as though we had died and had been resuscitated. All the first part of the voyage, the Indian Ocean on the other side of the Cape, all that was lost in a haze, like an ineradicable suspicion of some previous existence. It had ended—then there were blank hours: a livid blurr—and again we lived! Singleton was possessed of sinister truth; Mr. Creighton of a damaged leg; the cook of fame—and shamefully abused the opportunities of his distinction. Donkin had an added grievance. He went about repeating with insistence:—"'E said 'e would brain me—did yer 'ear? They are goin' to murder us now for the least little thing." We began at last to think it was rather awful. And we were conceited! We boasted of our pluck, of our capacity for work, of our energy. We remembered honourable episodes: our devotion, our indomitable perseverance—and were proud of them as though they had been the outcome of our unaided impulses. We remembered our danger, our toil—and conveniently forgot our horrible scare. We decried our officers—who had done nothing—and listened to the fascinating Donkin. His care for our rights, his disinterested concern for our dignity, were not discouraged by the invariable contumely of our words, by the disdain of our looks. Our contempt for him was unbounded—and we could not but listen with interest to that consummate artist. He told us we were good men—a "bloomin' condemned lot of good men." Who thanked us? Who took any notice of our wrongs? Didn't we lead a "dorg's loife for two poun' ten a month?"* Did we think that miserable pay enough to compensate us for the risk to our lives and for the loss of our clothes? "We've lost every rag!" he cried. He made us forget that he, at any rate, had lost nothing of his own. The younger men listened, thinking—

this 'ere Donkin's a long-headed chap, though no kind
of man, anyhow. The Scandinavians were frightened
at his audacities; Wamibo did not understand; and the
older seamen thoughtfully nodded their heads making
the thin gold earrings glitter in the fleshy lobes of hairy
ears. Severe, sunburnt faces were propped meditatively on tattooed forearms. Veined, brown fists held
in their knotted grip the dirty white clay of smouldering pipes. They listened, impenetrable, broad-backed,
with bent shoulders, and in grim silence. He talked
with ardour, despised and irrefutable. His picturesque
and filthy loquacity flowed like a troubled stream from
a poisoned source. His beady little eyes danced, glancing right and left, ever on the watch for the approach
of an officer. Sometimes Mr. Baker going forward to
take a look at the head sheets would roll with his uncouth gait through the sudden stillness of the men; or
Mr. Creighton limped along, smooth-faced, youthful,
and more stern than ever, piercing our short silence
with a keen glance of his clear eyes. Behind his back
Donkin would begin again darting stealthy, sidelong
looks.—" 'Ere's one of 'em. Some of yer 'as made 'im
fast that day. Much thanks yer got for it. Ain't 'ee
a-drivin' yer wusse'n ever? . . . Let 'im slip
overboard. . . . Vy not? It would 'ave been
less trouble. Vy not?" He advanced confidentially,
backed away with great effect; he whispered, he
screamed, waved his miserable arms no thicker than
pipe-stems—stretched his lean neck—spluttered—
squinted. In the pauses of his impassioned orations
the wind sighed quietly aloft, the calm sea unheeded
murmured in a warning whisper along the ship's side.
We abominated the creature and could not deny the
luminous truth of his contentions. It was all so obvious. We were indubitably good men; our deserts were

great and our pay small. Through our exertions we had saved the ship and the skipper would get the credit of it. What had he done? we wanted to know. Donkin asked:—"What 'ee could do without hus?" and we could not answer. We were oppressed by the injustice of the world, surprised to perceive how long we had lived under its burden without realising our unfortunate state, annoyed by the uneasy suspicion of our undiscerning stupidity. Donkin assured us it was all our "good 'eartedness," but we would not be consoled by such shallow sophistry. We were men enough courageously to admit to ourselves our intellectual shortcomings; though from that time we refrained from kicking him, tweaking his nose, or from accidentally knocking him about, which last, after we had weathered the Cape, had been rather a popular amusement. Davis ceased to talk at him provokingly about black eyes and flattened noses. Charley, much subdued since the gale, did not jeer at him. Knowles deferentially and with a crafty air propounded questions such as:—"Could we all have the same grub as the mates? Could we all stop ashore till we got it? What would be the next thing to try for if we got that?" He answered readily with contemptuous certitude; he strutted with assurance in clothes that were much too big for him as though he had tried to disguise himself. These were Jimmy's clothes mostly—though he would accept anything from anybody; but nobody, except Jimmy, had anything to spare. His devotion to Jimmy was unbounded. He was for ever dodging in the little cabin, ministering to Jimmy's wants, humouring his whims, submitting to his exacting peevishness, often laughing with him. Nothing could keep him away from the pious work of visiting the sick, especially when there was some heavy hauling to be done on deck. Mr. Baker had on two occasions jerked him out from there by the scruff of the neck to our inexpressible scandal. Was a sick chap to be left without attendance? Were we to be ill-used for attending a shipmate?—"What?" growled Mr. Baker, turning menacingly at the mutter, and the whole half-circle like one man stepped back a pace. "Set the topmast stunsail. Away aloft, Donkin, overhaul the gear," ordered the mate inflexibly. "Fetch the sail along; bend the down-haul clear. Bear a hand." Then, the sail set, he would go slowly aft and stand looking at the compass for a long time, careworn, pensive, and breathing hard as if stifled by the taint of unaccountable ill-will that pervaded the ship. "What's up amongst them?" he thought. "Can't make out this hanging back and growling. A good crowd, too, as they go nowadays." On deck the men exchanged bitter words, suggested by a silly exasperation against something unjust and irremediable that would not be denied, and would whisper into their ears long after Donkin had ceased speaking. Our little world went on its curved and unswerving path carrying a discontented and aspiring population. They found comfort of a gloomy kind in an interminable and conscientious analysis of their unappreciated worth; and inspired by Donkin's hopeful doctrines they dreamed enthusiastically of the time when every lonely ship would travel over a serene sea, manned by a wealthy and well-fed crew of satisfied skippers.

It looked as if it would be a long passage. The south-east trades, light and unsteady, were left behind; and then, on the equator and under a low grey sky, the ship, in close heat, floated upon a smooth sea that resembled a sheet of ground glass. Thunder squalls hung on the horizon, circled round the ship, far off and

growling angrily, like a troop of wild beasts afraid to
charge home. The invisible sun, sweeping above the
upright masts, made on the clouds a blurred stain of
rayless light, and a similar patch of faded radiance
kept pace with it from east to west over the unglittering
level of the waters. At night, through the impenetrable darkness of earth and heaven, broad sheets of
flame* waved noiselessly; and for half a second the be-
calmed craft stood out with its masts and rigging, with
every sail and every rope distinct and black in the cen-
tre of a fiery outburst, like a charred ship enclosed in a
glove of fire. And, again, for long hours she remained
lost in a vast universe of night and silence where gentle
sighs wandering here and there like forlorn souls, made
the still sails flutter as in sudden fear, and the ripple
of a beshrouded ocean whisper its compassion afar—
in a voice mournful, immense, and faint. . . .

When the lamp was put out, and through the door
thrown wide open, Jimmy, turning on his pillow, could
see vanishing beyond the straight line of top-gallant
rail, the quick, repeated visions of a fabulous world
made up of leaping fire and sleeping water. The lightning gleamed in his big sad eyes that seemed in a red
flicker to burn themselves out in his black face, and
then he would lie blinded and invisible in the midst of
an intense darkness. He could hear on the quiet deck
soft footfalls, the breathing of some man lounging on
the doorstep; the low creak of swaying masts; or the
calm voice of the watch-officer reverberating aloft,
hard and loud, amongst the unstirring sails. He listened with avidity, taking a rest in the attentive perception of the slightest sound from the fatiguing wander-
ings of his sleeplessness. He was cheered by the rattling of blocks, reassured by the stir and murmur of the

watch, soothed by the slow yawn of some sleepy and weary seaman settling himself deliberately for a snooze on the planks. Life seemed an indestructible thing. It went on in darkness, in sunshine, in sleep; tireless, it hovered affectionately round the imposture of his ready death. It was bright, like the twisted flare of lightning, and more full of surprises than the dark night. It made him safe, and the calm of its overpowering darkness was as precious as its restless and dangerous light.

But in the evening, in the dog-watches, and even far into the first night-watch, a knot of men could always be seen congregated before Jimmy's cabin. They leaned on each side of the door peacefully interested and with crossed legs; they stood astride the doorstep discoursing, or sat in silent couples on his sea-chest; while against the bulwark along the spare topmast, three or four in a row stared meditatively; with their simple faces lit up by the projected glare of Jimmy's lamp. The little place, repainted white, had, in the night, the brilliance of a silver shrine where a black idol, reclining stiffly under a blanket, blinked its weary eyes and received our homage. Donkin officiated. He had the air of a demonstrator showing a phenomenon, a manifestation bizarre, simple, and meritorious that, to the beholders, should be a profound and an everlasting lesson. "Just look at 'im, 'ee knows what's what—never fear!" he exclaimed now and then, flourishing a hand hard and fleshless like the claw of a snipe. Jimmy, on his back, smiled with reserve and without moving a limb. He affected the languor of extreme weakness, so as to make it manifest to us that our delay in hauling him out from his horrible confinement, and then that night spent on the poop among our selfish neglect of his needs, had "done for him." He rather liked to talk about it, and of course we were always interested. He spoke spasmodically, in fast rushes with long pauses between, as a tipsy man walks. . . . "Cook had just given me a pannikin* of hot coffee. . . . Slapped it down there, on my chest— banged the door to. . . . I felt a heavy roll coming; tried to save my coffee, burnt my fingers . . . and fell out of my bunk. . . . She went over so quick. . . . Water came in through the ventilator. . . . I couldn't move the door . . . dark as a grave . . . tried to scramble up into the upper berth. . . . Rats . . . a rat bit my finger as I got up. . . . I could hear him swimming below me. . . . I thought you would never come. . . . I thought you were all gone overboard . . . of course. . . . Could hear nothing but the wind. . . . Then you came . . . to look for the corpse, I suppose. A little more and . . . ."

"Man! But ye made a rare lot of noise in here," observed Archie, thoughtfully.

"You chaps kicked up such a confounded row above. . . . Enough to scare any one. . . . I didn't know what you were up to. . . . Bash in the blamed planks . . . my head. . . . Just what a silly, scary gang of fools would do. . . . Not much good to me anyhow. . . . Just as well . . . drown. . . . Pah."

He groaned, snapped his big white teeth, and gazed with scorn. Belfast lifted a pair of dolorous eyes, with a broken-hearted smile, clenched his fists stealthily; blue-eyed Archie caressed his red whiskers with a hesitating hand; the boatswain at the door stared a moment, and brusquely went away with a loud guffaw. Wamibo dreamed. . . . Donkin felt all over his sterile chin for the few rare hairs, and said, triumphantly, with a sidelong glance at Jimmy:—"Look at 'im! Wish I was 'arf has 'ealthy as 'ee is—I do." He jerked a short thumb over his shoulder towards the after end of the ship. "That's the blooming way to do 'em!" he yelped, with forced heartiness. Jimmy said:—"Don't be a dam' fool," in a pleasant voice. Knowles, rubbing his shoulder against the doorpost, remarked shrewdly:—"We can't all go an' be took sick —it would be mutiny."—"Mutiny—gawn!"* jeered Donkin, "there's no bloomin' law against bein' sick."— "There's six weeks' hard for refoosing dooty," argued Knowles, " I mind I once seed in Cardiff the crew of an overloaded ship—leastways she weren't overloaded, only a fatherly old gentleman with a white beard and an umbreller came along the quay and talked to the hands. Said as how it was crool hard to be drownded in winter just for the sake of a few pounds more for the owner—he said. Nearly cried over them—he did; and he had a square mainsail coat,* and a gaff-topsail hat* too—all proper. So they chaps they said they wouldn't go to be drownded in winter—depending upon that 'ere Plimsoll* man to see 'em through the court. They thought to have a bloomin' lark and two or three days' spree. And the beak*giv' 'em six weeks—coss the ship warn't overloaded. Anyways they made it out in court that she wasn't. There wasn't one overloaded ship in Penarth Dock*at all. 'Pears that old coon*he was only on pay and allowance from some kind people, under orders to look for overloaded ships, and he couldn't see no further than the length of his umbreller. Some of us in the boarding-house, where I live when I'm looking for a ship in Cardiff, stood by to duck that old weeping spunger in the dock. We kept a good look-out, too—but he topped his boom* directly he was outside the court. . . . Yes. They got six weeks' hard. . . ."

They listened, full of curiosity, nodding in the pauses their rough pensive faces. Donkin opened his mouth once or twice, but restrained himself. Jimmy lay still with open eyes and not at all interested. A seaman emitted the opinion that after a verdict of atrocious partiality "the bloomin' beaks go an' drink at the skipper's expense." Others assented. It was clear, of course. Donkin said:—"Well, six weeks ain't much trouble. You sleep all night in, reg'lar, in chokey. Do it on my 'ead." "You are used to it ainch'ee, Donkin?" asked somebody. Jimmy condescended to laugh. It cheered up every one wonderfully. Knowles, with surprising mental agility, shifted his ground. "If we all went sick what would become of the ship? eh?" He posed the problem and grinned all round. —"Let 'er go to 'ell," sneered Donkin. "Damn 'er. She ain't yourn."—"What? Just let her drift?" insisted Knowles in a tone of unbelief.—"Aye! Drift, an' be blowed," affirmed Donkin with fine recklessness. The other did not see it—meditated.—"The stores would run out," he muttered, "and . . . never get anywhere . . . and what about pay-day?" he added with greater assurance.—"Jack likes a good pay-day," exclaimed a listener on the doorstep. "Aye, because then the girls put one arm round his neck an' t'other in his pocket, and call him ducky. Don't they, Jack?"—"Jack, you're a terror with the gals."—"He takes three of 'em in tow at once, like one of 'em Watkinses*two-funnel tugs waddling away with three schooners* behind."—"Jack, you're a lame scamp."—"Jack, tell us about that one with a blue eye and a black eye. Do."—"There's plenty of girls with one black eye along the Highway by . . ."

—"No, that's a speshul one—come Jack." Donkin
looked severe and disgusted; Jimmy very bored; a grey-
haired sea-dog shook his head slightly, smiling at the
bowl of his pipe, discreetly amused. Knowles turned
about bewildered; stammered first at one, then at
another.—"No! . . . I never! . . . can't
talk sensible sense midst you. . . . Always
on the kid." He retired bashfully—muttering and
pleased. They laughed hooting in the crude light,
around Jimmy's bed, where on a white pillow his hol-
lowed black face moved to and fro restlessly. A puff
of wind came, made the flame of the lamp leap, and
outside, high up, the sails fluttered, while near by the
block of the foresheet struck a ringing blow on the
iron bulwark. A voice far off cried, "Helm up!"
another, more faint, answered, "Hard-up, sir!" They
became silent—waited expectantly. The grey-haired
seaman knocked his pipe on the doorstep and stood up.
The ship leaned over gently and the sea seemed to wake
up, murmuring drowsily. "Here's a little wind comin',"
said some one very low. Jimmy turned over slowly
to face the breeze. The voice in the night cried loud
and commanding:—"Haul the spanker out." The
group before the door vanished out of the light. They
could be heard tramping aft while they repeated with
varied intonations:—"Spanker out!" . . . "Out
spanker, sir!" Donkin remained alone with Jimmy.
There was a silence. Jimmy opened and shut his lips
several times as if swallowing draughts of fresher air;
Donkin moved the toes of his bare feet and looked at
them thoughtfully.

"Ain't you going to give them a hand with the sail?"
asked Jimmy.

"No. If six ov 'em ain't 'nough beef to set that
blamed, rotten spanker, they ain't fit to live," an-

swered Donkin in a bored, far-away voice, as though he had been talking from the bottom of a hole. Jimmy considered the conical, fowl-like profile with a queer kind of interest; he was leaning out of his bunk with the calculating, uncertain expression of a man who reflects how best to lay hold of some strange creature that looks as though it could sting or bite. But he said only:—"The mate will miss you—and there will be ructions."

Donkin got up to go. "I will do for 'im some dark night; see if I don't," he said over his shoulder.

Jimmy went on quickly:—"You're like a poll-parrot, like a screechin' poll-parrot." Donkin stopped and cocked his head attentively on one side. His big ears stood out, transparent and veined, resembling the thin wings of a bat.

"Yuss?" he said, with his back towards Jimmy.

"Yes! Chatter out all you know—like . . . like a dirty white cockatoo."

Donkin waited. He could hear the other's breathing, long and slow; the breathing of a man with a hundredweight or so on the breastbone. Then he asked calmly:—"What do I know?"

"What? . . . What I tell you . . . not much. What do you want . . . to talk about my health so . . ."

"It's a blooming imposyshun. A bloomin', stinkin', first-class imposyshun—but it don't tyke me in. Not it."

Jimmy kept still. Donkin put his hands in his pockets, and in one slouching stride came up to the bunk.

"I talk—what's the odds. They ain't men 'ere—sheep they are. A driven lot of sheep. I 'old you up . . . Vy not? You're well orf."

"I am . . . I don't say anything about that. . . ."

"Well. Let 'em see it. Let 'em larn what a man can do. I am a man, I know all about yer. . . ." Jimmy threw himself further away on the pillow; the other stretched out his skinny neck, jerked his bird face down at him as though pecking at the eyes. "I am a man. I've seen the inside of every chokey in the Colonies rather'n give up my rights. . . ."

"You are a jail-prop,"*said Jimmy, weakly.

"I am . . . an' proud of it, too. You! You 'aven't the bloomin' nerve—so you inventyd this 'ere dodge. . . ." He paused; then with marked afterthought accentuated slowly:—"Yer ain't sick—are yer?"

"No," said Jimmy, firmly. "Been out of sorts now and again this year," he mumbled with a sudden drop in his voice.

Donkin closed one eye, amicable and confidential. He whispered:—"Ye 'ave done this afore 'aven'tchee?" Jimmy smiled—then as if unable to hold back he let himself go:—"Last ship—yes. I was out of sorts on the passage. See? It was easy. They paid me off in Calcutta, and the skipper made no bones about it either. . . . I got my money all right. Laid up fifty-eight days! The fools! O Lord! The fools! Paid right off." He laughed spasmodically. Donkin chimed in giggling. Then Jimmy coughed violently. "I am as well as ever," he said, as soon as he could draw breath.

Donkin made a derisive gesture. "In course," he said, profoundly, "any one can see that."—"They don't," said Jimmy, gasping like a fish.—"They would swallow any yarn," affirmed Donkin.—"Don't you let on too much," admonished Jimmy in an exhausted

voice.—"Your little gyme? Eh?" commented Donkin,
jovially. Then with sudden disgust: "Yer all for
yerself, s'long as ye're right. . . ."

So charged with egoism James Wait pulled the blanket up to his chin and lay still for awhile. His heavy
lips protruded in an everlasting black pout. "Why
are you so hot on making trouble?" he asked without
much interest.

"'Cos it's a bloomin' shayme. We are put upon
. . . bad food, bad pay . . . I want us
to kick up a bloomin' row; a blamed 'owling row
that would make 'em remember! Knocking people
about . . . brain us . . . indeed! Ain't
we men?" His altruistic indignation blazed. Then
he said calmly:—"I've been airing yer clothes."—
"All right," said Jimmy, languidly, "bring them in."—
"Giv' us the key of your chest, I'll put 'em away for
yer," said Donkin with friendly eagerness.—"Bring
'em in, I will put them away myself," answered James
Wait with severity. Donkin looked down, muttering. . . . "What d'you say? What d'you say?"
inquired Wait anxiously.—"Nothink. The night's
dry, let 'em 'ang out till the morning," said Donkin, in
a strangely trembling voice, as though restraining
laughter or rage. Jimmy seemed satisfied.—"Give me
a little water for the night in my mug—there," he said.
Donkin took a stride over the doorstep.—"Git it yerself," he replied in a surly tone. "You can do it, unless
you *are* sick."—"Of course I can do it," said Wait,
"only . . . "—"Well, then, do it," said Donkin,
viciously, "if yer can look after yer clothes, yer can
look after yerself." He went on deck without a look
back.

Jimmy reached out for the mug. Not a drop. He
put it back gently with a faint sigh—and closed his

eyes. He thought:—That lunatic Belfast will bring
me some water if I ask. Fool. I am very thirsty.
. . . It was very hot in the cabin, and it seemed
to turn slowly round, detach itself from the ship, and
swing out smoothly into a luminous, arid space where
a black sun shone, spinning very fast. A place without
any water! No water! A policeman with the face
of Donkin drank a glass of beer by the side of an empty
well, and flew away flapping vigorously. A ship whose
mastheads protruded through the sky and could not
be seen, was discharging grain, and the wind whirled
the dry husks in spirals along the quay of a dock with
no water in it. He whirled along with the husks—very
tired and light. All his inside was gone. He felt
lighter than the husks—and more dry. He expanded
his hollow chest. The air streamed in carrying away
in its rush a lot of strange things that resembled houses,
trees, people, lamp-posts. . . . No more! There
was no more air—and he had not finished drawing his
long breath. But he was in jail! They were locking
him up. A door slammed. They turned the key
twice, flung a bucket of water over him—Phoo! What
for?

He opened his eyes, thinking the fall had been very
heavy for an empty man—empty—empty. He was
in his cabin. Ah! All right! His face was streaming
with perspiration, his arms heavier than lead. He saw
the cook standing in the doorway, a brass key in one
hand and a bright tin hook-pot in the other.

"I have locked up the galley for the night," said the
cook, beaming benevolently. "Eight-bells just gone.
I brought you a pot of cold tea for your night's drinking,
Jimmy. I sweetened it with some white cabin sugar,
too. Well—it won't break the ship."

He came in, hung the pot on the edge of the bunk,

asked perfunctorily, "How goes it?" and sat down on
the box.—"H'm," grunted Wait, inhospitably. The
cook wiped his face with a dirty cotton rag, which,
afterwards, he tied round his neck.—"That's how them
firemen do in steamboats," he said, serenely, and much
pleased with himself. "My work is as heavy as theirs
—I'm thinking—and longer hours. Did you ever see
them down the stokehold?* Like fiends they look—
firing—firing—firing—down there."

He pointed his forefinger at the deck. Some gloomy
thought darkened his shining face, fleeting, like the
shadow of a travelling cloud over the light of a peaceful
sea. The relieved watch tramped noisily forward,
passing in a body across the sheen of the doorway.
Some one cried, "Good-night!" Belfast stopped for
a moment and looked at Jimmy, quivering and speechless with repressed emotion. He gave the cook a glance
charged with dismal foreboding, and vanished. The
cook cleared his throat. Jimmy stared upwards and
kept as still as a man in hiding.

The night was clear, with a gentle breeze. Above
the mastheads the resplendent curve of the Milky Way
spanned the sky like a triumphal arch of eternal light,
thrown over the dark pathway of the earth. On the
forecastle head a man whistled with loud precision a
lively jig, while another could be heard faintly, shuffling
and stamping in time. There came from forward a
confused murmur of voices, laughter—snatches of song.
The cook shook his head, glanced obliquely at Jimmy,
and began to mutter. "Aye. Dance and sing. That's
all they think of. I am surprised that Providence don't
get tired. . . . They forget the day that's sure
to come . . . but you. . . . "

Jimmy drank a gulp of tea, hurriedly, as though he
had stolen it, and shrank under his blanket, edging

away towards the bulkhead. The cook got up, closed the door, then sat down again and said distinctly:—

"Whenever I poke my galley fire I think of you chaps —swearing, stealing, lying, and worse—as if there was no such thing as another world. . . . Not bad fellows, either, in a way," he conceded, slowly; then, after a pause of regretful musing, he went on in a resigned tone:—"Well, well. They will have a hot time of it. Hot! Did I say? The furnaces of one of them White Star boats ain't nothing to it."

He kept very quiet for a while. There was a great stir in his brain; an addled vision of bright outlines; an exciting row of rousing songs and groans of pain. He suffered, enjoyed, admired, approved. He was delighted, frightened, exalted—as on that evening (the only time in his life—twenty-seven years ago; he loved to recall the number of years) when as a young man he had—through keeping bad company—become intoxicated in an East-end music-hall. A tide of sudden feeling swept him clean out of his body. He soared. He contemplated the secret of the hereafter. It commended itself to him. It was excellent; he loved it, himself, all hands, and Jimmy. His heart overflowed with tenderness, with comprehension, with the desire to meddle, with anxiety for the soul of that black man, with the pride of possessed eternity, with the feeling of might. Snatch him up in his arms and pitch him right into the middle of salvation. . . . The black soul—blacker—body—rot—Devil. No! Talk— strength—Samson. . . . There was a great din as of cymbals in his ears; he flashed through an ecstatic jumble of shining faces, lilies, prayer-books, unearthly joy, white shirts, gold harps, black coats, wings. He saw flowing garments, clean shaved faces, a sea of light—a lake of pitch. There were sweet scents, a smell of sulphur—red tongues of flame licking a white mist. An awesome voice thundered! . . . It lasted three seconds.

"Jimmy!" he cried in an inspired tone. Then he hesitated. A spark of human pity glimmered yet through the infernal fog of his supreme conceit.

"What?" said James Wait, unwillingly. There was a silence. He turned his head just the least bit, and stole a cautious glance. The cook's lips moved without a sound; his face was rapt, his eyes turned up. He seemed to be mentally imploring deck beams, the brass hook of the lamp, two cockroaches.

"Look here," said Wait, "I want to go to sleep. I I think I could."

"This is no time for sleep!" exclaimed the cook, very loud. He had prayerfully divested himself of the last vestige of his humanity. He was a voice—a fleshless and sublime thing, as on that memorable night —the night when he went walking over the sea to make coffee for perishing sinners. "This is no time for sleeping," he repeated with exaltation. "*I* can't sleep."

"Don't care damn," said Wait, with factitious energy. "I can. Go an' turn in."

"Swear . . . in the very jaws! . . . In the very jaws! Don't you see the everlasting fire . . . don't you feel it? Blind, chockfull of sin! Repent, repent! I can't bear to think of you. I hear the call to save you. Night and day. Jimmy, let me save you!" The words of entreaty and menace broke out of him in a roaring torrent. The cockroaches ran away. Jimmy perspired, wriggling stealthily under his blanket. The cook yelled. . . . "Your days are numbered! . . . "—"Get out of this," boomed Wait, courageously.—"Pray with me! . . . "—"I won't! . . . The little cabin was as hot as an oven. It contained an immensity of fear and pain; an atmosphere of shrieks and moans; prayers vociferated like blasphemies and whispered curses. Outside, the men called by Charley, who informed them in tones of delight that there was a holy row going on in Jimmy's place, crowded before the closed door, too startled to open it. All hands were there. The watch below had jumped out on deck in their shirts, as after a collision. Men running up, asked:—"What is it?" Others said:—"Listen!" The muffled screaming went on:—"On your knees! On your knees!"—"Shut up!"—"Never! You are delivered into my hands. . . . Your life has been saved. . . . Purpose. . . . Mercy. . . . Repent." —"You are a crazy fool! . . . "—"Account of you . . . you . . . Never sleep in this world, if I . . . "—"Leave off."—"No! . . . stokehold . . . only think! . . . " Then an impassioned screeching babble where words pattered like hail.—"No!" shouted Wait.—"Yes. You are! . . . No help. . . . Everybody says so."— "You lie!"—"I see you dying this minnyt . . . before my eyes . . . as good as dead already."— "Help!" shouted Jimmy, piercingly.—"Not in this valley. . . . look upwards," howled the other.— "Go away! Murder! Help!" clamoured Jimmy. His voice broke. There were moanings, low mutters, a few sobs.

"What's the matter now?" said a seldom-heard voice.—"Fall back, men! Fall back, there!" repeated Mr. Creighton, sternly, pushing through.—"Here's the old man," whispered some.—"The cook's in there, sir," exclaimed several, backing away. The door clattered open; a broad stream of light darted out on wondering faces; a warm whiff of vitiated air passed. The two mates towered head and shoulders above the spare, grey-haired man who stood revealed between them, in shabby clothes, stiff and angular, like a small carved figure, and with a thin, composed face. The cook got up from his knees. Jimmy sat high in the bunk, clasping his drawn-up legs. The tassel of the blue night-cap almost imperceptibly trembled over his knees. They gazed astonished at his long, curved back, while the white corner of one eye gleamed blindly at them. He was afraid to turn his head, he shrank within himself; and there was an aspect astounding and animal-like in the perfection of his expectant immobility. A thing of instinct—the unthinking stillness of a scared brute.

"What are you doing here?" asked Mr. Baker, sharply.—"My duty," said the cook, with ardour.— "Your . . . what?" began the mate. Captain Allistoun touched his arm lightly.—"I know his caper," he said, in a low voice. "Come out of that, Podmore," he ordered, aloud.

The cook wrung his hands, shook his fists above his head, and his arms dropped as if too heavy. For a moment he stood distracted and speechless.—"Never," he stammered, "I . . . he . . . I."— "What—do—you—say?" pronounced Captain Allistoun. "Come out at once—or . . . "—"I am going," said the cook, with a hasty and sombre resignation. He strode over the doorstep firmly—hesitated —made a few steps. They looked at him in silence.— "I make you responsible!" he cried, desperately, turning half round. "That man is dying. I make you . . . "—"You there yet?" called the master in a threatening tone.—"No, sir," he exclaimed, hurriedly, in a startled voice. The boatswain led him away by the arm; some one laughed; Jimmy lifted his head for a stealthy glance, and in one unexpected leap sprang out of his bunk; Mr. Baker made a clever catch and felt him very limp in his arms; the group at the door grunted with surprise.—"He lies," gasped Wait, "he talked about black devils—he is a devil—a white devil—I am all right." He stiffened himself, and Mr. Baker, experimentally, let him go. He staggered a pace or two; Captain Allistoun watched him with a quiet and penetrating gaze; Belfast ran to his support. He did not appear to be aware of any one near him; he stood silent for a moment, battling single-handed with a legion of nameless terrors, amidst the eager looks of excited men who watched him far off, utterly alone in the impenetrable solitude of his fear. The sea gurgled through the scuppers as the ship heeled over to a short puff of wind.

"Keep him away from me," said James Wait at last in his fine baritone voice, and leaning with all his weight on Belfast's neck. "I've been better this last week . . . I am well . . . I was going back to duty . . . to-morrow—now if you like—Captain." Belfast hitched his shoulders to keep him upright.

"No," said the master, looking at him, fixedly.

Under Jimmy's armpit Belfast's red face moved uneasily. A row of eyes gleaming stared on the edge of light. They pushed one another with elbows, turned their heads, whispered. Wait let his chin fall on his breast and, with lowered eyelids, looked round in a suspicious manner.

"Why not?" cried a voice from the shadows, "the man's all right, sir."

"I am all right," said Wait, with eagerness. "Been sick . . . better . . . turn-to now." He sighed.—"Howly Mother!" exclaimed Belfast with a heave of the shoulders, "stand up, Jimmy."—

"Keep away from me then," said Wait, giving Belfast a petulant push, and reeling fetched against the door-post. His cheekbones glistened as though they had been varnished. He snatched off his night-cap, wiped his perspiring face with it, flung it on the deck. "I am coming out," he declared without stirring.

"No. You don't," said the master, curtly. Bare feet shuffled, disapproving voices murmured all round; he went on as if he had not heard:—"You have been skulking nearly all the passage and now you want to come out. You think you are near enough to the pay-table now. Smell the shore, hey?"

"I've been sick . . . now—better," mumbled Wait, glaring in the light.—"You have been shamming sick," retorted Captain Allistoun with severity; "Why . . ." he hesitated for less than half a second. "Why, anybody can see that. There's nothing the matter with you, but you choose to lie-up to please yourself—and now you shall lie-up to please me. Mr. Baker, my orders are that this man is not to be allowed on deck to the end of the passage."

There were exclamations of surprise, triumph, indignation. The dark group of men swung across the light. "What for?" "Told you so . . ." "Bloomin' shame . . ."—"We've got to say somethink about that," screeched Donkin from the rear.—"Never mind, Jim—we will see you righted," cried several together. An elderly seaman stepped to the front. "D'ye mean to say, sir," he asked, ominously, "that a sick chap ain't allowed to get well in this 'ere hooker?" Behind him Donkin whispered excitedly amongst a staring crowd where no one spared him a glance, but Captain Allistoun shook a forefinger at the angry bronzed face of the speaker.—"You— you hold your tongue," he said, warningly.—"This

isn't the way," clamoured two or three younger men.—
"Are we bloomin' masheens?" inquired Donkin in a
piercing tone, and dived under the elbows of the front
rank.—"Soon show 'im we ain't boys . . . "—
"The man's a man if he is black."—"We ain't goin'
to work this bloomin' ship shorthanded if Snowball's
all right . . . "—"He says he is."—"Well then,
strike, boys, strike!"—"That's the bloomin' ticket."
Captain Allistoun said sharply to the second mate:
"Keep quiet, Mr. Creighton," and stood composed in
the tumult, listening with profound attention to mixed
growls and screeches, to every exclamation and every
curse of the sudden outbreak. Somebody slammed the
cabin door to with a kick; the darkness full of menacing
mutters leaped with a short clatter over the streak of
light, and the men became gesticulating shadows that
growled, hissed, laughed excitedly. Mr. Baker whispered:—"Get away from them, sir." The big shape of
Mr. Creighton hovered silently about the slight figure
of the master.—"We have been imposed upon all this
voyage," said a gruff voice, "but this 'ere fancy takes
the cake."—"That man is a shipmate."—"Are we
bloomin' kids?"—"The port watch will refuse duty."
Charley carried away by his feeling whistled shrilly,
then yelped:—"Giv' us our Jimmy!" This seemed to
cause a variation in the disturbance. There was a
fresh burst of squabbling uproar. A lot of quarrels
were set going at once.—"Yes."—"No."—"Never been
sick."—"Go for them to once."—"Shut yer mouth,
youngster—this is men's work."—"Is it?" muttered
Captain Allistoun, bitterly. Mr. Baker grunted:
"Ough! They're gone silly. They've been simmering
for the last month."—"I did notice," said the master.
—"They have started a row amongst themselves now,"
said Mr. Creighton with disdain, "better get aft, sir.

We will soothe them.—"Keep your temper, Creighton," said the master. And the three men began to move slowly towards the cabin door.

In the shadows of the fore rigging a dark mass stamped, eddied, advanced, retreated. There were words of reproach, encouragement, unbelief, execration. The elder seamen, bewildered and angry, growled their determination to go through with something or other; but the younger school of advanced thought exposed their and Jimmy's wrongs with confused shouts, arguing amongst themselves. They clustered round that moribund carcass, the fit emblem of their aspirations, and encouraging one another they swayed, they tramped on one spot, shouting that they would not be "put upon." Inside the cabin, Belfast, helping Jimmy into his bunk, twitched all over in his desire not to miss all the row, and with difficulty restrained the tears of his facile emotion. James Wait, flat on his back under the blanket, gasped complaints.—"We will back you up, never fear," assured Belfast, busy about his feet.— "I'll come out to-morrow morning——take my chance ——you fellows must——" mumbled Wait, "I come out to-morrow——skipper or no skipper." He lifted one arm with great difficulty, passed the hand over his face; "Don't you let that cook . . . " he breathed out. —"No, no," said Belfast, turning his back on the bunk, "I will put a head on*him if he comes near you."—"I will smash his mug!" exclaimed faintly Wait, enraged and weak; "I don't want to kill a man, but . . ." He panted fast like a dog after a run in sunshine. Some one just outside the door shouted, "He's as fit as any ov us!" Belfast put his hand on the door-handle.— "Here!" called James Wait, hurriedly, and in such a clear voice that the other spun round with a start. James Wait, stretched out black and deathlike in the dazzling

light, turned his head on the pillow. His eyes stared at
Belfast, appealing and impudent. "I am rather weak
from lying-up so long," he said, distinctly. Belfast
nodded. "Getting quite well now," insisted Wait.—
"Yes. I noticed you getting better this . . . last
month," said Belfast, looking down. "Hallo! What's
this?" he shouted and ran out.

He was flattened directly against the side of the house
by two men who lurched against him. A lot of disputes
seemed to be going on all round. He got clear and saw
three indistinct figures standing alone in the fainter
darkness under the arched foot of the mainsail, that
rose above their heads like a convex wall of a high
edifice. Donkin hissed:—"Go for them . . . it's
dark!" The crowd took a short run aft in a body—
then there was a check. Donkin, agile and thin, flitted
past with his right arm going like a windmill—and then
stood still suddenly with his arm pointing rigidly above
his head. The hurtling flight of some heavy object
was heard; it passed between the heads of the two
mates, bounded heavily along the deck, struck the after
hatch with a ponderous and deadened blow. The
bulky shape of Mr. Baker grew distinct. "Come to
your senses, men!" he cried, advancing at the arrested
crowd. "Come back, Mr. Baker!" called the master's
quiet voice. He obeyed unwillingly. There was a
minute of silence, then a deafening hubbub arose.
Above it Archie was heard energetically:—"If ye do oot
ageen I wull tell!" There were shouts. "Don't!" —
"Drop it!"—"We ain't that kind!" The black cluster
of human forms reeled against the bulwark, back again
towards the house. Ringbolts rang under stumbling
feet.—"Drop it!"—"Let me!"—"No!"—"Curse you
. . . hah!" Then sounds as of some one's face
being slapped; a piece of iron fell on the deck; a short

scuffle, and some one's shadowy body scuttled rapidly
across the main hatch before the shadow of a kick. A
raging voice sobbed out a torrent of filthy language
. . . —"Throwing things—good God!" grunted
Mr. Baker in dismay.—"That was meant for me," said
the master, quietly; "I felt the wind of that thing;
what was it—an iron belaying-pin?"—"By Jove!"
muttered Mr. Creighton. The confused voices of men
talking amidships mingled with the wash of the sea,
ascended between the silent and distended sails—
seemed to flow away into the night, further than the
horizon, higher than the sky. The stars burned
steadily over the inclined mastheads. Trails of light
lay on the water, broke before the advancing hull, and,
after she had passed, trembled for a long time as if in
awe of the murmuring sea.

Meantime the helmsman, anxious to know what the
row was about, had let go the wheel, and, bent double,
ran with long, stealthy footsteps to the break of the
poop. The *Narcissus*, left to herself, came up gently
to the wind without any one being aware of it. She
gave a slight roll, and the sleeping sails woke suddenly,
coming all together with a mighty flap against the
masts, then filled again one after another in a quick
succession of loud reports that ran down the lofty spars,
till the collapsed mainsail flew out last with a violent
jerk. The ship trembled from trucks to keel; the sails
kept on rattling like a discharge of musketry; the chain
sheets and loose shackles jingled aloft in a thin peal;
the gin blocks groaned. It was as if an invisible hand
had given the ship an angry shake to recall the men that
peopled her decks to the sense of reality, vigilance, and
duty.—"Helm up!" cried the master, sharply. "Run
aft, Mr. Creighton, and see what that fool there is up
to."—"Flatten in the head sheets. Stand by the

weather fore-braces," growled Mr. Baker. Startled
men ran swiftly repeating the orders. The watch below, abandoned all at once by the watch on deck,
drifted towards the forecastle in twos and threes,
arguing noisily as they went—"We shall see to-morrow!" cried a loud voice, as if to cover with a menacing
hint an inglorious retreat. And then only orders were
heard, the falling of heavy coils of rope, the rattling of
blocks. Singleton's white head flitted here and there
in the night, high above the deck, like the ghost of a
bird.—"Going off, sir!" shouted Mr. Creighton from
aft.—"Full again."—"All right. . . . "—"Ease
off the head sheets. That will do the braces. Coil
the ropes up," grunted Mr. Baker, bustling about.

Gradually the tramping noises, the confused sound of
voices, died out, and the officers, coming together on the
poop, discussed the events. Mr. Baker was bewildered
and grunted; Mr. Creighton was calmly furious; but
Captain Allistoun was composed and thoughtful. He
listened to Mr. Baker's growling argumentation, to
Creighton's interjected and severe remarks, while looking down on the deck he weighed in his hand the iron
belaying-pin—that a moment ago had just missed his
head—as if it had been the only tangible fact of the
whole transaction. He was one of those commanders
who speak little, seem to hear nothing, look at no one—
and know everything, hear every whisper, see every
fleeting shadow of their ship's life. His two big officers
towered above his lean, short figure; they talked over
his head; they were dismayed, surprised, and angry,
while between them the little quiet man seemed to have
found his taciturn serenity in the profound depths of a
larger experience. Lights were burning in the forecastle; now and then a loud gust of babbling chatter
came from forward, swept over the decks, and became

faint, as if the unconscious ship, gliding gently through
the great peace of the sea, had left behind and for ever
the foolish noise of turbulent mankind. But it was re-
newed again and again. Gesticulating arms, profiles
of heads with open mouths appeared for a moment in
the illuminated squares of doorways; black fists darted
—withdrew. . . . "Yes.   It was most damn-
able to have such an unprovoked row sprung on one,"
assented the master. . . . A tumult of yells rose
in the light, abruptly ceased. . . . He didn't
think there would be any further trouble just then.
. . . A bell was struck aft, another, forward, answered in a deeper tone, and the clamour of ringing
metal spread round the ship in a circle of wide vibrations that ebbed away into the immeasurable night of an
empty sea. . . . Didn't he know them! Didn't
he! In past years. Better men, too. Real men to
stand by one in a tight place. Worse than devils too
sometimes—downright, horned devils. Pah! This—
nothing. A miss as good as a mile. . . . The
wheel was being relieved in the usual way.—"Full
and by," said, very loud, the man going off.—"Full
and by," repeated the other, catching hold of the spokes.
—"This head wind is my trouble," exclaimed the
master, stamping his foot in sudden anger; "head
wind! all the rest is nothing." He was calm again in a
moment. "Keep them on the move to-night, gentlemen; just to let them feel we've got hold all the time—
quietly, you know. Mind you keep your hands off
them, Creighton. To-morrow I will talk to them like a
Dutch Uncle.* A crazy crowd of tinkers! Yes, tinkers!
I could count the real sailors amongst them on the
fingers of one hand. Nothing will do but a row—if—
you—please." He paused. "Did you think I had
gone wrong there, Mr. Baker?" He tapped his fore-

head, laughed short. "When I saw him standing there, three parts dead and so scared—black amongst that gaping lot—no grit to face what's coming to us all—the notion came to me all at once, before I could think. Sorry for him—like you would be for a sick brute. If ever creature was in a mortal funk to die! . . . I thought I would let him go out in his own way. Kind of impulse. It never came into my head, those fools. . . . H'm! Stand to it now—of course." He stuck the belaying-pin in his pocket, seemed ashamed of himself, then sharply:—"If you see Podmore at his tricks again tell him I will have him put under the pump. Had to do it once before. The fellow breaks out like that now and then. Good cook tho'." He walked away quickly, came back to the companion. The two mates followed him through the starlight with amazed eyes. He went down three steps, and changing his tone, spoke with his head near the deck:—"I shan't turn in to-night, in case of anything; just call out if . . . Did you see the eyes of that sick nigger, Mr. Baker? I fancied he begged me for something. What? Past all help. One lone black beggar amongst the lot of us, and he seemed to look through me into the very hell. Fancy, this wretched Podmore! Well, let him die in peace. I am master here after all. Let him be. He might have been half a man once . . . Keep a good look-out." He disappeared down below, leaving his mates facing one another, and more impressed than if they had seen a stone image shed a miraculous tear of compassion over the incertitudes of life and death. . . .

In the blue mist spreading from twisted threads that stood upright in the bowls of pipes, the forecastle appeared as vast as a hall. Between the beams a heavy cloud stagnated; and the lamps surrounded by halos

burned each at the core of a purple glow in two lifeless flames without rays. Wreaths drifted in denser
wisps. Men sprawled about on the deck, sat in negli-
gent poses, or, bending a knee, drooped with one
shoulder against a bulkhead. Lips moved, eyes
flashed, waving arms made sudden eddies in the smoke.
The murmur of voices seemed to pile itself higher and
higher as if unable to run out quick enough through the
narrow doors. The watch below in their shirts, and
striding on long white legs, resembled raving somnam-
bulists; while now and then one of the watch on deck
would rush in, looking strangely over-dressed, listen a
moment, fling a rapid sentence into the noise and run
out again; but a few remained near the door, fascinated,
and with one ear turned to the deck. "Stick together,
boys," roared Davis. Belfast tried to make himself
heard. Knowles grinned in a slow, dazed way. A
short fellow with a thick clipped beard kept on yelling
periodically:—"Who's afeard? Who's afeard?" Another one jumped up, excited, with blazing eyes, sent
out a string of unattached curses and sat down quietly.
Two men discussed familiarly, striking one another's
breast in turn, to clinch arguments. Three others,
with their heads in a bunch, spoke all together with a
confidential air, and at the top of their voices. It was
a stormy chaos of speech where intelligible fragments
tossing, struck the ear. One could hear:—"In the last
ship"—"Who cares? Try it on any one of us if——."
"Knock under"*—"Not a hand's turn"—"He says he
is all right"—"I always thought"—"Never mind.
. . ." Donkin, crouching all in a heap against the
bowsprit, hunched his shoulderblades as high as his ears,
and hanging a peaked nose, resembled a sick vulture
with ruffled plumes. Belfast, straddling his legs, had a
face red with yelling, and with arms thrown up, figured

a Maltese cross. The two Scandinavians, in a corner, had the dumbfounded and distracted aspect of men gazing at a cataclysm. And, beyond the light, Singleton stood in the smoke, monumental, indistinct, with his head touching the beam; like a statue of heroic size in the gloom of a crypt.

He stepped forward, impassive and big. The noise subsided like a broken wave: but Belfast cried once more with uplifted arms:—"The man is dying I tell ye!" then sat down suddenly on the hatch and took his head between his hands. All looked at Singleton, gazing upwards from the deck, staring out of dark corners, or turning their heads with curious glances. They were expectant and appeased as if that old man, who looked at no one, had possessed the secret of their uneasy indignations and desires, a sharper vision, a clearer knowledge. And indeed standing there amongst them, he had the uninterested appearance of one who had seen multitudes of ships, had listened many times to voices such as theirs, had already seen all that could happen on the wide seas. They heard his voice rumble in his broad chest as though the words had been rolling towards them out of a rugged past. "What do you want to do?" he asked. No one answered. Only Knowles muttered—"Aye, aye," and somebody said low:—"It's a bloomin' shame." He waited, made a contemptuous gesture.—"I have seen rows aboard ship before some of you were born," he said, slowly, "for something or nothing; but never for such a thing." —"The man is dying, I tell ye," repeated Belfast, woefully, sitting at Singleton's feet.—"And a black fellow, too," went on the old seaman, "I have seen them die like flies." He stopped, thoughtful, as if trying to recollect gruesome things, details of horrors, hecatombs of niggers. They looked at him fascinated. He was

old enough to remember slavers, bloody mutinies,
pirates perhaps; who could tell through what violences
and terrors he had lived! What would he say? He
said:—"You can't help him; die he must." He made
another pause. His moustache and beard stirred. He
chewed words, mumbled behind tangled white hairs;
incomprehensible and exciting, like an oracle behind a
veil. . . .—"Stop ashore——sick.——Instead——
bringing all this head wind. Afraid. The sea will have her
own.——Die in sight of land. Always so. They know it
——long passage——more days, more dollars.——You
keep quiet.——What do you want? Can't help him."
He seemed to wake up from a dream. "You can't
help yourselves," he said, austerely, "Skipper's no fool.
He has something in his mind. Look out—I say! I
know 'em!" With eyes fixed in front he turned his
head from right to left, from left to right, as if inspecting
a long row of astute skippers.—"'Ee said 'ee would
brain me!" cried Donkin in a heartrending tone.
Singleton peered downwards with puzzled attention, as
though he couldn't find him.—"Damn you!" he said,
vaguely, giving it up. He radiated unspeakable wisdom, hard unconcern, the chilling air of resignation.
Round him all the listeners felt themselves somehow
completely enlightened by their disappointment, and
mute, they lolled about with the careless ease of men
who can discern perfectly the irremediable aspect of
their existence. He, profound and unconscious, waved
his arm once, and strode out on deck without another
word.

Belfast was lost in a round-eyed meditation. One
or two vaulted heavily into upper berths, and, once
there, sighed; others dived head first inside lower bunks
—swift, and turning round instantly upon themselves,
like animals going into lairs. The grating of a knife

scraping burnt clay was heard. Knowles grinned no more. Davies said, in a tone of ardent conviction:— "Then our skipper's looney." Archie muttered:— "My faith! we haven't heard the last of it yet!" Four bells were struck.—"Half our watch below gone!" cried Knowles in alarm, then reflected. "Well, two hours' sleep is something towards a rest," he observed, consolingly. Some already pretended to slumber; and Charley, sound asleep, suddenly said a few slurred words in an arbitrary, blank voice.— "This blamed boy has worrums!" commented Knowles from under a blanket, in a learned manner. Belfast got up and approached Archie's berth.—"We pulled him out," he whispered, sadly.—"What?" said the other, with sleepy discontent.—"And now we will have to chuck him overboard," went on Belfast, whose lower lip trembled.—"Chuck what?" asked Archie.— "Poor Jimmy," breathed out Belfast.—"He be blowed!" said Archie with untruthful brutality, and sat up in his bunk; "It's all through him. If it hadn't been for me, there would have been murder on board this ship!"—"'Tain't his fault, is it?" argued Belfast, in a murmur; "I've put him to bed . . . an' he ain't no heavier than an empty beef-cask," he added, with tears in his eyes. Archie looked at him steadily, then turned his nose to the ship's side with determination. Belfast wandered about as though he had lost his way in the dim forecastle, and nearly fell over Donkin. He contemplated him from on high for a while. "Ain't ye going to turn in?" he asked. Donkin looked up hopelessly.—"That black 'earted Scotch son of a thief kicked me!" he whispered from the floor, in a tone of utter desolation.—"And a good job, too!" said Belfast, still very depressed; "You were as near hanging as damn-it to-night, sonny. Don't you play

any of your murthering games around my Jimmy!
You haven't pulled him out. You just mind! 'Cos if
I start to kick you"—he brightened up a bit—"if I
start to kick you, it will be Yankee fashion—to break
something!" He tapped lightly with his knuckles the
top of the bowed head. "You moind that, my bhoy!"
he concluded, cheerily. Donkin let it pass.—"Will
they split on me?" he asked, with pained anxiety.—
"Who—split?" hissed Belfast, coming back a step.
"I would split your nose this minyt if I hadn't Jimmy
to look after! Who d'ye think we are?" Donkin
rose and watched Belfast's back lurch through the doorway. On all sides invisible men slept, breathing
calmly. He seemed to draw courage and fury from the
peace around him. Venomous and thin-faced, he
glared from the ample misfit of borrowed clothes as if
looking for something he could smash. His heart
leaped wildly in his narrow chest. They slept! He
wanted to wring necks, gouge eyes, spit on faces. He
shook a dirty pair of meagre fists at the smoking
lights. "Ye're no men!" he cried, in a deadened tone.
No one moved. "Yer 'aven't the pluck of a mouse!"
His voice rose to a husky screech. Wamibo darted
out a dishevelled head, and looked at him wildly.
"Ye're sweepings ov ships! I 'ope you will all rot
before you die!" Wamibo blinked, uncomprehending
but interested. Donkin sat down heavily; he blew with
force through quivering nostrils, he ground and snapped his teeth, and, with the chin pressed hard against
the breast, he seemed busy gnawing his way through it,
as if to get at the heart within. . . .

In the morning the ship, beginning another day of
her wandering life, had an aspect of sumptuous freshness, like the spring-time of the earth. The washed

decks glistened in a long clear stretch; the oblique sunlight struck the yellow brasses in dazzling splashes, darted over the polished rods in lines of gold, and the single drops of salt water forgotten here and there along the rail were as limpid as drops of dew, and sparkled more than scattered diamonds. The sails slept, hushed by a gentle breeze. The sun, rising lonely and splendid in the blue sky, saw a solitary ship gliding close-hauled on the blue sea.

The men pressed three deep abreast of the mainmast and opposite the cabin-door. They shuffled, pushed, had an irresolute mien and stolid faces. At every slight movement Knowles lurched heavily on his short leg. Donkin glided behind backs, restless and anxious, like a man looking for an ambush. Captain Allistoun came out on the quarter-deck suddenly. He walked to and fro before the front. He was grey, slight, alert, shabby in the sunshine, and as hard as adamant. He had his right hand in the side-pocket of his jacket, and also something heavy in there that made folds all down that side. One of the seamen cleared his throat ominously.—"I haven't till now found fault with you men," said the master, stopping short. He faced them with his worn, steely gaze, that by an universal illusion looked straight into every individual pair of the twenty pairs of eyes before his face. At his back Mr. Baker, gloomy and bull-necked, grunted low; Mr. Creighton, fresh as paint, had rosy cheeks and a ready, resolute bearing. "And I don't now," continued the master; "but I am here to drive this ship and keep every man-jack aboard of her up to the mark. If you knew your work as well as I do mine, there would be no trouble. You've been braying in the dark about 'See to-morrow morning!' Well, you see me now. What do you want?" He waited, stepping quickly to and fro, giving them searching glances. What did they want? They shifted from foot to foot, they balanced their bodies; some, pushing back their caps, scratched their heads. What did they want? Jimmy was forgotten; no one thought of him, alone forward in his cabin, fighting great shadows, clinging to brazen lies, chuckling painfully over his transparent deceptions. No, not Jimmy; he was more forgotten than if he had been dead. They wanted great things. And suddenly all the simple words they knew seemed to be lost for ever in the immensity of their vague and burning desire. They knew what they wanted, but they could not find anything worth saying. They stirred on one spot, swinging, at the end of muscular arms, big tarry hands with crooked fingers. A murmur died out.— "What is it—food?" asked the master, "you know the stores have been spoiled off the Cape."—"We know that, sir," said a bearded shell-back in the front rank.— "Work too hard—eh? Too much for your strength?" he asked again. There was an offended silence.— "We don't want to go shorthanded, sir," began at last Davies in a wavering voice, "and this 'ere black— . . ."—"Enough!" cried the master. He stood scanning them for a moment, then walking a few steps this way and that began to storm at them coldly, in gusts violent and cutting like the gales of those icy seas that had known his youth.—"Tell you what's the matter? Too big for your boots. Think yourselves damn good men. Know half your work. Do half your duty. Think it too much. If you did ten times as much it wouldn't be enough."—"We did our best by her, sir," cried some one with shaky exasperation.—"Your best," stormed on the master; "You hear a lot on shore, don't you? They don't tell you there your best isn't much to boast of. I tell you—your best is no better than bad.

You can do no more? No, I know, and say nothing.
But you stop your caper or I will stop it for you. I am
ready for you! Stop it!" He shook a finger at the
crowd. "As to that man," he raised his voice very
much; "as to that man, if he puts his nose out on deck
without my leave I will clap him in irons. There!"
The cook heard him forward, ran out of the galley
lifting his arms, horrified, unbelieving, amazed, and
ran in again. There was a moment of profound silence
during which a bow-legged seaman, stepping aside,
expectorated decorously into the scupper. "There is
another thing," said the master, calmly. He made a
quick stride and with a swing took an iron belaying-
pin out of his pocket. "This!" His movement was so
unexpected and sudden that the crowd stepped back.
He gazed fixedly at their faces, and some at once put on
a surprised air as though they had never seen a belaying-pin before. He held it up. "This is my affair.
I don't ask you any questions, but you all know it; it
has got to go where it came from." His eyes became
angry. The crowd stirred uneasily. They looked
away from the piece of iron, they appeared shy, they
were embarrassed and shocked as though it had been
something horrid, scandalous, or indelicate, that in
common decency should not have been flourished like
this in broad daylight. The master watched them
attentively. "Donkin," he called out in a short, sharp
tone.

Donkin dodged behind one, then behind another,
but they looked over their shoulders and moved aside.
The ranks kept on opening before him, closing behind,
till at last he appeared alone before the master as though
he had come up through the deck. Captain Allistoun
moved close to him. They were much of a size, and at
short range the master exchanged a deadly glance with

the beady eyes. They wavered.—"You know this,"
asked the master.—"No, I don't," answered the other
with cheeky trepidation.—"You are a cur. Take
it," ordered the master. Donkin's arms seemed glued
to his thighs; he stood, eyes front, as if drawn on parade.
"Take it," repeated the master, and stepped closer;
they breathed on one another. "Take it," said Captain Allistoun again, making a menacing gesture.
Donkin tore away one arm from his side.—"Vy are
yer down on me?" he mumbled with effort and as if his
mouth had been full of dough.—"If you don't . . ."
began the master. Donkin snatched at the pin as
though his intention had been to run away with it, and
remained stock still holding it like a candle. "Put it
back where you took it from," said Captain Allistoun,
looking at him fiercely. Donkin stepped back opening
wide eyes. "Go, you blackguard, or I will make you,"
cried the master, driving him slowly backwards by a
menacing advance. He dodged, and with the dangerous iron tried to guard his head from a threatening fist.
Mr. Baker ceased grunting for a moment.—"Good!
By Jove," murmured appreciatively Mr. Creighton in
the tone of a connoisseur.—"Don't tech me," snarled
Donkin, backing away.—"Then go. Go faster."—
"Don't yer 'it me. . . . I will pull yer up afore the
magistryt. . . . I'll show yer up." Captain Allistoun made a long stride, and Donkin, turning his back
fairly, ran off a little, then stopped and over his shoulder
showed yellow teeth.—"Further on, fore-rigging,"
urged the master, pointing with his arm.—"Are yer
goin' to stand by and see me bullied," screamed Donkin at the silent crowd that watched him. Captain
Allistoun walked at him smartly. He started off
again with a leap, dashed at the fore-rigging, rammed
the pin into its hole violently. "I'll be even with yer

yet," he screamed at the ship at large and vanished beyond the foremast. Captain Allistoun spun round and walked back aft with a composed face, as though he had already forgotten the scene. Men moved out of his way. He looked at no one.—"That will do, Mr. Baker. Send the watch below," he said, quietly. "And you men try to walk straight for the future," he added in a calm voice. He looked pensively for a while at the backs of the impressed and retreating crowd. "Breakfast, steward," he called in a tone of relief through the cabin door.—"I didn't like to see you— Ough!—give that pin to that chap, sir," observed Mr. Baker; "he could have bust—Ough!—bust your head like an eggshell with it.—"O! he!" muttered the master, absently. "Queer lot," he went on in a low voice. "I suppose it's all right now. Can never tell tho', nowadays, with such a . . . Years ago—I was a young master then—one China voyage I had a mutiny; real mutiny, Baker. Different men tho'. I knew what they wanted: they wanted to broach the cargo and get at the liquor. Very simple. . . . We knocked them about for two days, and when they had enough—gentle as lambs. Good crew. And a smart trip I made." He glanced aloft at the yards braced sharp up. "Head wind day after day," he exclaimed, bitterly. "Shall we never get a decent slant this passage?"—"Ready, sir," said the steward, appearing before them as if by magic and with a stained napkin in his hand.—"Ah! All right. Come along, Mr. Baker —it's late—with all this nonsense."

CHAPTER FIVE

A HEAVY atmosphere of oppressive quietude pervaded the ship. In the afternoon men went about washing clothes and hanging them out to dry in the unprosperous breeze with the meditative languor of disenchanted philosophers. Very little was said. The problem of life seemed too voluminous for the narrow limits of human speech, and by common consent it was abandoned to the great sea that had from the beginning enfolded it in its immense grip; to the sea that knew all, and would in time infallibly unveil to each the wisdom hidden in all the errors, the certitude that lurks in doubts, the realm of safety and peace beyond the frontiers of sorrow and fear. And in the confused current of impotent thoughts that set unceasingly this way and that through bodies of men, Jimmy bobbed up upon the surface, compelling attention, like a black buoy chained to the bottom of a muddy stream. Falsehood triumphed. It triumphed through doubt, through stupidity, through pity, through sentimentalism. We set ourselves to bolster it up, from compassion, from recklessness, from a sense of fun. Jimmy's steadfastness to his untruthful attitude in the face of the inevitable truth had the proportions of a colossal enigma—of a manifestation grand and incomprehensible that at times inspired a wondering awe; and there was also, to many, something exquisitely droll in fooling him thus to the top of his bent.* The latent egoism of tenderness to suffering appeared in the developing anxiety not to see him die. His obstinate non-recognition of the only certitude whose approach we could watch from day to day was as disquieting as the failure of some law of nature. He was so utterly wrong about himself that one could not but suspect him of having access to some source of supernatural knowledge. He was absurd to the point of inspiration. He was unique, and as fascinating as only something inhuman could be; he seemed to shout his denials already from beyond the awful border. He was becoming immaterial like an apparition; his cheekbones rose, the forehead slanted more; the face was all hollows, patches of shade; and the fleshless head resembled a disinterred black skull, fitted with two restless globes of silver in the sockets of eyes. He was demoralising. Through him we were becoming highly humanised, tender, complex, excessively decadent: we understood the subtlety of his fear, sympathised with all his repulsions, shrinkings, evasions, delusions—as though we had been over-civilised, and rotten, and without any knowledge of the meaning of life. We had the air of being initiated in some infamous mysteries; we had the profound grimaces of conspirators, exchanged meaning glances, significant short words. We were inexpressibly vile and very much pleased with ourselves. We lied to him with gravity, with emotion, with unction, as if performing some moral trick with a view to an eternal reward. We made a chorus of affirmation to his wildest assertions, as though he had been a millionaire, a politician, or a reformer—and we a crowd of ambitious lubbers.* When we ventured to question his statements we did it after the manner of obsequious sycophants, to the end that his glory should be augmented by the flattery of our dissent. He influenced the moral tone of our world as though he had it in his power to distribute honours, treasures, or pain; and he could give us nothing but his contempt. It was immense; it seemed to grow gradually larger, as his body day by day shrank a little more, while we looked. It was the only thing about him—of him—that gave the impression of durability and vigour. It lived within him with an unquenchable life. It spoke through the eternal pout of his black lips; it looked at us through the impertinent mournfulness of his languid and enormous stare. We watched him intently. He seemed unwilling to move, as if distrustful of his own solidity. The slightest gesture must have disclosed to him (it could not surely be otherwise) his bodily weakness, and caused a pang of mental suffering. He was chary of movements. He lay stretched out, chin on blanket, in a kind of sly, cautious immobility. Only his eyes roamed over faces: his eyes disdainful, penetrating and sad.

It was at that time that Belfast's devotion—and also his pugnacity—secured universal respect. He spent every moment of his spare time in Jimmy's cabin. He tended him, talked to him; was as gentle as a woman, as tenderly gay as an old philanthropist, as sentimentally careful of his nigger as a model slave-owner. But outside he was irritable, explosive as gunpowder, sombre, suspicious, and never more brutal than when most sorrowful. With him it was a tear and a blow: a tear for Jimmy, a blow for any one who did not seem to take a scrupulously orthodox view of Jimmy's case. We talked about nothing else. The two Scandinavians, even, discussed the situation—but it was impossible to know in what spirit, because they quarrelled in their own language. Belfast suspected one of them of irreverence, and in this incertitude thought that there was no option but to fight them both. They became very much terrified by his truculence, and henceforth lived amongst us, dejected, like a pair of mutes. Wamibo never spoke intelligibly, but he was as smileless as an animal—seemed to know much less about it all than the cat—and consequently was safe. Moreover, he had belonged to the chosen band of Jimmy's rescuers, and was above suspicion. Archie was silent generally, but often spent an hour or so talking to Jimmy quietly with an air of proprietorship. At any time of the day and often through the night some man could be seen sitting on Jimmy's box. In the evening, between six and eight, the cabin was crowded, and there was an interested group at the door. Every one stared at the nigger.

He basked in the warmth of our interest. His eyes gleamed ironically, and in a weak voice he reproached us with our cowardice. He would say, "If you fellows had stuck out for me I would be now on deck." We hung our heads. "Yes, but if you think I am going to let them put me in irons just to show you sport. . . . Well, no. . . . It ruins my health, this lying-up, it does. You don't care." We were as abashed as if it had been true. His superb impudence carried all before it. We would not have dared to revolt. We didn't want to, really. We wanted to keep him alive till home—to the end of the voyage.

Singleton as usual held aloof, appearing to scorn the insignificant events of an ended life. Once only he came along, and unexpectedly stopped in the doorway. He peered at Jimmy in profound silence, as if desirous to add that black image to the crowd of Shades that peopled his old memory. We kept very quiet, and for a long time Singleton stood there as though he had come by appointment to call for some one, or to see some important event. James Wait lay perfectly still, and apparently not aware of the gaze scrutinising him with a steadiness full of expectation. There was a sense of a contest in the air. We felt the inward strain of men watching a wrestling bout. At last Jimmy with perceptible apprehension turned his head on the pillow.— "Good evening," he said in a conciliating tone.— "H'm," answered the old seaman, grumpily. For a moment longer he looked at Jimmy with severe fixity, then suddenly went away. It was a long time before any one spoke in the little cabin, though we all breathed more freely as men do after an escape from some dangerous situation. We all knew the old man's ideas about Jimmy, and nobody dared to combat them. They were unsettling, they caused pain; and, what was worse, they might have been true for all we knew. Only once did he condescend to explain them fully, but the impression was lasting. He said that Jimmy was the cause of head winds. Mortally sick men—he maintained—linger till the first sight of land, and then die; and Jimmy knew that the very first land would draw his life from him. It is so in every ship. Didn't we know it? He asked us with austere contempt: what did we know? What would we doubt next? Jimmy's desire encouraged by us and aided by Wamibo's (he was a Finn—wasn't he? Very well!) by Wamibo's spells delayed the ship in the open sea. Only lubberly fools couldn't see it. Whoever heard of such a run of calms and head winds? It wasn't natural. . . . We could not deny that it was strange. We felt uneasy. The common saying, "More days, more dollars," did not give the usual comfort because the stores were running short. Much had been spoiled off the Cape, and we were on half allowance of biscuit. Peas, sugar and tea had been finished long ago. Salt meat was giving out. We had plenty of coffee but very little water to make it with. We took up another hole in our belts and went on scraping, polishing, painting

the ship from morning to night. And soon she looked
as though she had come out of a band-box; but hunger
lived on board of her. Not dead starvation, but steady,
living hunger that stalked about the decks, slept in the
forecastle; the tormentor of waking moments, the dis-
turber of dreams. We looked to windward for signs
of change. Every few hours of night and day we put
her round with the hope that she would come up on
that tack at last! She didn't. She seemed to have forgotten the way home; she rushed to and fro, heading
northwest, heading east; she ran backwards and forwards, distracted, like a timid creature at the foot of
a wall. Sometimes, as if tired to death, she would
wallow languidly for a day in the smooth swell of an
unruffled sea. All up the swinging masts the sails
trashed furiously through the hot stillness of the calm.
We were weary, hungry, thirsty; we commenced to
believe Singleton, but with unshaken fidelity dissembled
to Jimmy. We spoke to him with jocose allusiveness,
like cheerful accomplices in a clever plot; but we looked
to the westward over the rail with longing eyes for a
sign of hope, for a sign of fair wind; even if its first
breath should bring death to our reluctant Jimmy.
In vain! The universe conspired with James Wait.
Light airs from the northward sprang up again; the sky
remained clear; and round our weariness the glittering
sea, touched by the breeze, basked voluptuously in the
great sunshine, as though it had forgotten our life and
trouble.

Donkin looked out for a fair wind along with the rest.
No one knew the venom of his thoughts now. He was
silent, and appeared thinner, as if consumed slowly
by an inward rage at the injustice of men and of fate.
He was ignored by all and spoke to no one, but his
hate for every man dwelt in his furtive eyes. He talked

with the cook only, having somehow persuaded the good man that he—Donkin—was a much calumniated and persecuted person. Together they bewailed the immorality of the ship's company. There could be no greater criminals than we, who by our lies conspired to send the unprepared soul of a poor ignorant black man to everlasting perdition. Podmore cooked what there was to cook, remorsefully, and felt all the time that by preparing the food of such sinners he imperilled his own salvation. As to the Captain—he had sailed with him for seven years, now, he said, and would not have believed it possible that such a man . . . "Well. Well . . . There it was . . . Can't get out of it. Judgment capsized all in a minute . . . Struck in all his pride . . . More like a sudden visitation than anything else." Donkin, perched sullenly on the coal-locker, swung his legs and concurred. He paid in the coin of spurious assent for the privilege to sit in the galley; he was disheartened and scandalised; he agreed with the cook; could find no words severe enough to criticise our conduct; and when in the heat of reprobation he swore at us, Podmore, who would have liked to swear also if it hadn't been for his principles, pretended not to hear. So Donkin, unrebuked, cursed enough for two, cadged for matches, borrowed tobacco, loafed for hours and very much at home before the stove. From there he could hear us on the other side of the bulkhead, talking to Jimmy. The cook knocked the saucepans about, slammed the oven door, muttered prophesies of damnation for all the ship's company; and Donkin, who did not admit of any hereafter (except for purposes of blasphemy) listened, concentrated and angry, gloating fiercely over a called-up image of infinite torment—as men gloat over the accursed images of cruelty and revenge, of greed, and of power. . . .

On clear evenings the silent ship, under the cold
sheen of the dead moon, took on a false aspect of
passionless repose resembling the winter of the earth.
Under her a long band of gold barred the black disc
of the sea. Footsteps echoed on her quiet decks. The
moonlight clung to her like a frosted mist, and the
white sails stood out in dazzling cones as of stainless
snow. In the magnificence of the phantom rays
the ship appeared pure like a vision of ideal beauty,
illusive like a tender dream of serene peace. And
nothing in her was real, nothing was distinct and solid
but the heavy shadows that filled her decks with their
unceasing and noiseless stir: the shadows darker than
the night and more restless than the thoughts of men.

Donkin prowled spiteful and alone amongst the
shadows, thinking that Jimmy too long delayed to die.
That evening land had been reported from aloft, and
the master, while adjusting the tubes of the long glass,
had observed with quiet bitterness to Mr. Baker that,
after fighting our way inch by inch to the Western
Islands,* there was nothing to expect now but a spell
of calm. The sky was clear and the barometer high.
The light breeze dropped with the sun, and an enormous
stillness, forerunner of a night without wind, descended
upon the heated waters of the ocean. As long as daylight lasted, the hands collected on the forecastle-head
watched on the eastern sky the island of Flores,* that
rose above the level expanse of the sea with irregular and
broken outlines like a sombre ruin upon a vast and
deserted plain. It was the first land seen for nearly
four months. Charley was excited, and in the midst of
general indulgence took liberties with his betters. Men
strangely elated without knowing why, talked in groups,
and pointed with bared arms. For the first time that
voyage Jimmy's sham existence seemed for a moment

forgotten in the face of a solid reality. We had got so far anyhow. Belfast discoursed, quoting imaginary examples of short homeward runs from the Islands. "Them smart fruit schooners do it in five days," he affirmed. "What do you want?—only a good little breeze." Archie maintained that seven days was the record passage, and they disputed amicably with insulting words. Knowles declared he could already smell home from there, and with a heavy list on his short leg laughed fit to split his sides. A group of grizzled sea-dogs looked out for a time in silence and with grim absorbed faces. One said suddenly— " 'Tain't far to London now."—"My first night ashore, blamme if I haven't steak and onions for supper . . . and a pint of bitter," said another.—"A barrel ye mean," shouted someone.—"Ham an' eggs three times a day. That's the way I live!" cried an excited voice. There was a stir, appreciative murmurs; eyes began to shine; jaws champed; short, nervous laughs were heard. Archie smiled with reserve all to himself. Singleton came up, gave a careless glance, and went down again without saying a word, indifferent, like a man who had seen Flores an incalculable number of times. The night travelling from the East blotted out of the limpid sky the purple stain of the high land. "Dead calm," said somebody quietly. The murmur of lively talk suddenly wavered, died out; the clusters broke up; men began to drift away one by one, descending the ladders slowly and with serious faces as if sobered by that reminder of their dependence upon the invisible. And when the big yellow moon ascended gently above the sharp rim of the clear horizon it found the ship wrapped up in a breathless silence; a fearless ship that seemed to sleep profoundly, dreamlessly on the bosom of the sleeping and terrible sea.

Donkin chafed at the peace—at the ship—at the sea that stretching away on all sides merged into the illimitable silence of all creation. He felt himself pulled up sharp by unrecognised grievances. He had been physically cowed, but his injured dignity remained indomitable, and nothing could heal his lacerated feelings. Here was land already—home very soon—a bad pay-day—no clothes—more hard work. How offensive all this was. Land. The land that draws away life from sick sailors. That nigger there had money—clothes—easy times; and would not die. Land draws life away. . . . He felt tempted to go and see whether it did. Perhaps already . . . It would be a bit of luck. There was money in the beggar's chest. He stepped briskly out of the shadows into the moonlight, and, instantly, his craving, hungry face from sallow became livid. He opened the door of the cabin and had a shock. Sure enough, Jimmy was dead! He moved no more than a recumbent figure with clasped hands, carved on the lid of a stone coffin. Donkin glared with avidity. Then Jimmy, without stirring, blinked his eyelids, and Donkin had another shock. Those eyes were rather startling. He shut the door behind his back with gentle care, looking intently the while at James Wait as though he had come in there at a great risk to tell some secret of startling importance. Jimmy did not move but glanced languidly out of the corners of his eyes.—"Calm?" he asked.—"Yuss," said Donkin, very disappointed, and sat down on the box.

Jimmy was used to such visits at all times of night or day. Men succeeded one another. They spoke in clear voices, pronounced cheerful words, repeated old jokes, listened to him; and each, going out, seemed to leave behind a little of his own vitality, surrender some of his own strength, renew the assurance of life—the indestructible thing! He did not like to be alone in his cabin, because, when he was alone, it seemed to him as if he hadn't been there at all. There was nothing. No pain. Not now. Perfectly right—but he couldn't enjoy his healthful repose unless some one was by to see it. This man would do as well as anybody. Donkin watched him stealthily:—"Soon home now," observed Wait.—"Vy d'yer whisper?" asked Donkin with interest, "can't yer speak up?" Jimmy looked annoyed and said nothing for a while; then in a lifeless, unringing voice:—"Why should I shout? You ain't deaf that I know."—"Oh! I can 'ear right enough," answered Donkin in a low tone, and looked down. He was thinking sadly of going out when Jimmy spoke again.— "Time we did get home . . . to get something decent to eat . . . I am always hungry." Donkin felt angry all of a sudden.—"What about me," he hissed, "I am 'ungry too an' got ter work. You, 'ungry!"—"Your work won't kill you," commented Wait, feebly; "there's a couple of biscuits in the lower bunk there—you may have one. I can't eat them." Donkin dived in, groped in the corner and when he came up again his mouth was full. He munched with ardour. Jimmy seemed to doze with open eyes. Donkin finished his hard bread and got up.—"You're not going?" asked Jimmy, staring at the ceiling.— "No," said Donkin, impulsively, and instead of going out leaned his back against the closed door. He looked at James Wait, and saw him long, lean, dried up, as though all his flesh had shrivelled on his bones in the heat of a white furnace; the meagre fingers of one hand moved lightly upon the edge of the bunk playing an endless tune. To look at him was irritating and fatiguing; he could last like this for days; he was outrageous—belonging wholly neither to death nor life, and perfectly invulnerable in his apparent ignorance of both. Donkin felt tempted to enlighten him.— "What are yer thinkin' of?" he asked, surlily. James Wait had a grimacing smile that passed over the death-like impassiveness of his bony face, incredible and frightful as would, in a dream, have been the sudden smile of a corpse.

"There is a girl," whispered Wait. . . . "Canton Street* girl.——She chucked a third engineer of a Rennie boat*——for me. Cooks oysters just as I like . . . She says——she would chuck——any toff—— for a coloured gentleman. . . . That's me. I am kind to wimmen," he added, a shade louder.

Donkin could hardly believe his ears. He was scandalised—"Would she? Yer wouldn't be any good to 'er," he said with unrestrained disgust. Wait was not there to hear him. He was swaggering up the East India Dock Road;* saying kindly, " Come along for a treat," pushing glass swing-doors, posing with superb assurance in the gaslight above a mahogany counter.—"D'yer think yer will ever get ashore?" asked Donkin, angrily. Wait came back with a start. —"Ten days," he said, promptly, and returned at once to the regions of memory that know nothing of time. He felt untired, calm, and safely withdrawn within himself beyond the reach of every grave incertitude. There was something of the immutable quality of eternity in the slow moments of his complete restfulness. He was very quiet and easy amongst his vivid reminiscences which he mistook joyfully for images of an undoubted future. He cared for no one. Donkin felt this vaguely like a blind man feeling in his darkness the fatal antagonism of all the surrounding existences, that to him shall for ever remain irrealisable, unseen and enviable. He had a desire to assert his importance, to break, to crush; to be even with everybody for everything; to tear the veil, unmask, expose, leave no refuge—a perfidious desire of truthfulness! He laughed in a mocking splutter and said:

"Ten days. Strike me blind if I ever! . . . You will be dead by this time to-morrow p'r'aps. Ten days!" He waited for a while. "D'ye 'ear me? Blamme if yer don't look dead already."

Wait must have been collecting his strength for he said almost aloud—"You're a stinking, cadging liar. Every one knows you." And sitting up, against all probability, startled his visitor horribly. But very soon Donkin recovered himself. He blustered,

"What? What? Who's a liar? You are—the crowd are—the skipper—everybody. I ain't! Putting on airs! Who's yer?" He nearly choked himself with indignation. "Who's yer to put on airs," he repeated, trembling. "'Ave one—'ave one, says 'ee—an' cawn't eat 'em 'isself. Now I'll 'ave both. By Gawd—I will! Yer nobody!"

He plunged into the lower bunk, rooted in there and brought to light another dusty biscuit. He held it up before Jimmy—then took a bite defiantly.

"What now?" he asked with feverish impudence. "Yer may take one—says yer. Why not giv' me both? No. I'm a mangy dorg. One fur a mangy dorg. I'll tyke both. Can yer stop me? Try. Come on. Try."

Jimmy was clasping his legs and hiding his face on the knees. His shirt clung to him. Every rib was visible. His emaciated back was shaken in repeated jerks by the panting catches of his breath.

"Yer won't? Yer can't! What did I say?" went on Donkin, fiercely. He swallowed another dry mouthful with a hasty effort. The other's silent helplessness, his weakness, his shrinking attitude exasperated him. "Ye're done!" he cried. "Who's yer to be lied to; to be waited on 'and an' foot like a bloomin' ymperor. Yer nobody! Yer no one at all!" he spluttered with such a strength of unerring conviction that it shook him from head to foot in coming out, and left him vibrating like a released string.

James Wait rallied again. He lifted his head and turned bravely at Donkin, who saw a strange face, an unknown face, a fantastic and grimacing mask of despair and fury. Its lips moved rapidly; and hollow, moaning, whistling sounds filled the cabin with a vague mutter full of menace, complaint and desolation, like the far-off murmur of a rising wind. Wait shook his head; rolled his eyes; he denied, cursed, threatened— and not a word had the strength to pass beyond the sorrowful pout of those black lips. It was incomprehensible and disturbing: a gibberish of emotions, a frantic dumb show of speech pleading for impossible things, promising a shadowy vengeance. It sobered Donkin into a scrutinising watchfulness.

"Yer can't oller. See? What did I tell yer?" he said, slowly, after a moment of attentive examination. The other kept on headlong and unheard, nodding passionately, grinning with grotesque and appalling flashes of big white teeth. Donkin, as if fascinated by the dumb eloquence and anger of that black phantom, approached, stretching his neck out with distrustful curiosity; and it seemed to him suddenly that he was looking only at the shadow of a man crouching high in the bunk on the level with his eyes.—"What? What?" he said. He seemed to catch the shape of some words in the continuous panting hiss. "Yer will tell Belfast! Will yer? Are yer a bloomin' kid?" He trembled with alarm and rage, "Tell yer gran'mother! Yer afeard! Who's yer ter be afeard more'n any one?" His passionate sense of his own importance ran away with a last remnant of caution. "Tell an' be damned! Tell, if yer can!" he cried. "I've been treated worser'n a dorg by your blooming back-lickers. They 'as set me on, only to turn aginst me. I am the only man 'ere. They clouted me, kicked me—an' yer laffed—yer black, rotten incumbrance, you! You will pay fur it. They giv' yer their grub, their water—yer will pay fur it to me, by Gawd! Who axed me ter 'ave a drink of water? They put their bloomin' rags on yer that night, an' what did they giv' ter me—a clout on the bloomin' mouth—blast their . . . S'elp me! . . . Yer will pay fur it with yer money. I'm goin' ter 'ave it in a minyte; as soon as ye're dead, yer bloomin' useless fraud. That's the man I am. An' ye're a thing—a bloody thing. Yah—you corpse!"

He flung at Jimmy's head the biscuit he had been all the time clutching hard, but it only grazed, and striking with a loud crack the bulkhead beyond burst like a hand-grenade into flying pieces. James Wait, as if wounded mortally, fell back on the pillow. His lips ceased to move and the rolling eyes became quiet and stared upwards with an intense and steady persistence. Donkin was surprised; he sat suddenly on the chest, and looked down, exhausted and gloomy. After a moment, he began to mutter to himself, "Die, you beggar—die. Somebody'll come in . . . I wish I was drunk . . . Ten days . . . oysters . . ." He looked up and spoke louder. "No . . . No more for yer . . . no more bloomin' gals that cook oysters . . . Who's yer? It's my turn now . . . I wish I was drunk; I would soon giv' you a leg up. That's where yer bound to go.

Feet fust, through a port . . . Splash! Never see yer any more. Overboard! Good 'nuff fur yer."

Jimmy's head moved slightly and he turned his eyes to Donkin's face; a gaze unbelieving, desolated and appealing, of a child frightened by the menace of being shut up alone in the dark. Donkin observed him from the chest with hopeful eyes; then, without rising, tried the lid. Locked. "I wish I was drunk," he muttered and getting up listened anxiously to the distant sound of footsteps on the deck. They approached—ceased. Some one yawned interminably just outside the door, and the footsteps went away shuffling lazily. Donkin's fluttering heart eased its pace, and when he looked towards the bunk again Jimmy was staring as before at the white beam.—"'Ow d'yer feel now?" he asked.— "Bad," breathed out Jimmy.

Donkin sat down patient and purposeful. Every half-hour the bells spoke to one another ringing along the whole length of the ship. Jimmy's respiration was so rapid that it couldn't be counted, so faint that it couldn't be heard. His eyes were terrified as though he had been looking at unspeakable horrors; and by his face one could see that he was thinking of abominable things. Suddenly with an incredibly strong and heart-breaking voice he sobbed out:

"Overboard! . . . I! . . . My God!"

Donkin writhed a little on the box. He looked unwillingly. James Wait was mute. His two long bony hands smoothed the blanket upwards, as though he had wished to gather it all up under his chin. A tear, a big solitary tear, escaped from the corner of his eye and, without touching the hollow cheek, fell on the pillow. His throat rattled faintly.

And Donkin, watching the end of that hateful nigger, felt the anguishing grasp of a great sorrow on his heart at the thought that he himself, some day, would have to go through it all—just like this—perhaps! His eyes became moist. "Poor beggar," he murmured. The night seemed to go by in a flash; it seemed to him he could hear the irremediable rush of precious minutes. How long would this blooming affair last? Too long surely. No luck. He could not restrain himself. He got up and approached the bunk. Wait did not stir. Only his eyes appeared alive and his hands continued their smoothing movement with a horrible and tireless industry. Donkin bent over.

"Jimmy," he called low. There was no answer, but the rattle stopped. "D'yer see me?" he asked, trembling. Jimmy's chest heaved. Donkin, looking away, bent his ear to Jimmy's lips, and heard a sound like the rustle of a single dry leaf driven along the smooth sand of a beach. It shaped itself.

"Light . . . the lamp . . . and . . . go," breathed out Wait.

Donkin, instinctively, glanced over his shoulder at the brilliant flame; then, still looking away, felt under the pillow for a key. He got it at once and for the next few minutes remained on his knees shakily but swiftly busy inside the box. When he got up, his face —for the first time in his life—had a pink flush—perhaps of triumph.

He slipped the key under the pillow again, avoiding to glance at Jimmy, who had not moved. He turned his back squarely from the bunk, and started to the door as though he were going to walk a mile. At his second stride he had his nose against it. He clutched the handle cautiously, but at that moment he received the irresistible impression of something happening behind his back. He spun round as though he had been tapped on the shoulder. He was just in time to see Wait's eyes blaze up and go out at once, like two lamps overturned together by a sweeping blow. Something resembling a scarlet thread hung down his chin out of the corner of his lips—and he had ceased to breathe.

Donkin closed the door behind him gently but firmly. Sleeping men, huddled under jackets, made on the lighted deck shapeless dark mounds that had the appearance of neglected graves. Nothing had been done all through the night and he hadn't been missed. He stood motionless and perfectly astounded to find the world outside as he had left it; there was the sea, the ship—sleeping men; and he wondered absurdly at it, as though he had expected to find the men dead, familiar things gone for ever: as though, like a wanderer returning after many years, he had expected to see bewildering changes. He shuddered a little in the penetrating freshness of the air, and hugged himself forlornly. The declining moon drooped sadly in the western board as if withered by the cold touch of a pale dawn. The ship slept. And the immortal sea stretched away, immense and hazy, like the image of life, with a glittering surface and lightless depths. Donkin gave it a defiant glance and slunk off noiselessly as if judged and cast out by the august silence of its might.

Jimmy's death, after all, came as a tremendous surprise. We did not know till then how much faith we had put in his delusions. We had taken his chances of life so much at his own valuation that his death, like the death of an old belief, shook the foundations of our society. A common bond was gone; the strong, effective and respectable bond of a sentimental lie. All that day we mooned at our work, with suspicious looks and a disabused air. In our hearts we thought that in the matter of his departure Jimmy had acted in a perverse and unfriendly manner. He didn't back us up, as a shipmate should. In going he took away with himself the gloomy and solemn shadow in which our folly had posed, with humane satisfaction, as a tender arbiter of fate. And now we saw it was no such thing. It was just common foolishness; a silly and ineffectual meddling with issues of majestic import—that is, if Podmore was right. Perhaps he was? Doubt survived Jimmy; and, like a community of banded criminals disintegrated by a touch of grace, we were profoundly scandalised with each other. Men spoke unkindly to their best chums. Others refused to speak at all. Singleton only was not surprised. "Dead—is he? Of course," he said, pointing at the island right abeam: for the calm still held the ship spell-bound within sight of Flores. Dead—of course. *He* wasn't surprised. Here was the land, and there, on the fore-hatch and waiting for the sailmaker—there was that corpse. Cause and effect. And for the first time that voyage, the old seaman became quite cheery and garru-lous, explaining and illustrating from the stores of ex-perience how, in sickness, the sight of an island (even a very small one) is generally more fatal than the view of a continent. But he couldn't explain why.

Jimmy was to be buried at five, and it was a long day till then—a day of mental disquiet and even of physical disturbance. We took no interest in our work and, very properly, were rebuked for it. This, in our con-stant state of hungry irritation, was exasperating. Donkin worked with his brow bound in a dirty rag, and looked so ghastly that Mr. Baker was touched with compassion at the sight of this plucky suffering.— "Ough! You, Donkin! Put down your work and go lay-up this watch. You look ill."—"I am bad, sir— in my 'ead," he said in a subdued voice, and vanished

speedily. This annoyed many, and they thought the
mate "bloomin' soft to-day." Captain Allistoun
could be seen on the poop watching the sky to the
southwest, and it soon got to be known about the decks
that the barometer had begun to fall in the night, and
that a breeze might be expected before long. This,
by a subtle association of ideas, led to violent quar-
relling as to the exact moment of Jimmy's death. Was
it before or after "that 'ere glass started down?"
It was impossible to know, and it caused much contemptuous growling at one another. All of a sudden
there was a great tumult forward. Pacific Knowles and
good-tempered Davies had come to blows over it. The
watch below interfered with spirit, and for ten minutes
there was a noisy scrimmage round the hatch, where,
in the balancing shade of the sails, Jimmy's body, wrapped up in a white blanket, was watched over by the
sorrowful Belfast, who, in his desolation, disdained the
fray. When the noise had ceased, and the passions had
calmed into surly silence, he stood up at the head of the
swathed body, lifting both arms on high, cried with
pained indignation:—"You ought to be ashamed of
yourselves! . . ." We were.

Belfast took his bereavement very hard. He gave
proofs of unextinguishable devotion. It was he, and no
other man, who would help the sailmaker to prepare
what was left of Jimmy for a solemn surrender to the
insatiable sea. He arranged the weights carefully at
the feet: two holystones, an old anchor-shackle without
its pin, some broken links of a worn-out stream cable.
He arranged them this way, then that. "Bless my
soul! you aren't afraid he will chafe his heel?" said
the sailmaker, who hated the job. He pushed the
needle, puffing furiously, with his head in a cloud of
tobacco smoke; he turned the flaps over, pulled at the

stitches, stretched at the canvas.—"Lift his shoulders. . . . Pull to you a bit. . . . So—o—o. Steady." Belfast obeyed, pulled, lifted, overcome with sorrow, dropping tears on the tarred twine.— "Don't you drag the canvas too taut over his poor face, Sails," he entreated, tearfully.—"What are you fashing yourself*for? He will be comfortable enough," assured the sailmaker, cutting the thread after the last stitch, which came about the middle of Jimmy's forehead. He rolled up the remaining canvas, put away the needles. "What makes you take on so?" he asked. Belfast looked down at the long package of grey sailcloth.—"I pulled him out," he whispered, "and he did not want to go. If I had sat up with him last night he would have kept alive for me . . . but something made me tired." The sailmaker took vigorous draws at his pipe and mumbled:—"When I . . . West India Station . . . In the *Blanche* frigate* . . . Yellow Jack* . . . sewed in twenty men a week . . . Portsmouth-Devonport* men—townies—knew their fathers, mothers, sisters—the whole boiling of 'em. Thought nothing of it. And these niggers like this one—you don't know where it comes from. Got nobody. No use to nobody. Who will miss him?"—"I do—I pulled him out," mourned Belfast dismally.

On two planks nailed together and apparently resigned and still under the folds of the Union Jack with a white border, James Wait, carried aft by four men, was deposited slowly, with his feet pointing at an open port. A swell had set in from the westward, and following on the roll of the ship, the red ensign, at half-mast, darted out and collapsed again on the grey sky, like a tongue of flickering fire; Charley tolled the bell; and at every swing to starboard the whole vast semicircle of steely waters visible on that side seemed to come up with a rush to the edge of the port, as if impatient to get at our Jimmy. Every one was there but Donkin, who was too ill to come; the Captain and Mr. Creighton stood bareheaded on the break of the poop; Mr. Baker, directed by the master, who had said to him gravely:—"You know more about the prayer book than I do," came out of the cabin door quickly and a little embarrassed. All the caps went off. He began to read in a low tone, and with his usual harmlessly menacing utterance, as though he had been for the last time reproving confidentially that dead seaman at his feet. The men listened in scattered groups; they leaned on the fife rail, gazing on the deck; they held their chins in their hands thoughtfully, or, with crossed arms and one knee slightly bent, hung their heads in an attitude of upright meditation. Wamibo dreamed. Mr. Baker read on, grunting reverently at the turn of every page. The words, missing the unsteady hearts of men, rolled out to wander without a home upon the heartless sea; and James Wait, silenced for ever, lay uncritical and passive under the hoarse murmur of despair and hopes.

Two men made ready and waited for those words that send so many of our brothers to their last plunge. Mr. Baker began the passage. "Stand by," muttered the boatswain. Mr. Baker read out: "To the deep," and paused. The men lifted the inboard end of the planks, the boatswain snatched off the Union Jack, and James Wait did not move.—"Higher," muttered the boatswain angrily. All the heads were raised; every man stirred uneasily, but James Wait gave no sign of going. In death and swathed up for all eternity, he yet seemed to cling to the ship with the grip of an undying fear. "Higher! Lift!" whispered the boatswain, fiercely.—"He won't go," stammered one of the men, shakily, and both appeared ready to drop everything. Mr. Baker waited, burying his face in the book, and shuffling his feet nervously. All the men looked profoundly disturbed; from their midst a faint humming noise spread out—growing louder. . . . "Jimmy!" cried Belfast in a wailing tone, and there was a second of shuddering dismay.

"Jimmy, be a man!" he shrieked, passionately. Every mouth was wide open, not an eyelid winked. He stared wildly, twitching all over; he bent his body forward like a man peering at an horror. "Go!" he shouted, and sprang out of the crowd with his arm extended. "Go, Jimmy!—Jimmy, go! Go!" His fingers touched the head of the body, and the grey package started reluctantly to whizz off the lifted planks all at once, with the suddenness of a flash of lightning. The crowd stepped forward like one man; a deep Ah—h—h! came out vibrating from the broad chests. The ship rolled as if relieved of an unfair burden; the sails flapped. Belfast, supported by Archie, gasped hysterically; and Charley, who anxious to see Jimmy's last dive, leaped headlong on the rail, was too late to see anything but the faint circle of a vanishing ripple.

Mr. Baker, perspiring abundantly, read out the last prayer in a deep rumour of excited men and fluttering sails. "Amen!" he said in an unsteady growl, and closed the book.

"Square the yards!" thundered a voice above his head. All hands gave a jump; one or two dropped their caps; Mr. Baker looked up surprised. The master, standing on the break of the poop, pointed to the westward. "Breeze coming," he said, "Man the weather braces." Mr. Baker crammed the book hurriedly into his pocket.—"Forward, there—let go the

foretack!" he hailed joyfully, bareheaded and brisk;
"Square the foreyard, you port-watch!"—"Fair wind
—fair wind," muttered the men going to the braces.—
"What did I tell you?" mumbled old Singleton, flinging down coil after coil with hasty energy; "I knowed it
—he's gone, and here it comes."

It came with the sound of a lofty and powerful sigh.
The sails filled, the ship gathered way, and the waking
sea began to murmur sleepily of home to the ears of
men.

That night, while the ship rushed foaming to the
Northward before a freshening gale, the boatswain un-
bosomed himself to the petty officers' berth:—"The
chap was nothing but trouble," he said, "from the moment he came aboard—d'ye remember—that night in
Bombay? Been bullying all that softy crowd—cheeked
the old man—we had to go fooling all over a half-
drowned ship to save him. Dam' nigh a mutiny all
for him—and now the mate abused me like a pickpocket
for forgetting to dab a lump of grease on them planks.
So I did, but you ought to have known better, too,
than to leave a nail sticking up—hey, Chips?"*

"And you ought to have known better than to chuck
all my tools overboard for 'im, like a skeary greenhorn,"* retorted the morose carpenter. "Well—he's
gone after 'em now," he added in an unforgiving tone.
—"On the China Station,* I remember once, the Ad-
miral he says to me . . ." began the sailmaker.

A week afterwards the *Narcissus* entered the chops
of the Channel.*

Under white wings she skimmed low over the blue sea
like a great tired bird speeding to its nest. The clouds
raced with her mastheads; they rose astern enormous
and white, soared to the zenith, flew past, and, falling

down the wide curve of the sky, seemed to dash headlong into the sea—the clouds swifter than the ship, more
free, but without a home. The coast to welcome her
stepped out of space into the sunshine. The lofty
headlands trod masterfully into the sea; the wide bays
smiled in the light; the shadows of homeless clouds ran
along the sunny plains, leaped over valleys, without a
check darted up the hills, rolled down the slopes; and the
sunshine pursued them with patches of running bright-
ness. On the brows of dark cliffs white lighthouses
shone in pillars of light. The Channel glittered like
a blue mantle shot with gold and starred by the silver
of the capping seas. The *Narcissus* rushed past the
headlands and the bays. Outward-bound vessels
crossed her track, lying over, and with their masts
stripped for a slogging fight with the hard sou'wester.
And, inshore, a string of smoking steamboats waddled,
hugging the coast, like migrating and amphibious mon-
sters, distrustful of the restless waves.

At night the headlands retreated, the bays advanced
into one unbroken line of gloom. The lights of the
earth mingled with the lights of heaven; and above the
tossing lanterns of a trawling fleet a great lighthouse
shone steadily, like an enormous riding light burning above a vessel of fabulous dimensions. Below its
steady glow, the coast, stretching away straight and
black, resembled the high side of an indestructible craft
riding motionless upon the immortal and unresting sea.
The dark land lay alone in the midst of waters, like
a mighty ship bestarred with vigilant lights—a ship
carrying the burden of millions of lives—a ship freighted
with dross and with jewels, with gold and with steel.
She towered up immense and strong, guarding priceless
traditions and untold suffering, sheltering glorious
memories and base forgetfulness, ignoble virtues and

splendid transgressions. A great ship! For ages had
the ocean battered in vain her enduring sides; she was
there when the world was vaster and darker, when the
sea was great and mysterious, and ready to surrender
the prize of fame to audacious men. A ship mother of
fleets and nations! The great flagship of the race;
stronger than the storms! and anchored in the open sea.

The *Narcissus*, heeling over to off-shore gusts,
rounded the South Foreland,* passed through the
Downs,* and, in tow, entered the river. Shorn of the
glory of her white wings, she wound obediently after the
tug through the maze of invisible channels. As she
passed them the red-painted light-vessels, swung at
their moorings, seemed for an instant to sail with
great speed in the rush of tide, and the next moment
were left hopelessly behind. The big buoys on the tails
of banks slipped past her sides very low, and, dropping
in her wake, tugged at their chains like fierce watch-
dogs. The reach narrowed; from both sides the land
approached the ship. She went steadily up the river.
On the riverside slopes the houses appeared in groups—
seemed to stream down the declivities at a run to see her
pass, and, checked by the mud of the foreshore, crowded
on the banks. Further on, the tall factory chimneys
appeared in insolent bands and watched her go by, like
a straggling crowd of slim giants, swaggering and upright under the black plummets of smoke, cavalierly
aslant. She swept round the bends; an impure breeze
shrieked a welcome between her stripped spars; and the
land, closing in, stepped between the ship and the sea.

A low cloud hung before her—a great opalescent and
tremulous cloud, that seemed to rise from the steaming
brows of millions of men. Long drifts of smoky
vapours soiled it with livid trails; it throbbed to the beat
of millions of hearts, and from it came an immense

and lamentable murmur—the murmur of millions of lips praying, cursing, sighing, jeering—the undying murmur of folly, regret, and hope exhaled by the crowds of the anxious earth. The *Narcissus* entered the cloud; the shadows deepened; on all sides there was the clang of iron, the sound of mighty blows, shrieks, yells. Black barges drifted stealthily on the murky stream. A mad jumble of begrimed walls loomed up vaguely in the smoke, bewildering and mournful, like a vision of disaster. The tugs backed and filled in the stream, to hold the ship steady at the dock-gates; from her bows two lines went through the air whistling, and struck at the land viciously, like a pair of snakes. A bridge broke in two before her, as if by enchantment; big hydraulic capstans began to turn all by themselves, as though animated by a mysterious and unholy spell. She moved through a narrow lane of water between two low walls of granite, and men with check-ropes in their hands kept pace with her, walking on the broad flag-stones. A group waited impatiently on each side of the vanished bridge: rough heavy men in caps; sallow-faced men in high hats; two bareheaded women; ragged children, fascinated, and with wide eyes. A cart coming at a jerky trot pulled up sharply. One of the women screamed at the silent ship—"Hallo, Jack!" without looking at any one in particular, and all hands looked at her from the forecastle head.—"Stand clear! Stand clear of that rope!" cried the dockmen, bending over stone posts. The crowd murmured, stamped where they stood.—"Let go your quarter-checks! Let go!" sang out a ruddy-faced old man on the quay. The ropes splashed heavily falling in the water, and the *Narcissus* entered the dock.

The stony shores ran away right and left in straight lines, enclosing a sombre and rectangular pool.* Brick

walls rose high above the water—soulless walls, staring
through hundreds of windows as troubled and dull as the
eyes of over-fed brutes. At their base monstrous iron
cranes crouched, with chains hanging from their long
necks, balancing cruel-looking hooks over the decks of
lifeless ships. A noise of wheels rolling over stones,
the thump of heavy things falling, the racket of feverish
winches, the grinding of strained chains, floated on the
air. Between high buildings the dust of all the continents soared in short flights; and a penetrating smell of
perfumes and dirt, of spices and hides, of things costly
and of things filthy, pervaded the space, made for it an
atmosphere precious and disgusting. The *Narcissus*
came gently into her berth; the shadows of soulless
walls fell upon her, the dust of all the continents leaped
upon her deck, and a swarm of strange men, clambering
up her sides, took possession of her in the name of the
sordid earth. She had ceased to live.

A toff in a black coat and high hat scrambled with
agility, came up to the second mate, shook hands, and
said:—"Hallo, Herbert." It was his brother. A lady
appeared suddenly. A real lady, in a black dress and
with a parasol. She looked extremely elegant in the
midst of us, and as strange as if she had fallen there from
the sky. Mr. Baker touched his cap to her. It was
the master's wife. And very soon the Captain, dressed
very smartly and in a white shirt, went with her over
the side. We didn't recognise him at all till, turning
on the quay, he called to Mr. Baker:—"Don't forget to
wind up the chronometers to-morrow morning."
An underhand lot of seedy-looking chaps with shifty
eyes wandered in and out of the forecastle looking for a
job—they said.—"More likely for something to steal,"
commented Knowles, cheerfully. Poor beggars. Who
cared? Weren't we home! But Mr. Baker went for

one of them who had given him some cheek, and we were
delighted. Everything was delightful.—"I've finished
aft, sir," called out Mr. Creighton.—"No water in the
well, sir," reported for the last time the carpenter,
sounding-rod in hand. Mr. Baker glanced along the
decks at the expectant group of sailors, glanced aloft at
the yards.—"Ough! That will do, men," he grunted.
The group broke up. The voyage was ended.

Rolled-up beds went flying over the rail; lashed
chests went sliding down the gangway—mighty few of
both at that. "The rest is having a cruise off the
Cape," explained Knowles enigmatically to a dock-
loafer with whom he had struck a sudden friendship.
Men ran, calling to one another, hailing utter strangers
to "lend a hand with the dunnage," then with sudden
decorum approached the mate to shake hands before
going ashore.—"Good-bye, sir," they repeated in
various tones. Mr. Baker grasped hard palms, grunted
in a friendly manner at every one, his eyes twinkled.—
"Take care of your money, Knowles. Ough! Soon
get a nice wife if you do." The lame man was delighted.—"Good-bye, sir," said Belfast, with emotion,
wringing the mate's hand, and looked up with swimming eyes. "I thought I would take 'im ashore with
me," he went on, plaintively. Mr. Baker did not understand, but said kindly:—"Take care of yourself,
Craik," and the bereaved Belfast went over the rail
mourning and alone.

Mr. Baker, in the sudden peace of the ship, moved
about solitary and grunting, trying door-handles, peering into dark places, never done—a model chief mate!
No one waited for him ashore. Mother dead; father
and two brothers, Yarmouth fishermen, drowned together on the Dogger Bank;* sister married and unfriendly. Quite a lady. Married to the leading tailor

of a little town, and its leading politician, who did not think his sailor brother-in-law quite respectable enough for him. Quite a lady, quite a lady, he thought, sitting down for a moment's rest on the quarter-hatch. Time enough to go ashore and get a bite and sup, and a bed somewhere. He didn't like to part with a ship. No one to think about then. The darkness of a misty evening fell, cold and damp, upon the deserted deck; and Mr. Baker sat smoking, thinking of all the successive ships to whom through many long years he had given the best of a seaman's care. And never a command in sight. Not once!—"I haven't somehow the cut of a skipper about me," he meditated, placidly, while the shipkeeper (who had taken possession of the galley), a wizened old man with bleared eyes, cursed him in whispers for "hanging about so."—"Now, Creighton," he pursued the unenvious train of thought, "quite a gentleman . . . swell friends . . . will get on. Fine young fellow . . . a little more experience." He got up and shook himself. "I'll be back first thing to-morrow morning for the hatches. Don't you let them touch anything before I come, shipkeeper," he called out. Then, at last, he also went ashore—a model chief mate!

The men scattered by the dissolving contact of the land came together once more in the shipping office.— "The *Narcissus* pays off," shouted outside a glazed door a brass-bound old fellow with a crown and the capitals B. T.* on his cap. A lot trooped in at once but many were late. The room was large, white-washed, and bare; a counter surmounted by a brass-wire grating fenced off a third of the dusty space, and behind the grating a pasty-faced clerk, with his hair parted in the middle, had the quick, glittering eyes and the vivacious, jerky movements of a caged bird. Poor Captain

Allistoun also in there, and sitting before a little table with piles of gold and notes on it, appeared subdued by his captivity. Another Board of Trade bird was perching on a high stool near the door: an old bird that did not mind the chaff of elated sailors. The crew of the *Narcissus*, broken up into knots, pushed in the corners. They had new shore togs, smart jackets that looked as if they had been shaped with an axe, glossy trousers that seemed made of crumpled sheet-iron, collarless flannel shirts, shiny new boots. They tapped on shoulders, button-holed one another, asked:— "Where did you sleep last night?" whispered gaily, slapped their thighs with bursts of subdued laughter. Most had clean, radiant faces; only one or two turned up dishevelled and sad; the two young Norwegians looked tidy, meek, and altogether of a promising material for the kind ladies who patronise the Scandinavian Home. Wamibo, still in his working clothes, dreamed, upright and burly in the middle of the room, and, when Archie came in, woke up for a smile. But the wide-awake clerk called out a name, and the paying-off business began.

One by one they came up to the pay-table to get the wages of their glorious and obscure toil. They swept the money with care into broad palms, rammed it trustfully into trousers' pockets, or, turning their backs on the table, reckoned with difficulty in the hollow of their stiff hands.—"Money right? Sign the release. There —there," repeated the clerk, impatiently. "How stupid those sailors are!" he thought. Singleton came up, venerable—and uncertain as to daylight; brown drops of tobacco juice hung in his white beard; his hands, that never hesitated in the great light of the open sea, could hardly find the small pile of gold in the profound darkness of the shore. "Can't write?" said the clerk, shocked. "Make a mark, then." Singleton painfully sketched in a heavy cross, blotted the page. "What a disgusting old brute," muttered the clerk. Somebody opened the door for him, and the patriarchal seaman passed through unsteadily, without as much as a glance at any of us.

Archie displayed a pocket-book. He was chaffed. Belfast, who looked wild, as though he had already luffed up*through a public-house or two, gave signs of emotion and wanted to speak to the Captain privately. The master was surprised. They spoke through the wires, and we could hear the Captain saying:—"I've given it up to the Board of Trade." "I should 've liked to get something of his," mumbled Belfast. "But you can't, my man. It's given up, locked and sealed, to the Marine Office,"*expostulated the master; and Belfast stood back, with drooping mouth and troubled eyes. In a pause of the business we heard the master and the clerk talking. We caught: "James Wait—deceased—found no papers of any kind—no relations—no trace—the Office must hold his wages then." Donkin entered. He seemed out of breath, was grave, full of business. He went straight to the desk, talked with animation to the clerk, who thought him an intelligent man. They discussed the account, dropping h's against one another as if for a wager—very friendly. Captain Allistoun paid. "I give you a bad discharge," he said, quietly. Donkin raised his voice:—"I don't want your bloomin' discharge—keep it. I'm goin' ter 'ave a job ashore." He turned to us. "No more bloomin' sea fur me," he said, aloud. All looked at him. He had better clothes, had an easy air, appeared more at home than any of us; he stared with assurance, enjoying the effect of his declaration. "Yuss. I'ave friends well off. That's more'n you got. But I am a man. Ye're' shipmates for all that. Who's comin fur a drink?"

No one moved. There was a silence; a silence of blank faces and stony looks. He waited a moment, smiled bitterly, and went to the door. There he faced round once more. "You won't? You bloomin' lot of yrpocrits. No? What 'ave I done to yer? Did I bully yer? Did I 'urt yer? Did I? . . . You won't drink? . . . No! . . . Then may ye die of thirst, every mother's son of yer! Not one of yer 'as the sperrit of a bug. Ye're the scum of the world. Work and starve!"

He went out, and slammed the door with such violence that the old Board of Trade bird nearly fell off his perch.

"He's mad," declared Archie. "No! No! He's drunk," insisted Belfast, lurching about, and in a maudlin tone. Captain Allistoun sat smiling thoughtfully at the cleared pay-table.

Outside, on Tower Hill,* they blinked, hesitated clumsily, as if blinded by the strange quality of the hazy light, as if discomposed by the view of so many men; and they who could hear one another in the howl of gales seemed deafened and distracted by the dull roar of the busy earth.—"To the Black Horse! To the Black Horse!"*cried some. "Let us have a drink together before we part." They crossed the road, clinging to one another. Only Charley and Belfast wandered off alone. As I came up I saw a red-faced, blowsy woman, in a grey shawl, and with dusty, fluffy hair, fall on Charley's neck. It was his mother. She slobbered over him:—"O, my boy! My boy!"— "Leggo of me," said Charley, "Leggo, mother!" I was passing him at the time, and over the untidy head of the

blubbering woman he gave me a humorous smile and a
glance ironic, courageous, and profound, that seemed to
put all my knowledge of life to shame. I nodded and
passed on, but heard him say again, good-naturedly:—
"If you leggo of me this minyt—ye shall 'ave a bob for a
drink out of my pay." In the next few steps I came
upon Belfast. He caught my arm with tremulous
enthusiasm.—"I couldn't go wi' 'em," he stammered,
indicating by a nod our noisy crowd, that drifted
slowly along the other sidewalk. "When I think of
Jimmy . . . Poor Jim! When I think of him I
have no heart for drink. You were his chum, too
. . . but I pulled him out . . . didn't I?
Short wool he had. . . . Yes. And I stole the
blooming pie. . . . He wouldn't go. . . . He
wouldn't go for nobody." He burst into tears. "I
never touched him—never—never!" he sobbed. "He
went for me like . . . like . . . a lamb."

I disengaged myself gently. Belfast's crying fits
generally ended in a fight with some one, and I wasn't
anxious to stand the brunt of his inconsolable sorrow.
Moreover, two bulky policemen stood near by, looking
at us with a disapproving and incorruptible gaze.—
"So long!" I said, and went on my way.

But at the corner I stopped to take my last look at
the crew of the *Narcissus*. They were swaying irresolute and noisy on the broad flagstones before the
Mint.* They were bound for the Black Horse, where
men, in fur caps with brutal faces and in shirt sleeves,
dispense out of varnished barrels the illusions of
strength, mirth, happiness; the illusion of splendour and
poetry of life, to the paid-off crews of southern-going
ships. From afar I saw them discoursing, with jovial
eyes and clumsy gestures, while the sea of life thundered
into their ears ceaseless and unheeded. And swaying

about there on the white stones, surrounded by the
hurry and clamour of men, they appeared to be creatures
of another kind—lost, alone, forgetful, and doomed;
they were like castaways, like reckless and joyous castaways, like mad castaways making merry in the storm
and upon an insecure ledge of a treacherous rock. The
roar of the town resembled the roar of topping breakers,
merciless and strong, with a loud voice and cruel purpose; but overhead the clouds broke; a flood of sunshine
streamed down the walls of grimy houses. The dark
knot of seamen drifted in sunshine. To the left of them
the trees in Tower Gardens* sighed, the stones of the
Tower gleaming, seemed to stir in the play of light, as if
remembering suddenly all the great joys and sorrows of
the past, the fighting prototypes of these men; press-
gangs; mutinous cries; the wailing of women by the
riverside, and the shouts of men welcoming victories.
The sunshine of heaven fell like a gift of grace on the
mud of the earth, on the remembering and mute stones,
on greed, selfishness; on the anxious faces of forgetful
men. And to the right of the dark group the stained
front of the Mint, cleansed by the flood of light, stood
out for a moment dazzling and white like a marble
palace in a fairy tale. The crew of the *Narcissus*
drifted out of sight.

I never saw them again. The sea took some, the
steamers took others, the graveyards of the earth will
account for the rest. Singleton has no doubt taken with
him the long record of his faithful work into the peaceful
depths of an hospitable sea. And Donkin, who never
did a decent day's work in his life, no doubt earns his
living by discoursing with filthy eloquence upon the
right of labour to live. So be it! Let the earth and
the sea each have its own.

A gone shipmate, like any other man, is gone for ever;

and I never met one of them again. But at times the spring-flood of memory sets with force up the dark River of the Nine Bends.* Then on the waters of the forlorn stream drifts a ship—a shadowy ship manned by a crew of Shades. They pass and make a sign, in a shadowy hail. Haven't we, together and upon the immortal sea, wrung out a meaning from our sinful lives? Good-bye, brothers! You were a good crowd. As good a crowd as ever fisted with wild cries the beating canvas of a heavy foresail; or tossing aloft, invisible in the night, gave back yell for yell to a westerly gale.

THE END

THE PREFACE TO THE
NIGGER OF THE 'NARCISSUS'

BY a happy coincidence Conrad's *Preface* has become as much of
a classic in its genre as the novel it introduces. It offers itself, of
course, as an apology for fiction, and the position it assumes is
characteristic of such apologies: that those who write fiction are
not indulging themselves in careless, capricious or irresponsible
activity, but performing a conscious and voluntary action,
demanding sincerity in the writer and seriousness in the reader.
It rests its case on the well-known paradox that the story-teller's
art is the art of truth-telling.

In what sense can fiction be said to be a form of truth? In the
course of the ten paragraphs of the *Preface* Conrad makes no less
than three attempts to answer the question. He begins by
asserting (paragraph 1) that the essential purpose of art is to
bring to light the 'truth, manifold and one' underlying every
'aspect' of the 'visible universe', and to discover in all these
aspects 'what of each is fundamental, what is enduring and
essential—their one illuminating and convincing quality—the
very truth of their existence'. He appears, then, to be distinguishing between some surface 'truth' of nature (which is
manifold, transient and contingent) and some fundamental
'truth' (which is single, enduring and significant), associating
true art with the latter. But the strained, insistent repetition of
the very proposition that is in question ('illuminating', 'convincing', 'the very truth') betrays an anxiety about the effectiveness of the argument; and quite soon he feels the need to attempt
a second definition. This time (paragraph 5) he suggests that it is
the artist's individual 'temperament' that has the power of
'endowing passing events with their true meaning'. Again the
distinction is between transience and permanence; but now

'permanent truth' is less a property perceived in the world than a quality visited upon it. How this idealist-sounding formulation relates to the platonizing definition offered earlier is not at all apparent. So Conrad returns to the problem for a third time, arguing (paragraph 7) that the artist's true task is to snatch a 'fragment' from the rush of time in order to exhibit 'its vibration, its colour, its form', thus disclosing its 'inspiring secret: the stress and passion within the core of each convincing moment'. Once more we are exhorted to distinguish between change and permanence and between a surface and an inner reality; but once again the emphasis shifts. If the first definition was concerned with the object-in-itself, and the second with the object-as-perceived, the third concentrates on the object-in-time.

What are we to make of this? For it is obvious that Conrad's definitions, either singly or conjointly, would not long survive the test of strict intelligibility. Leaving aside the problem of their consistency with each other, how are we to construe each individual proposition? Conrad's appeal to 'cores' and 'essences' and 'substances' and 'fundamentals', which offers so much and gives so little, has all the symptoms of a misapplication of theory. Its compulsive reiteration of inert abstractions betrays the strained obstinacy of a man using the wrong tool for the job. Yet to dismiss Conrad, as some have done, as a vacuous rhetorician from whom nothing can be learnt would be a serious mistake.[1] As a novelist he knows what he is talking about, even if he may not always know how to talk about it. It is unproductive to approach the *Preface* in an attitude of logical scepticism. The question one should bring to it is not 'What does he get wrong?' but 'What is he trying to get at?' Thus one will see that the *Preface* does not merely consist of unitary definitions; it also exploits a variety of indirect methods—notably that of the comparison, which becomes the main tactic of its argument. Its conception of art as truth acquires substance by being placed in differential relation first with the so-called discursive disciplines (science and philosophy), then with naïve theories of art (vulgar represen-

---

[1] For example, David Goldknopf, *The Life of the Novel*, Chicago University Press, 1972.

tation and vulgar expression). We shall look briefly at each of these in turn.[2]

Conrad begins by discovering in the activities of both the thinker-scientist and the artist a common basis. Both are confronted by the 'enigmatical spectacle' of the world, and both are drawn to resolve the enigma. This comparison already gives us a clue for interpreting the nagging dualism of the direct definitions. Here, surface and depth, the outer and the inner, are construable in terms of, on the one hand, the 'aspect of the world' which is by itself unintelligible (for the merely given does not carry its meaning on its face), and, on the other hand, the various significances and explanations—whether scientific, philosophical or artistic—that men discover and formulate.

Pursuit of the comparison reveals how these interpretative processes are able to take place. An intermediate medium is required: the scientist 'plunges' into facts, the thinker into 'ideas'. But how are these ideas and facts validated? The usual answer would invoke criteria; Conrad resorts to an appeal—to the community of mankind. Thinker and scientist earn their authority from what they can offer to men and women in their struggle to make a success of their lives: not only practically, by attempting to control nature and society, but also morally, through the passions that motivate these attempts—the desire for 'peace' or 'unrest', the drives of 'prejudices', 'fears', and 'egoism'—and even 'credulity', since success in life is unalterably short-term.

These tests or conditions of truth apply equally to the artist, for he too in his need to make sense of the enigmatical spectacle seeks an intermediary element. But he finds it by 'descending into himself'. At this point Conrad's argument does not make wholly clear how far this descent is meant to parallel the thinker-scientist's plunge into ideas and facts. But it does suggest that the artist must find a basis for his appeal to mankind quite

[2] In the most interesting essay I have come across on the subject, 'Conrad's Preface to *The Nigger of the "Narcissus"*', reprinted in the Norton ed., pp. 151–67, and in an amended form in *Conrad in the Nineteenth Century*, Chatto and Windus, 1980, pp. 76–88, Ian Watt rightly sets the *Preface* in a broad tradition of Romantic criticism.

different from the thinker-scientist's. By 'descending into himself' the artist sinks into a region of the self anterior to that which participates in the struggle for life. Accordingly what he finds there lacks the practical immediacy of what his rivals find; but Conrad believes that it will possess a more permanent appeal, for novels are less easily superseded than theories. The nature of this distinction will become clearer if we recall the list of qualities that the thinker-scientist addresses. It includes intelligence, egoism and fear—qualities that variously support man's engagement in the competition of life. The artist, however, appeals to a very different set: 'our capacity for delight and wonder . . . the sense of mystery surrounding our lives, our sense of pity and beauty and pain. . .' These constitute a new category consisting not of qualities that permit the control and amelioration of life, but that make possible an undesigning response to life as it is. We should note that the distinction between these sets is not that between the presence and absence of emotion. Both include the feelings; but they do so in very different ways—or, more accurately, they admit different kinds of feeling. The scientist appeals to what could be called the 'driving' emotions, the artist to the 'objective' emotions—that is, emotions directed towards an object from which they receive definition as they provide it with illumination. In this perspective, contrary to all normal expectations, it is science that becomes the more 'emotional' of the two disciplines.

If man's task is to 'render justice . . . to the visible universe', the artist performs it by making this universe subjectively real to himself. But to see the world in which we live as 'real' is to belong to it as a part belongs to the whole. Hence in addressing 'our sense of pity, and beauty, and pain', the artist is addressing our 'latent feeling of fellowship with all creation'; more profoundly, since the world we inhabit is not only mediated but constituted by human history, he is also appealing to 'the subtle but invincible conviction of solidarity . . . which binds together all humanity—the dead to the living and the living to the unborn'. This may not yet constitute a sufficient test of artistic truth, but at least it shows that the artist's descent into the self is the reverse of an act of solipsism, for what he is seeking is *what*

he really feels about the world. In this context, Conrad's term for
the deeper self—'temperament' (paragraph 5)—cannot retain
the connotation that generations of primadonnas have given it. It
is restored to its more neutral sense of 'subjective individuality'
—individuality in its perceiving or experiencing mode. Nor, for
that matter, can the censoring decorum which classifies this or
that subject as more or less worthy of artistic regard survive
either, for the sense of solidarity with the whole of creation
renders every part of it fit for creative attention (paragraph 4).

Conrad's first major comparison, then, produces a distinction
between the business of living and the appreciation of life. From
this he is able to derive two stipulations for artistic truth: creative
activity, and communal assent. He has not yet shown us,
however, what these terms might mean for the novelist in
particular. For this he has to turn to his second major comparison, which is less explicit but no less operative than the
first—that between what could be called the 'imaginative' view of
literature,[3] and stock referential and emotive theories of literature.

Reference to the thinker-scientist has allowed Conrad to show
that artistic activity need not be solipsistic; but it has not
permitted him to clarify the nature of this activity, for it has left
his conception of art very general. Once a particular art is
identified, however, the specific medium that differentiates it
becomes visible. This new focus enables him to deal with what
we saw to be the inadequacy of his account of the descent into
the self. He can now complete his original parallel. Just as the
thinker and the scientist cannot interpret the world without
remaining faithful to the logic of ideas and the integrity of facts,

---

[3] cf. *A Personal Record*, Dent, 1946: 'Only in men's imagination does
every truth find an effective and undeniable existence. Imagination,
not invention, is the supreme master of art as of life' (p. 25); and conversely,
he speaks of 'the band ... of the totally unimaginative, of those
unfortunate beings in whose empty and unseeing gaze (as a great
French writer has it) "the whole universe vanishes into a blank
nothingness"' (p. 92). A considerable proportion of *A Personal Record*,
but especially Chapter V, constitutes a mature reworking of the ideas of
the *Preface*.

so the novelist cannot make the world real to himself without 'unflinching' devotion to the practice of his craft. Conrad is no mere copier of reality, because he does not believe in unmediated perception. For him, the world present to habitual perception is not an automatic given, but something mediated by habitual language—what he calls 'the old, old words, worn thin, defaced by ages of careless usage'. A heightening of perception, there-fore, requires a heightening of the medium of perception. More-over, Conrad is no realist either: fidelity to the medium involves more than attention to the referential uses of language. In order to become a creative mode of representation, language must be exploited in all its expressive properties—suggestive, plastic, pictorial, sensuous, auditory (paragraph 5).[4] The reasons for this are complex, and Conrad does not go into them, except to suggest that the novelist must aim at nothing less than 'the perfect blending of form and content'. In other words, for him representation and perception cannot be regarded as indepen-dent activities; if they were so, his task would be reduced to mere technique—the recording of ready-mades in which means and ends would be quite separate elements in a two-stage process. Given this emphasis, it should not surprise us that the only artistic doctrine that Conrad is prepared to acknowledge as 'encouraging' (and that only 'faintly') is 'Art for Art' (paragraph 8)—here without its usual aesthetizing overtones.[5]

Having distinguished his conception of fictional truth from crude realism, Conrad goes on to contrast it with crude emotiv-ism (paragraphs 6 and 7). For him, the goal of the novelist cannot be the *arousal* of emotion. Those who, looking for 'immediate profit', demand to be 'edified, consoled, amused ... improved, or encouraged, or frightened, or shocked, or charmed' have

[4] This provides an explanation of Conrad's subtle qualification of Arnold Bennett's *Man from the North*: 'I would quarrel not with the truth of your conception but with the realism thereof. You stop just short of being absolutely real because you are faithful to your dogmas of realism.' (G. Jean Aubry, *Joseph Conrad, Life and Letters*, vol. i, p. 303.)

[5] This seems to me to define the nature and limits of Conrad's indebtedness to Walter Pater, a matter perceptively broached by Ian Watt (op. cit., pp. 164–5).

fallen prey to utilitarian expectations. What then is the novelist's goal? It is in response to this question that Conrad produces his famous declaration: 'My task . . . is, by the power of the written word, to make you hear, to make you feel—it is, before all, to make you *see!*' What makes this sentence memorable is not its incantatory tone (as some have suggested) but its contextual conclusiveness: art is not rhetorical but visionary.[6] It is memorable too because of its precision: the sequence of verbs is not haphazard, but virtually enacts the process it is defining. Sensory perception ('to make you hear') merges into affective engagement ('to make you feel'), which in turn yields to visionary perception ('to make you see'). Thus the feelings play a constituent part in a seamless process that starts with the senses and ends with the mind, fulfilling itself in the achieved work deliberately defined by Conrad as 'the *presented vision* of regret or pity, of terror or mirth' (my italics).

This 'vision', if it arouses emotions, does so only *contingently*; according to Conrad, what the reader feels in this sense is determined by his 'deserts'. What it does *necessarily* is something else: it awakens 'that feeling of unavoidable solidarity' to which we have already referred. That this motif should return here, at the climax of the peroration, is surely no accident. I see as implicit in the conduct of the whole argument that if there is a necessary connection between 'visionary truth' and 'human solidarity' it is because the latter is the test of the former. The thinker, we are told, finds his justification 'in the clear logic of a triumphant conclusion', the scientist 'in the unveiling of . . . the Laws of Nature' (paragraph 10); both are verifiable in terms of public criteria. In contrast, art repairs the defects not of falsehood but of unreality. Concerned with the truth of images rather than propositions, it can only be justified by acts of recognition. Hence its test can only be its capacity to make its vision that of the reader's. It would scarcely force Conrad's meaning to suggest that what we have here is a further extension of the idea

---

[6] cf. W. B. Yeats's 'Ego Dominus Tuus': 'The rhetorician would deceive his neighbours, / The sentimentalist himself; while art / Is but a vision of reality'. For Conrad's repudiation of the emotive theory of art see 'A Familiar Preface' to *A Personal Record*.

of solidarity, for the community of writer and readers (which is in
principle not less than humanity itself) may be understood as
art's version of the problem that exercised Conrad in his opening
paragraph: how to derive the one from the many, or to generate
the universal out of the particular.

Any attempt to define 'presented vision' in terms of an explicit
formula must end in vacuousness, for it rests on a failure to
appreciate the special character of artistic truth. I have argued
that the flaws in Conrad's argument, such as they are, can be
accounted for in this way. In case this sounds patronizing I
should emphasize that it is from the *Preface* itself that I have
derived the means of diagnosing its errors. For certainly its
conclusion (which for some reason has been found syntactically
puzzling[7]) is in line with its abiding claims: that the 'truth of life'
art affords is 'a moment of vision, a sigh, a smile—and the return
to an eternal rest'—in other words, that art, like life, consists of
an effort of attention, poignant or appreciative, that raises us
above the essential inertia to which we invariably, and in due
course permanently, return.

[7] See Watt, op. cit., pp. 162–3, and Goldknopf, op. cit., p. 83.

EXPLANATORY NOTES

For all nautical terms relating to the *Narcissus* see the Glossary. Reference is made in the notes below to Gerald Morgan, 'The Book of the Ship *"Narcissus"*' in Robert Kimbrough (ed.), *The Nigger of the 'Narcissus'*, Norton, 1979 (Morgan), and to Kimbrough's Notes to that edition (Kimbrough).

Title-page. Edward Garnett: reader for Fisher Unwin, who published Conrad's first two novels, and Conrad's literary adviser and friend in the first part of his literary career. Looking for better terms for Conrad than Unwin was willing to offer, Garnett recommended *The Nigger* to Heinemann, who published it in book form on 2 December 1897.

3 *Narcissus*: on 28 April 1884 Conrad was signed on in Bombay as second mate of the *Narcissus*, a full-rigged iron sailing-ship of 1336 tons built in Glasgow in 1876. The ship sailed on 3 June and berthed at Dunkirk on 16 October. For a full account of Conrad's transmutation of this experience into the novel, see Morgan.

muster: to assemble the ship's company in order to check their names against the official list.

4 *maul*: a heavy wooden hammer.

liberty-men: men allowed on shore on a 'liberty day'.

rupee: monetary unit of India, represented by a silver coin currently valued at fifty pence; *anna*: coin valued at one sixteenth of a rupee; *pice*: copper coin equal to one fourth of an anna.

Bombay Harbour: not the Bombay docks, but the name of the capital of the Island of Bombay.

5 *Puget Sound*: great inlet of the Pacific Ocean on the north-west coast of the state of Washington, USA, which has a government naval yard.

hooker: derogatory name for a ship.

Jack (Jack tar): familiar name for a sailor.

6 *Pelham: Pelham: or Adventures of a Gentleman*, a novel by E. Bulwer Lytton published in 1828, which created a fashion for the figure of the dandy. Bulwer Lytton's novels were indeed popular with seamen. Kimbrough cites Richard Dana in *Two Years before the Mast*.

8 *Board of Trade*: ministry supervising commerce and industry, divided into seven departments. The Marine Department, founded in 1850, had a variety of responsibilities, including the compulsory examinations of masters and mates, and shipping offices for the engagement and discharge of seamen.

10 *American ship*: US merchant ships were notorious for the severity of discipline aboard.

shellback: jocular name for a hardened, experienced sailor.

11 *take your shirt off*: to offer to fight.

jump my guts out: colourful variant of 'jump upon': to come down crushingly on (cf. p. 21, lines 18–19: 'jump down a fellow's throat').

13 *blanked*: euphemism for 'bloody'. Editorial pressure was put on Conrad to bowdlerize sailors' talk. He softened a number of expressions, e.g. 'blamed Finn' (p. 69) and 'cursed nigger' (p. 165), but a number escaped censorship, e.g. 'bloody black beast' (p. 69) and 'a bloody thing' (p. 152).

square-head: derogatory term for a Scandinavian, German or Dutch immigrant.

Whitechapel: district in the East End of London, notorious for its raffishness and crime.

15 *Byculla*: a district west of the Bombay docks.

18 *shipped*: to ship is to take service on a ship.

19 *dunnage*: protective mats stowed under and between the cargo; hence, by unflattering association, a slang term for sailors' luggage.

doctor: nickname of the ship's cook, who was responsible for administering first aid.

21 *costermonger*: man who sells fruit and vegetables from a street barrow.

Western Ocean: the North Atlantic. The epithet was applied to deep sea, as opposed to coastal, sailors.

26 *incult*: rough, untrimmed. Conrad's language bears frequent marks of French idiom (see note to p. 68).

28 *dhow*: traditional Arabian Sea ship, lateen-rigged (i.e. with triangular sails on long diagonal spars).

monsoon: seasonal wind of India and the Indian Ocean blowing from the south-east in Summer and from the north-east in Winter. It is caused by seasonal differences in temperature between sea and land.

30 *Pentland Firth*: a channel to the north-east of Scotland separating the Orkneys from the mainland. It is notable for its rough seas.

Peterhead whalers: seaport in Aberdeenshire, Scotland, from which whaling was carried out. Kimbrough notes that Allistoun's early promotion to the rank of harpooner was 'no mean feat'.

East Indian Trade: the British East India Company, founded by Elizabeth I in 1600, controlled all British trade to India and the East Indies until the nineteenth century, when its monopolies were gradually removed and its administration finally dissolved in 1873.

31 *Mauritius*: a tropical island in the Indian Ocean, east of Madagascar.

37 *St. Kitts*: a small archipelago near Barbados in the former British West Indies.

38 *to bone*: slang for 'to steal'.

41 *savoir vivre*: French for 'to know how to live'; viz., to possess the art of life, in the worldly sense.

45 *paregoric*: camphorated solution of opium used as an analgesic.

49 *cape of storms*: name given by Bartholomew Diaz, its discoverer, to the cape now known as the Cape of Good Hope.

westerly: the Westerlies are the prevailing winds of the southern latitudes. Known as 'the Roaring Forties' on the 40th parallel, they form one of the great wind belts of the world.

50 *Clyde*: the great ship-building yards on the River Clyde, east of Glasgow.

51 *crank*: liable to capsize.

57 *right as a trivet*: colloquial for 'in perfectly good condition' (a trivet is an iron tripod for holding cooking vessels over heat).

66 *adze*: tool with an arched blade at right angles to the handle for cutting away the surface of wood.

bear a hand: lend a hand, take part in an action.

68 *inabordable*: French word, unnaturally anglicized, meaning 'unapproachable, unmanageable, inaccessible'.

81 *milch-cow*: cow kept for milk. Animals were regularly taken on a voyage: the *Narcissus* had a pigsty, and a cat.

83 *north-east trade*: the trade wind in the Atlantic north of the equator. Trade winds are caused by cold air flowing from the northern and southern latitudes towards the tropical zone where rising warm air creates low pressure. They are deflected eastwards by the rotation of the earth, and constitute major wind belts.

86 *earn your salt*: salt is taken as a type of a necessary condiment for food.

90 *a fair wind*: the south-east trade (see note to p. 83).

95 *chummed*: colloquial for 'shared'.

99 *south-easter*: the south-east trade (see note to p. 83).

100 *two poun' ten a month*: in his edition of *The Nigger* for Everyman's Library (Dent, 1974) Norman Sherry notes that on the original *Narcissus* able seamen earned £3 per month, ordinary seamen £2, and the second mate (Conrad himself) £5.

103 *on the equator*: in the doldrums, a region of calms, electric storms, and light, unpredictable winds caused by the vertical ascent of air and the neutralizing of the meeting trade winds.

104 *sheets of flame*: sheet lightning.

106 *pannikin*: small metal drinking vessel.

    gawn: phonetic cockney for 'go on'.

    square mainsail coat . . . gaff-topsail hat: frock coat and top hat (see Glossary).

    Plimsoll: Samuel Plimsoll, a radical member of Parliament for 1868–80, maintained an aggressive, and sometimes uninformed, campaign against ship owners who disregarded the safety of their employees by such practices as overloading. He was responsible for bills enforcing a maximum 'load-line' known as the 'Plimsoll mark'.

    beak: slang for 'magistrate', originally thieves' cant.

    Penarth Dock: seaport in South Wales.

    coon: derogatory term for a Negro, from racoon.

    topped his boom: got drunk (see Glossary).

108 *chokey*: slang for 'prison'; originally Anglo Indian (from Hindi 'chauki' meaning 'shed').

    Watkinses: William Watkins founded one of the first steam tug companies on the River Thames.

    schooners: fore-and-aft rigged vessels with two masts (see Glossary).

110 *poll parrot*: tame parrot, hence user of conventional words and ideas.

111 *jail-prop*: a prop is the upholder of an institution.

114 *stokehold*: compartment in which a steamer's furnace is tended.

115 *White Star*: passenger line between Liverpool and New York, established in the mid-nineteenth century and now merged with Cunard.

122 *put a head on*: punched on the head.

126 *talk . . . like a Dutch uncle*: lecture with moralizing severity.

128 *Knock under*: to submit.

138 *to the top of his bent*: to the limit (cf. *Hamlet*, III.ii.375 [Arden]: 'They fool me to the top of my bent'; probably from the extent to which a bow may be bent).

139 *lubbers*: clumsy seamen.

143 *band-box*: box of paper-covered cardboard or thin wood, originally for neck-bands, now for millinery; hence *looked as though she had come out of a band box*: looking extremely neat.

145 *Western Islands*: the Azores, a Portuguese group of islands about 900 miles west of Lisbon.

   Flores: the most north-westerly of the Azores.

149 *Canton Street*: red-light street parallel to the East India Dock Road (see below).

   Rennie boat: John Rennie (1761–1821) introduced steam to the Royal Navy; his son George (1791–1866) designed marine engines for the Navy; hence a screw-driven navy steam vessel.

   East India Dock Road: main street servicing the two principal London docks.

158 *fashing yourself*: Scottish for 'bothering' or 'troubling' yourself.

   Blanche frigate: later name of the *Tilkhurst*, a ship in which Conrad served in 1885 (Kimbrough).

   Yellow Jack: (i) yellow fever, a tropical virus disease with fever and jaundice; (ii) the yellow quarantine flag signalling contagious disease on board.

   Devonport: originally named Plymouth Dock, a naval town at the head of Plymouth Sound.

   red ensign: the red flag of the British Merchant Navy.

161 *Chips*: nautical slang for ship's carpenter.

   skeary greenhorn: 'skeary' is a dialectal form of 'scary'; hence a frightened ignoramus or novice.

   China Station: Royal Navy service in the China Sea.

   chops of the Channel: the entrance from the Atlantic Ocean into the English Channel.

163 *South Foreland*: the Kent headland marking the entrance to the Thames.

   Downs: the part of the Channel between the Kentish coast and the Goodwin Sands lying opposite the eastern termination of the North Downs; a famous rendezvous for ships.

164 *pool*: part of the Thames just below London Bridge.

166 *Dogger Bank*: submerged sand-shoal in the North Sea fifty miles east of the Yorkshire coast.

167 *B.T.*: Board of Trade (see note to p. 8).

168 *Scandinavian Home*: Kimbrough notes that this was the Scandinavian Sailors' Temperance Home, by West India Dock, founded in 1880.

169 *luffed up*: 'slouched' or 'staggered' (see Glossary).

   Marine Office: section of the Board of Trade (see note to p. 6), located on Tower Hill (see following note), supervising the signing on, paying off and treatment of seamen.

170 *Tower Hill*: name of the high ground behind the Tower of London.

   Black Horse: Kimbrough notes that this public house formerly faced the Board of Trade building.

171 *the Mint*: on Tower Hill, where until recently the currency of the realm was coined.

172 *Tower Gardens*: public gardens between the Tower of London and Tower Hill.

173 *River of the Nine Bends*: the Thames, with suggestions of the River Styx in the Underworld.

GLOSSARY

OF NAUTICAL TERMS

The terms listed below refer exclusively to the structure, equipment, manning and operation of the *Narcissus*, as they appear in the text of the novel. I am particularly indebted to Eric Newby's *The Last Grain Race* (1956), which provides a vividly intelligible account of how a full-rigged ship is actually worked.

abaft: in the *stern* (q.v.) half of the ship

abeam: on a line at right angles to the ship's length

accommodation ladder: a removable ladder let down a ship's side to a small boat or a quay

aft: towards the *stern* (q.v.) of a ship

amidships: in the middle of a ship

astern: (i) beyond the *stern* (q.v.) of a ship; (ii) backwards

athwart: across the ship, from side to side

backstay: rope or wire from a mast-head to the rear of the ship for supporting the masts against wind-pressure

battens: wooden slats for securing tarpaulins over *hatches* (q.v.). Hence, *to batten (down)*.

beam: the maximum width of a ship (from the horizontal cross-timbers supporting the deck and joining the sides). Hence *on beam ends*: ship laid on her side.

beating to the wind: sailing to windward (against the wind) by means of *tacks* (q.v.)

belay: to coil or fix a running rope round a *cleat* (q.v.) or *pin* (see next entry)

belaying pin: short solid tube of wood or iron secured in a socket for *belaying* (see previous entry) ropes

bells: sounded to mark the half-hour divisions of a four-hour *watch* (q.v.). Hence *four bells*: half the watch; *eight bells*: the whole watch.

bend: to tie a sail to a *spar* (q.v.) or *halyard* (q.v.)

bight: a loop of rope

binnacle: receptacle for a ship's compass, fitted with a *binnacle lamp*, and mounted on a *binnacle stand*

block: pulley or pulleys mounted in a case

boatswain (bo'sun): officer responsible for the sails and rigging, and for summoning the crew to duty

bolster: circular metal casing near the bows, through which the *anchor chain* (see *cable*) passes

boom: a *spar* (q.v.) fixed to the mast at one end, to support the sail foot

bows: fore end of a ship from the point at which it begins to curve to the *stem* (q.v.). Hence *on the bows*: within forty-five degrees of the point straight ahead.

bowsprit: *spar* (q.v.) projecting forwards from the *stem* (q.v.) to which the *forestays* (q.v.) are fastened

brace: rope attached to a *yard* (q.v.) for adjusting it

break of the poop: the fore partition of the poop, where it drops to meet the main deck

bridge: raised rear deck from which the ship is directed

bridge-stanchion: see *stanchion*

bulkhead: upright partitions separating compartments below deck and creating watertight areas in the hull

bulwarks: ship's sides above the deck

buntline: a rope attached to the sail foot to confine a bunt or baggy cavity when furling a sail

cabin: officers' quarters in the *quarterdeck* (q.v.)

cable: anchor chain

capstan: revolving barrel on a vertical axis for winding up the *cable* (q.v.) or a rope

catch a turn: to loop a rope (see *nip*)

chain, chain-cable: see *cable*

chain compressor: an iron lever for checking the running of the *cable* (q.v.)

chain-tie: a chain for hoisting a *yard* (q.v.)

cleat: anvil-shaped piece of wood or iron bolted down for securing ropes *clew*: lower corner of a square sail, or the aftermost corner of a fore-and-aft sail (see *spanker*)

close-hauled: with sails and *yards* (q.v.) hauled close (i.e. away from square) in order to sail as nearly against the wind as is consistent with using its force (opposite of *flowing sheet*: with *sheets* (q.v.) eased for running before the wind).

come (up) to the wind: to veer into (against) the wind

companion: raised frame on the *quarterdeck* (q.v.) for lighting the cabins below. Hence *companionway* or *companion-ladder*: staircase to the cabins.

counter: curved part of the *stern* (q.v.) of the ship

crew: the ship's company, other than the three *officers* and *petty officers* (qq.v.), divided into *special crew* (the cook and the steward), and able and ordinary *seamen* (q.v.). (In addition to the cook Podmore and the anonymous steward, the *Narcissus* seems to have recruited sixteen hands for the voyage: Barnes, Boy, Campbell, Charley, Craig [Belfast], Davis, Donkin, Hansen, Knowles, Maclean [Archie], Narrator, Nielsen, Singleton, Smith, Wait, Wamibo.)

cross-head: bar between the piston-rod and the connecting-rod in a steam engine

crossjack (crojeck): the main sail on the mizzen mast (see *mast*)

deadeye: round, flat, three-holed block for extending the *shrouds* (q.v.). Hence *lower deadeyes*: deadeyes for fixing shrouds to the deck railing.

deck: plank platform extending from side to side of a ship. (The *Narcissus* appears to have had three decks: the *main deck*, extending to every side of the hull; the *poop* [q.v.] deck, above the maindeck aft; and the *forecastle* [q.v.] deck, below the main deck, forward.)

deck-house: structure erected on the deck between the mainmast and the foremast. (In the *Narcissus* comprising the *galley* [q.v.], the carpenter's shop, and Wait's cabin.)

dogwatch: one of a pair of short half-watches of two hours each, from 4–6 p.m. and from 6–8 p.m.

downhaul: rope used for hauling sails downwards (opposite of *halyard* [q.v.])

earing: short rope fastening the upper corner of a sail to a *yard* (q.v.)

ease off the head sheets: see *close-hauled*

fife-rail: rail round the mainmast for holding *belaying pins* (q.v.)

flatten-in: to trim a sail more nearly in line with the direction of the ship

flukes: pair of broad triangular plates at the end of each anchor-arm for fixing the anchor to the sea floor

flywheel: heavy-rimmed wheel on a rotating shaft for regulating its movement

footrope: rope stretched below a *yard* (q.v.) for sailors to stand on when furling or *reefing* (q.v.)

forecastle (fo'c'sle): forward part of the ship under the upper deck where the crew has its quarters. (In the *Narcissus* it would have accommodated, moving away from the *forepeak* [q.v.]: the *bowsprit* [q.v.] *heel* flanked by the *cable compressors* [q.v.], then the *forepeak hatch* [q.v.], then the *windlass* [q.v.], then the *chain* [q.v.] *-locker hatch*.)

forepeak: end of the forward hold in the angle of the *bows* (q.v.)

foresail: see *sail*

forestay: a rope from the mast-head to the fore of the ship (cf. *backstay*)

foretack: rope by means of which the weather (windward) corner of the foresail is kept in place

full: having the sails filled with wind

full and by: sailing *close-hauled* (q.v.) to the wind

gaff: spar extending the top of a fore-and-aft sail (see *spanker*). Hence *gaff-topsail*: small sail having its foot on the gaff.

galley: ship's kitchen (in the *Narcissus* in the *deck-house* [q.v.])

gangway: opening in the *bulwarks* (q.v.) through which a ship may be entered or left

gantline: (usually *girtline*), a rope through a *block* (q.v.) attached to a lower mast-head to hoist up the rigging

gear: generic term for 'hoisting equipment'

gin block: small iron frame furnished with a swivel-hook and pulley for raising or lowering cargo

goose-wing: triangular segment of a mainsail or foresail (usually on the weather or windward side) left exposed when the other half of the sail is furled up to the middle of the *yard* (q.v.).

gunwale (gun'l): upper edge of a ship's side (cf. *bulwark*)

halyard: rope or tackle used for raising or lowering a sail or *yard* (q.v.) (cf. *downhaul*)

handspike: a wooden bar, shod with iron, used as a lever on shipboard

hatch: square opening on the deck to provide access below. (The *Narcissus* would have had three main hatches, located before each mast: the *fore hatch*, the *main hatch* and the *after hatch* or *quarter hatch*.)

haul out: to change a ship's course by *trimming* (q.v.) the sails (cf. *light to*)

hawse-pipes: the castings through which the *cable* (q.v.) runs, fitted to protect the bows in which the hawse, or holes, are pierced

head: front or top (cf. *heel*)

head-earings: see *earing*

headsheets: see *sheets*

heave short: to heave in on the anchor cable until the ship is nearly over her anchor

heel: rear or bottom (cf. *head*)

helm: wheel on the *bridge* (q.v.) by which the rudder is controlled. Hence *helm up*: to bring the rudder to *leeward* (q.v.); *helm down*: to bring the rudder to *windward* (q.v.).

high poop: see *poop*

holystone: soft sandstone used for scouring the decks

hull: the body of the ship excluding everything that is above the top decks

iron: nautical slang for 'anchor'

jib: triangular sail, stretched from the *bowsprit* (q.v.) to the mast heads (see *sail*)

jump out: (of a mast), to be pulled or jerked out of its socket below deck on the *keelson* (q.v.)

keel: lowest longitudinal timber of a ship from which the framework of the hull is built up *keelson*: internal keel fastening a ship's floor-timbers to her keel

kid: small wooden container for sailors' food

lanyard: short piece of rope, used especially to secure the *shrouds* (q.v.) and the *stays* (q.v.)

lashings: rope or cord fastenings, often criss-crossed over tarpaulin wrapping

lee (leeward): on the side away from the wind (cf. *windward*)

lifts: ropes from each mast-head to its yard-arms to suspend and steady the ends

light to: to move the ship into the wind

luffed up: to move a ship so close into the wind that the sails flap

mainmast: see *mast*

mainsail: see *sail*

marlinspike: pointed iron tool used for separating strands of rope in *splicing* (q.v.)

mast (familiar, *sticks*): a three-master like the *Narcissus* would have a *foremast* forward, a *mainmast* amidships and a *mizzenmast* aft. Each of these masts would be subdivided as follows (from the deck up): *lower mast*, *topmast*, *topgallant mast*, *royal mast* and *skysail mast*.

masthead: highest part of the *lower mast*, and sometimes of the other mast sections

mate: officer on a merchant ship who sees to the execution of the *master's* (captain's) commands. (On the *Narcissus*, the *chief mate* or *first mate* [Baker] would take charge in the master's absence; his next-in-command would be the *second mate* [Crighton]; the *master* [Allistoun] and the two mates would form the ship's officers [cf. *petty officers*].)

mizzenmast: see *mast*

mooring bitts: strong wooden posts inserted in pairs into the deck of a ship for fastening the moorings when she is alongside a quay

nip: grip of a rope when it is twisted round something; hence *to nip*: to give a loop or twist to a rope (cf. *catch a turn*)

ordinary seaman: see *seaman*

paid off: ship turned to *leeward* (q.v.) through a movement of the *helm* (q.v.) (cf. *went off*)

petty officers: minor officers ranked between the ship's officers and the crew consisting (on the *Narcissus*) of the *boatswain* (q.v.), the *carpenter* (or familiarly 'chips') and the *sail-maker*

pin: see *belaying pin*

poop: raised deck (or *mizzendeck*) in the *stern* (q.v.) of a ship containing the accommodation of the ship's officers

port: (i) left side of the ship, when facing forward (cf. *starboard*); (ii) opening in a ship's side for loading, or coming and going

port-hole: glazed circular window in a ship's side

pump: fitted on or just below deck, to empty the hold of sea water

quarter: either side of the ship, aft of the *beam* (q.v.). Hence *on the quarter*: between *astern* (q.v.) and *abeam* (q.v.).

quarter checks: when the ship is berthed, ropes extending from the *quarterdeck* to the dock walls on either side to keep the *stern* (q.v.) centred

quarterdeck: that quarter-length of the main deck between the *poop* (q.v.) and the *mainmast* (q.v.)

quarter hatch: see *hatch*

rail: often lining the top of the *bulkheads* (q.v.) or above the *break of the poop* (q.v.); *mast-rail*: fitted for seamen's protection round the heads of the *lower* and *topgallant* masts (see *mast*)

ratlines: small ropes fastened across the ship's *shrouds* (q.v.) like ladder rungs to permit access to the *mastheads* (q.v.)

reef: one of the horizontal portions of a sail which may be successively folded up or furled. Hence *reefing*: reduction of the extent of a sail by rolling up a part or the whole of it and securing it.

reeve: to thread a rope through a *block* (q.v.) or any aperture. Hence *reeve clear*.

riding light: white light carried in the bow of a ship at anchor

rig: the way in which the sailing apparatus (mast, sails, ropes) of a ship is arranged

rigging: collective term for the ropes of a vessel (cf. *stays* [*fore-* and *back-*], *shrouds*, *ratlines*, *halyards*, *downhauls*, *braces*, *sheets*, *lifts*)

roving (also *rove*): a length of fibrous material (e.g. hemp) drawn out and slightly twisted (cf. *spunyard*) *royal*: see *sails*

running: sailing before the wind, i.e. with the wind aft

sails: the *Narcissus* would have been equipped with twenty-five sails, as follows:

- (a) *bowsprit* to *foremast*, moving aft: *flying jib* (see *jib*), *outer jib*, *inner jib*, *fore topmast staysail* (see *staysail*);
- (b) *foremast*, moving from deck: *foresail*, *fore lower topsail*, *fore upper topsail*, *fore topgallant sail*, *fore royal*;
- (c) *foremast* to *mainmast*, moving from deck: *main topmast staysail*, *main topgallant staysail*;
- (d) *mainmast*, moving from deck: *mainsail*, *main lower topsail*, *main upper topsail*, *main topgallant sail*, *main royal*;
- (e) *mainmast* to *mizzenmast*, moving from deck: *mizzen topmast staysail*, *mizzen topgallant staysail*, *mizzen royal staysail*;
- (f) *mizzenmast*, moving from deck: *crossjack*, *mizzen lower topsail*, *mizzen upper topsail*, *mizzen topgallant sail*, *mizzen royal*;
- (g) *boom* (q.v.) from *mizzenmast*, pointing aft: *spanker*

scend: impulse given by a wave. Hence a ship's resulting plunge or *pitch* (fore-and-aft movement, as opposed to *roll*, side-to-side movement).

screw: a manually-operated winch for lifting loads. Hence *screw-brake*.

scupper: hole in a ship's sides to carry off water from the decks

seaman: sailor, usually below the rank of officer. An *able seaman*, ranked above the *ordinary seaman*, is one who can perform all duties without supervision.

shackle: U-shaped metal link closed by a bolt or 'pin' for connecting chains. Hence *anchor-shackle*.

sheet: rope at the lower corner of a sail for regulating its position

shipkeeper: caretaker of a ship in harbour after the crew has been paid off

shorten: to reduce the spread of sail

shrouds: ropes, usually in threes or pairs, stretching from the mastheads to both sides of the ship to support the masts against lateral strain

skids: deck-planks for supporting a boat

spanker: a fore-and-aft (i.e. in line with the ship's keel) sail, set on the after-side of the *mizzenmast* (q.v.) between the *boom* (q.v.) at the sail foot and the *gaff* (q.v.) at the sail head

spar: stout pole, as used for a mast, a *yard* (q.v.), a *boom* (q.v.), a *gaff* (q.v.), a *bowsprit* (q.v.)

splice: to join the ends of a rope by interweaving the strands

spunyard: line composed of rope-yarns twisted together

square rigged: *rig* (q.v.) in which the sails are suspended from horizontal *yards* (q.v.) set at right angles to the line of the keel, as distinct from fore-and-aft rig (cf. *spanker*)

square yards: *yards* (q.v.) set at right angles to the line of the keel in order to take advantage of a following wind. Hence *squaring the braces*: adjusting the *braces* (q.v.) so as to square the yards.

stanchions: upright posts supporting the *beams* (q.v.) or the *bulwarks* (q.v.)

starboard: on the right side, when facing forward (cf. *port*)

stay: long rope supporting a mast or *spar* (q.v.) extending from the mastheads downwards to the *bowsprit* (q.v.) or the *stern* (q.v.), or to another mast forward

staysail: a triangular sail hoisted on a stay

stem: curved timber to which the ship's sides are joined at the fore end

stern: the rear part of the ship's hull, especially the part projecting beyond the *stern-post* (the upright timber bearing the rudder)

steward: officers' waiter

stop: (i) a small piece of line used to fasten or secure anything; (ii) a projection at the upper part of a lower mast; hence *midship stop*. As the boatswain is kneeling on a yard (*NN*, p. 93) and the stop is located amidships, I conjecture that sense (ii) is meant.

stream cable: cable of the *stream-anchor* (a medium-sized anchor used for mooring a ship in a sheltered position)

studding sail (scudding sail): a sail set on a small extra *yard* (q.v.) projecting beyond the edge of the square sails in a fair wind

stunsail: contraction of *studding sail* (q.v.)

sweating up: to set a sail taut so as to increase the speed

tack: to make a zig-zag course against the wind by angling the *yards* (q.v.) alternately for each oblique run. In square-rigged ships this can be done in two ways: by bringing the head of the ship across the wind (*tacking*), or by turning her head away from the wind (*wearing ship*, q.v.) before putting her on the new course or tack. The *starboard tack* has the wind on the *starboard* (q.v.) side, the *port tack* on the *port* (q.v.) side. On the starboard tack the yards are angled so that the starboard yard-arms point in the direction from which the wind is blowing; on the port tack the angle of the yards is reversed.

tackle: any piece of the running *rigging* (q.v.) of a ship; hence, *fall of the relieving tackle*. The *fall* is the loose end of the tackle to which the force is applied; *relieving tackle* is used to reduce strain on the tiller in bad weather.

taffrail: the aftermost portion of the poop rail of a ship, following the curve of the stern

tally on: to haul taut the *lee sheets* (qq.v.)

tide rode (for *tide-ridden*): swung by the tide, as a ship at anchor (opposed to *wind rode*)

top: to top a *boom* (q.v.) is to slant it by raising one arm and lowering the other

topgallant: see *sail*

topsail: see *sail*

tow-rope: rope for towing a sailing-ship out of harbour

trim: to adjust the sails and *yards* (q.v.) with reference to the direction of the wind

truck: flat cap of wood, fixed at the head of a mast, with small holes for signal *halyards* (q.v.)

vang: one of a pair of ropes extending to the *stern* (q.v.) for steadying the *gaff* (q.v.)

waist: the middle part of the upper deck between the *quarter-deck* (q.v.) and the *forecastle* (q.v.)

washboard: board fastened above the bulwarks to prevent the seas breaking over

watch: four-hour periods, divided by *bells* (q.v.). During these periods each of the two divisions of a ship's company under the first and second mates respectively (the *port watch* and the *starboard watch*, so named from the position of their bunks in the forecastle) remains alternately on deck.

waterline: line of intersection of the surface of the water and the ship's hull

wear ship: to turn the head of a ship away from the wind

weigh: to raise from below the water (chiefly applied to the anchor)

well: vertical shaft protecting the pump below the deck in the hold

went off: to move along the line of a given direction (cf. *paid off*)

wheel box (*wheel house*): steersman's shelter

windlass: machine for hoisting the anchor, with a horizontal *barrel* about which the cable winds

windward: in the direction from which the wind blows (cf. *leeward*). Also known as the *weather side*.

yard: spar tapering at each end slung horizontally across the mast to support a square sail. Hence *yard-arm*: either half of the yard.

THE WORLD'S CLASSICS

A Select List

The Woman in White
Edited by Harvey Peter Sucksmith

JOSEPH CONRAD: Lord Jim
Edited by John Batchelor

Nostromo
Edited and with an introduction by Keith Carabine

The Secret Agent
Edited by Roger Tennant

Under Western Eyes
Edited by Jeremy Hawthorn

DANIEL DEFOE: Moll Flanders
Edited by G. A. Starr

Robinson Crusoe
Edited by J. Donald Crowley

Roxana
Edited by Jane Jack

FËDOR DOSTOEVSKY: Crime and Punishment
Translated by Jessie Coulson
With an introduction by John Jones

Memoirs from the House of the Dead
Translated by Jessie Coulson
Edited by Ronald Hingley

GEORGE ELIOT: The Mill on the Floss
Edited by Gordon S. Haight

GUSTAVE FLAUBERT: Madame Bovary
Translated by Gerard Hopkins
With an introduction by Terence Cave

ALEXANDER HERZEN: Childhood, Youth and Exile
With an introduction by Isaiah Berlin

JAMES HOGG: The Private Memoirs and
Confessions of a Justified Sinner
Edited by John Carey

HOMER: The Iliad
Translated by Robert Fitzgerald
With an introduction by G. S. Kirk

The Odyssey
Translated by Walter Shewring
With an introduction by G. S. Kirk

HENRIK IBSEN: Four Major Plays
Translated by James McFarlane and Jens Arup
With an introduction by James McFarlane

HENRY JAMES: The Aspern Papers and Other Stories
Edited by Adrian Poole

The Awkward Age
Edited by Vivien Jones

The Golden Bowl
Edited by Virginia Llewellyn Smith

The Portrait of a Lady
Edited by Nicola Bradbury
With an introduction by Graham Greene

Roderick Hudson
With an introduction by Tony Tanner

The Spoils of Poynton
Edited by Bernard Richards

Washington Square
Edited by Mark Le Fanu

What Maisie Knew
Edited by Douglas Jefferson

RICHARD JEFFERIES: After London *or* Wild England
With an introduction by John Fowles

KATHERINE MANSFIELD: Selected Stories
Edited by D. M. Davin

EDGAR ALLAN POE: Selected Tales
Edited by Julian Symons

ANN RADCLIFFE:
The Italian
Edited by Frederick Garber

A complete list of Oxford Paperbacks, including books in
The World's Classics, Past Masters, and OPUS Series,
can be obtained from the General Publicity Department,
Oxford University Press, Walton Street, Oxford OX2 6DP.